BRAZEN BRIDE

Maggie Harrington isn't about to let her tyrannical father "sell" her into a marriage for business purposes—and she will deal with the Devil himself to preserve her independence. So she makes condemned criminal Cade Chisk-Ko an offer he'd be foolish to refuse: if the handsome half-breed agrees to accompany her to Texas as a temporary husband, Maggie will gratefully rescue him from the gallows.

RED SKY WARRIOR

A drifter, a rogue, but no killer, Cade wants no part of the white world that betrayed him. But even a brief marriage to Maggie Harrington may prove as lethal as the hangman's rope. For the raven-haired hellion's passionate fire ignites a wanting that threatens to consume Cade's damaged soul . . . and kindles a love he would give his life to protect.

The COMANCHE Trilogy *by*
Genell Dellin
from Avon Books

COMANCHE WIND
COMANCHE FLAME
COMANCHE RAIN

The CHEROKEE Trilogy

CHEROKEE DAWN
CHEROKEE NIGHTS
CHEROKEE SUNDOWN

If You've Enjoyed This Book,
Be Sure to Read These Other
AVON ROMANTIC TREASURES

KISSED *by Tanya Anne Crosby*
LADY OF SUMMER *by Emma Merritt*
MY RUNAWAY HEART *by Miriam Minger*
RUNAWAY TIME *by Deborah Gordon*
TIMESWEPT BRIDE *by Eugenia Riley*

Coming Soon

SUNDANCER'S WOMAN *by Judith E. French*

GENELL DELLIN

RED SKY WARRIOR

An Avon Romantic Treasure

AVON BOOKS ◆ NEW YORK

RED SKY WARRIOR is an original publication of Avon Books. This work has never before appeared in book form. This work is a novel. Any similarity to actual persons or events is purely coincidental.

AVON BOOKS
A division of
The Hearst Corporation
1350 Avenue of the Americas
New York, New York 10019

Copyright © 1996 by Genell Smith Dellin
Inside back cover author photo by Loy's Photography
Published by arrangement with the author
Library of Congress Catalog Card Number: 95-94627
ISBN: 0-380-77526-3

First Avon Books Printing: January 1996

AVON TRADEMARK REG. U.S. PAT. OFF. AND IN OTHER COUNTRIES, MARCA REGISTRADA, HECHO EN U.S.A.

Printed in the U.S.A.

RA   10   9   8   7   6   5   4   3   2   1

For my dear son, David

Prologue

Kiamichi Mountains, New Choctaw Nation
October, 1856

Every muscle in the boy's body screamed to him to jump up and run. Instead, he squared his shoulders against the rock wall behind him and continued to stare out across the valley into the setting sun.

Soon. Surely it would come soon, he thought.

Sweat stung the scratches and cuts on his skin while hunger twisted his insides, but he didn't dare move. Ever since he'd left home he had been running, and ever since he'd slipped away from the white man's school he had been chasing the deer and racing the mountain lion, yet all those steps had not brought him the peace he had been seeking.

The old man Moshulatubbee was named for a great chief. Surely what he said was right, and he had said that Cade must sit entirely still until he had his answer. His name.

His blood hummed and his head floated from dizziness, but he didn't move. He had already flattened his ankles against the natural stone seat, where he sat with his legs crossed beneath him and his shoulders touching the mountain. He wouldn't fall off.

He couldn't bear the waiting much longer. It must come soon, his name, or he would go looking for it. He would run until he found it. Sitting entirely still allowed for too many terrible pictures to come back into his mind.

Moshulatubbee didn't know anything about the bad times he'd experienced, trapped in the white man's school. He had lived all his long, old life far back in the woods, first in the Choctaw country in the east and then in these mountains. He did not know how living with the white man's ways could drive an Indian to run without stopping.

The sunset sky swam in Cade's steadfast sight, then stopped and steadied. The great blazing eye of the sun would drop behind the mountains soon. How would he then be able to see a medicine animal or bird in the dark? How could he have an experience or do something worthy of giving him his name if he was sitting still as the mountain staring out into blackness?

If his name didn't come soon, he would leave. He knew that. All too often something in his soul told him to go, and he had no choice but to follow that command.

The sun rested at the very top of the western ridge, its lingering light growing bright red with every breath he took. It poured its redness over the top of the purple mountain.

Suddenly, the vermilion burst upward, in a great rising wave, and the whole sky opened up to swallow it. In the next instant, the sky turned red and yellow, bright as the autumn leaves on the trees, while the valley lay dark at the mountains' feet.

The sky glowed with every shade of red, and with purple from the mountain and many, many yellows, plus tiny touches of blue left from the daytime sky. But mostly it was deepest glowing crimson, a shimmering red that gleamed like rich velvet.

Then it grew brighter, the colors blazed, began dancing like flames with little blue tongues. Fire. The sky was on fire.

Fire big enough to burn up the world.

He widened his eyes and searched it, searched for his sign, searched for his name. Finally, in the midst of the conflagration, he saw white. White like a cloud. White in the shape of a buffalo.

He stared at it. He wasn't mistaken. It was the shape of a buffalo, even though that animal had long been gone from this place. Was that his sign?

He balled his fingers inside his sweating palms into fists. Was that his name?

He did not move. He barely breathed. He only watched until the fire had burned out, turning the sky into dark gray ash. As the last of the light faded, he saw Moshulatubbee halfway down the mountain, beckoning him.

Cade leaped to his feet and ran to him, jumping from boulder to boulder, his feet hardly touching the ground.

When he stood before the old man, Moshulatubbee reached out and laid both hands on Cade's naked shoulders.

"Red Sky," he called him.

Chapter 1

Near Van Buren, Arkansas
October, 1870

The hairs on the back of his neck stood up when Cade Chisk-Ko rode beneath the high, arching sign that proclaimed Argus Academy. It was written in wrought iron script.

Iron hard as the hearts of the white-eyed bastards who ran the place.

Cade shifted slightly in his silver-trimmed saddle and fought the feeling this place had implanted deep inside him on that first night he'd spent inside its fancy fence. *The feeling* had ruled his life since then. The terrifying sensation that he was floating loose in the air, needing to run back home but unable to set his feet steadfastly on the ground, made him feel torn out of the very arms of Mother Earth herself.

He had been eight years old that horrible night those twenty long years ago, and he hadn't been allowed to use the term *Mother Earth* for long. Headmaster John G. Haynes had knocked every Choctaw word right out of his head.

Cade's jaw tightened so quick and hard it made his teeth hurt. If the cruel son of a bitch was still alive and still here, no doubt he was slapping Cade's sister, Cotannah, around.

He touched a spur to the gray and sent him flying up the long, curving driveway, wracking his memory as to whether he'd ever seen Haynes hit a girl. He remembered that he used to publicly humiliate them for the slightest infraction of his countless rules. That alone would be enough to devastate Cade's shy, reserved little sister.

That alone had been enough to make Talihina Tuskahoma kill herself.

Sweat beaded on his forehead. He leaned forward, signaling his horse, Smoke, to break into an even faster gallop. *Damn it!* Why had Uncle Jumper and Aunt Ancie sent the child here when he had told them not to?

How could this place still be standing when the War Between the States had destroyed so many others like it?

The gray reached the foot of the steps leading up to the white-columned portico of the administration building. Cade sat back in the saddle and reined the horse to a sliding stop that threw gravel against the stone like scattered gunshots.

He leaped from Smoke's back onto the broad stairway and ran up, bootheels pounding.

At the top, a door swung open and a man stepped out.

"May I help you, sir?"

Cade took the last two steps, and then he was on the porch, looking down into the pinched face of Haynes's prissy secretary. Incredible! The sneak who had spied and tattled on the students twenty years ago, the scum who had watched with glee when they were whipped and taunted, was still here. Wrinkled and graying, but still here.

The secretary's tiny eyes widened as they roamed over the heavy boots, tight breeches, big-sleeved shirt, and up into Cade's face. His eyes hardened with prejudice.

Cade saw every one of his features reflected in those shining, stony eyes as the little man took stock of him.

Long black hair, bright copper skin, high cheekbones. Norris dropped all pretense of courtesy.

"What do you want?"

"I've come to take my sister home. Cotannah Chisk-Ko. Send for her."

"I'm sor-ry . . ." the familiar, singsong voice began.

"I won't argue with that," Cade drawled. His jaw tightened again, but he held his voice cool and level. "I never saw a sorrier excuse for a human being than you are, Norris, and I've gambled and fought my way up and down the Mississippi and to the Rio Grande and back."

"Well!"

Norris's skinny face went even whiter as the insult soaked in. "You savage! You needn't be impudent . . ."

"You needn't be talking. Not to me. Call your errand boy and send for Cotannah Chisk-Ko."

A greasy smile creased Norris's pale, thin face. The man was gloating.

"Miss Sarah Coates is in Headmaster Haynes's office at the moment. She is being disciplined for speaking at the breakfast table this morning in her vile native language."

Cade took a step forward, the little man slipped aside and Cade plunged through the door.

The office, no doubt, was still in the same place. Nothing about this hellhole of a prison for children had changed.

The wide hallway, filled with morning dimness, stretched endlessly back into the building. It stank with the harsh, dank smell of careful cruelty.

That smell hung heavier than the humid air outside. It permeated the cloth of his shirt and his breeches, chilling his skin and sending its cold all the way to his bones.

He hurled himself down the long corridor, found the right door, grabbed the big cut-glass knob, and twisted, wishing it was Haynes's fat neck.

The polished oak slab swung silently inward.

Cade made one long stride into the room before the sight before him stopped him dead in his tracks.

He froze. Who was that girl? She wasn't his sister. That wasn't Cotannah.

But it was. She had grown up!

And though Cade couldn't see his face, he knew it was Haynes who towered over her.

Cade realized the man hadn't heard him come in.

He was brandishing a buggy whip at Cotannah, talking to her in a menacing voice too loud for the short distance between them, a voice shaking with fury and excitement.

"If you won't let me unfasten your bodice, Miss Sarah, I will remove your buttons with the tiny tip end of Tommy the Whip."

Cade hurled himself across the room, desperate to reach Haynes and stop him before he could hurt his sister any more.

But, in a blur against the sunlight streaming through the double glass doors, Cade saw the whip flick fast as a snake's tongue at his little sister.

She screamed.

Cade went cold inside, cold as sleet, as he often did during a fight. In one glance he saw Haynes's astonished face. Then Cade was on him, driving him down, pounding at him with strength surging up into his muscles out of a bottomless well of rage.

He snapped his fingers around Haynes's wrist, raised the straining arm, and rammed the elbow against the floor once, twice, then again. The whip clattered away.

He glanced at Cotannah.

She was slumped against the wall, looking too dazed to ever move again. One ripe breast was entirely exposed, neat beads of blood standing in a straight line over the curve of it. She made no effort to cover herself. All she did was stare down at him.

Blankly, as if she didn't even recognize him.

Fear, a bright, raging fear, grabbed his guts and squeezed. "Put this on," he growled, tearing his shirt off with one hand while he held Haynes down with the other. "It's Cade, darlin', your brother. Don't you know me?"

He ripped the garment off and threw it in Cotannah's direction just before the bulky headmaster heaved up to look him square in the face. Cade let him come, then he grabbed Haynes's collar and jerked him to his feet. Before his boots were even solidly set against the polished floor, Cade swung his mighty fist and smashed it into the pale, sweating flesh of Haynes's face.

Outside the room, Norris's shrill scream echoed down the hallway.

"Help! Help! Roy, where are you? There's a savage in here attacking Mr. Haynes . . ."

Cade twisted his fingers harder into the handful of cloth he held, planted the heels of his boots on the floor, and held Haynes at the end of his stiffened arm.

"L-let go of me . . ."

Cade heard him, but suddenly he could no longer see him.

The world went red in front of his eyes, and fury exploded inside him. He spread his legs, set his weight on his heels, and lifted Haynes off the floor.

Then he drew back his fist and, with everything he had, he hit him again.

Norris screamed, "Roy! Get in here!"

The force of Cade's blow broke his grip on Haynes's shirtfront and the headmaster's head snapped backward. Haynes staggered, arms flailing. He fell against the square brick hearth jutting out from the wall with a sickening crack when his skull met the stone, then he lay still.

Cade spun away, looking for his sister.

Outside in the hallway, the sound of running footsteps pounded closer.

"I'm a-comin', Mr. Norris. I had to git my shotgun."

Cotannah huddled against the desk, staring at Cade with huge eyes still full of fear. They recognized him now, though.

Relief mixed with the adrenaline still pumping through him. It made his hands shake as he bent to grab his shirt, which had landed at her feet.

"Put this on, sweetheart," he said urgently as he slipped it over her head. "I want you to run. Get your horse and ride for home. Don't stop. Don't talk to anyone."

Her hands moved feebly toward her wound.

Cade caught them and thrust them into the billowing shirtsleeves as he glanced at the line of blood across her chest. The cut wasn't deep, but it would leave a scar.

"Haynes will come to any minute," he said, as the shirt fell down to cover her. "Go, now. Go home!"

She went.

Cade stood by the door to the hall, watching her retreating as she ran the few feet to the veranda doors.

Guilt tore at him. He should have stayed close enough to home to keep this from happening.

"He pushed his way past me and attacked Mr. Haynes in the office!" Norris screeched.

Cade turned to see the skinny secretary dashing across the room to the headmaster.

A burly man in overalls filled the doorway, holding the butt of a shotgun against his rounded stomach. Its muzzle pointed straight at Cade.

"Stay right where you are, Injun, and don't make any sudden moves or I'll let you have it with both barrels!"

Cade froze.

From the corner of his eye he saw Norris kneeling next to Haynes, trying to rouse him. Roy moved slowly into the room, walking toward Norris while holding the muzzle of the gun on Cade. The empty doorway filled up with curious white faces, and the air filled with horrified murmurings.

But Norris silenced them.

"He's *dead*!" he screamed. "Oh, God, that savage has killed Mr. Haynes! He's not taken a breath since I found him."

Haynes lay where he had fallen in exactly the same position. Norris lifted one of his hands, then let it drop lifelessly to the floor.

Cade stared at them, his head buzzing, his stomach churning. Could it be true? Could he actually have killed the slimy bastard?

"Somebody go for the sheriff!" Norris shouted at the people crowding the doorway.

Then he looked at Roy, and with a shaking finger pointed at Cade. "Tie him up!" he screamed.

"He's a big 'un," Roy muttered, "and a murderin' savage. I'd best keep my sights on him whilst you tie him with your belt."

"You'll rue the day you ever pushed me aside and bulled your way in here like the arrogant heathen you are!" Norris babbled, drawing his belt from its loops and advancing on Cade. "I've sent for the sheriff. Your red hide'll be sitting in the Van Buren jail before you know what hit you."

Cade's insides constricted. There was nothing, nothing on the face of the earth, that he hated more than confinement.

Especially in a white man's institution.

Jail in Van Buren, a Choctaw charged with killing a white man, would be a whole lot worse than this hell of a boarding school ever was.

"Murdering red savage," Norris ranted. "Turn around and put your hands together behind your back."

Cade didn't move.

Roy slid the pump on the gun.

Cade turned around. He'd certainly be no help to Cotannah lying dead on the ground. He squared his shoulders and put his hands, his fists, behind his back.

Then he looked out through the glass doors, swiftly searching the campus. There she was! Her slight form was running like the wind toward the horse pasture, his long shirttail billowing out behind her.

Norris slapped the leather belt around and around Cade's wrists, drawing it up and jerking it tighter than the knot that filled Cade's belly.

It squeezed the heart out of him. He should have let Roy shoot him, for he was a dead man anyway. He was a Choctaw who had killed a white man. He might as well get his mind around that.

He was going to hang.

Maggie pressed her fingertips to the cool, smooth top of the dry-goods counter at Brown and Young's Mercantile and looked at the picture in Godey's Lady's Book. Mrs. Brown was holding the book propped open against her ample bosom so that all of the Harrington girls and their mother could see it at the same time.

They were all looking at a lace-drenched

dress with a bustle. It could have had three sleeves and a skirt cut off above the knees for all Maggie cared, but she stared at it as hard as she could because that was better than looking at the pale, stricken face of her favorite sister, Emily.

"Don't you agree with me, Amanda Louise?" the merchant's wife asked Mama. "Won't these dresses go a long, long ways to make Emily's wedding the most spectacular that Van Buren, Arkansas, ever has seen?"

When she realized what she'd said, a pink flush stained her cheeks as she looked from Eustacia to Emma and back again, her lips twitching in her haste to soften the remark. "Except for your other daughters, of course!" she trilled. "You ladies know, now, that I thought that your weddings were absolutely beautiful! It's just that . . ."

Her darting brown eyes lit on Maggie.

"And yours will be, too, dear Margaret. Next year, it'll be your turn, won't it?"

The thought made Maggie's blood freeze.

Recently her father had started bringing dull, sloppy Neidell Kurtz, the banker's balding bookkeeper of a son, to dinner. In the same, sudden way he'd first brought in Asa Cunningham.

Poor Emily. How awful it would be to be married to Asa, a man older than — and nearly as mean as — her father.

"No," Maggie said clearly. "It won't be my

turn until *I* have decided who will be my groom."

Her three sisters and her mother all whipped their heads around to look at her. The smile froze on Mrs. Brown's face.

"Oh, my goodness," Mama exclaimed. "Maggie doesn't mean that the way it sounded!"

She assaulted Maggie with her sweetest smile and with tears that sprang suddenly into her large, hazel eyes. "Do you, Margaret Lea?"

Maggie didn't drop her gaze.

"I don't know how it sounded," she said stubbornly. "But I mean it."

"Oh, Maggie!" Emily cried. "You know you would seek Mama and Papa's advice on such a serious decision, just as all the rest of us girls have done! Why, honey, some rake might fool you . . ."

The tremor in her sister's voice made Maggie want to scream. Poor, scared Emily. Asa Cunningham was the farthest thing in the world from a rake. Emily, meek as she was, would give anything right now to be fooled by a rake. To be carried off by a rapscallion and ravished so that maybe Asa would refuse her.

Oh, dear God, Emily's wedding would take place soon, too soon. Thanksgiving was only six weeks away!

"Anybody can fool any of us and anybody can dictate to us, if we let them," Maggie said, looking from Emily's pale face to her mother's.

"Anybody can take our lives away and make us live them however they choose, if we allow it!"

"Maggie!"

Along with the tears, Mama's eyes began to fill with panic and horrified hurt.

Maggie laid her palms flat down on the unyielding glass and bit her tongue against all the fury inside her, raging to come out right here in the mercantile.

Mama set great store by what the people of Van Buren thought and said about the Harringtons. She was proud that theirs was one of the most prominent families in town, along with the Stones, of course. But shy Judge Stone and his mother, Miss Cordia, who were Old South aristocracy come west to Arkansas long before the war, were both old, and the judge was the last of his line. Mama had four young ladylike daughters and two grandchildren to carry on her social position, and she was proud of them. Mama was a proud person. Her reputation meant everything to her.

Even if she did let her husband boss her around every minute of her life as if she were his slave.

Her three oldest daughters followed in her footsteps.

Emily was younger and sweeter than Emma and Eustacia and she was the most pliable. She was going into this Thanksgiving wedding to old Asa Cunningham like a lamb to the slaughter.

Maggie reached around Eustacia and grabbed Emily by the arm.

"Mama, Mrs. Brown, excuse us for a moment, please," she said.

She ignored Eustacia and Emma. If either one had had the spunk to stand up to Pierce about choosing *their* own husbands, maybe Emily would have found the courage to refuse this obscene marriage.

Maggie tugged at Emily, pulling her away from the group huddled at the dry-goods counter.

"Come over here," she hissed into her sister's ear. "I have to say something or else I'll burst."

"Well!" She heard her mama say cheerfully for Mrs. Brown's benefit. "Let's look at the fabrics. The bride will be with us again in a minute, and we can have some choices lined out for her."

"Hear that?" Maggie demanded as she guided the hapless Emily as far as she could from the others, into the curve of the bay window that looked onto the street.

Emily jerked her arm free, but Maggie held onto her with her fierce gaze.

"At least Mama's going to give you a choice of fabrics," she said. "That's more than Pierce did when he picked your groom for you!"

"Maggie, if you don't quit calling Papa by his first name, you're going to go down below when you die!" Emily cried.

She glanced back at the others to see if they could overhear.

"I'll only call him Father when Mama makes me," Maggie snapped. "And I'll never call him Papa for as long as I live."

"B-but . . ."

"Hush up about that and listen to me!" Maggie whispered desperately. "Emily, you don't have to pick out these dresses and you don't have to marry Asa. I know that the very thought of it is making you sick! Refuse to do it. You're educated! You could run away from here and teach school!"

"B-but . . ." Emily stammered, as she always did when she was worried, which was most of the time, "I . . . I couldn't do that. Think of how *furious* Papa would be!"

"I'll help you! I'll stand with you, Emily, if you'll only stand up to him!"

For one shining second, hope flared in Emily's big brown eyes.

Then a tear drowned it.

"I can't, Sister," she said, through lips stiff with pain. "But thank you. Thanks, Maggie. I'll never forget that you offered, but you know as well as I do that if we ever did set out to go against Papa, we'd need the help of the Devil himself."

"Well, help or no help, *I'm* going to go against him!" Maggie cried. "I'll refuse to marry Mr. Pig as long as there's a breath in my body!"

Emily giggled through her tears.

"Maggie, someone may hear you call Neidell Mr. Pig, and he isn't even fat! I'll declare, you are so disrespectful, Sister!"

"No," Maggie said, imitating Neidell Kurtz's eager dinnertime expression to keep Emily chuckling. "I'm truthful. He's not fat but he's greedy, purely greedy. Anyone who's stuffing himself because the food is free, shoveling in English peas by sticking them to spoonfuls of sweet potatoes, deserves the name Mr. Pig."

Her heart leaped when Emily laughed, truly laughed, that time.

But just as quickly, she sobered.

"Neidell's only hungry for good food because he and his father batch and do for themselves," Emily said, determined as always, just like Mama, to put a good face on things. "If Neidell's mother was alive . . ."

"If they weren't tight as the bark on a tree they could hire a cook," Maggie snapped.

But Emily was no longer interested in the Kurtzes' eating habits.

"I can't defy Papa, Maggie," she said, sadly. "And I'm scared to death of what will happen to you if you do."

She grabbed both of Maggie's hands with her cold, trembling ones.

"You're so brave, Maggie, you're lots braver than I am," she whispered. "But please don't make a scene at the levee tonight. Mama has worked so hard on it and she'd be *crushed* if you embarrassed everyone!"

"I won't!" Maggie promised.

Then, suddenly, her whole body felt as if it would collapse. "It's making me crazy to see you so sick at heart!" she cried. "I can't stand it, Mimi, I just cannot bear it!"

Using the old pet name made them both start crying. Maggie fumbled in her empty pocket for a handkerchief.

Emily opened the small bag hanging from her wrist, took out a scrap of cloth and pressed it into Maggie's hand. She squeezed her sister's fingers just once, then she turned away.

"I never knew that just choosing the dresses for weddings could make people cry," she trilled, with a brittle little laugh that was so like Mama's when she was hiding *her* bad feelings. "Now, what fabrics have you all decided would be best?"

Maggie closed her ears and clamped her jaw shut. She wouldn't say another word.

But her heart filled to bursting with fear and fury.

Was Mimi truly lost, like Mama? Was there nothing Maggie could do to save her?

Well, if she couldn't save them, she could, by the grace of God, save herself. Thank goodness she had a whole year to figure out how to avoid marrying Mr. Pig!

She turned her back on the whole room and walked to the window, where she pressed her forehead against one of its square panes to cool herself down. At least the rain had stopped. Driving from their house on the hill to Main Street in that depressing downpour had made this horrid occasion even more pathetic.

"Murderer!"

The clarion shout came from someone in the street as a crowd poured down the hill. A phalanx of horsemen rode around the bank corner, the sheriff in the lead. As they came onto Main Street they slowed. A man sitting in a wagon suddenly stood up and shouted, his words carrying clearly into the mercantile through the open door.

"Sheriff, I say don't bother stoppin' at the jailhouse. Ride on down to the river and we'll hang that murderin' Choctaw from the big oak tree!" The man took a raw, gasping breath. "Ungrateful heathen! To think he was raised at th'academy there, and now he's come back and killed his own teachers!"

The sheriff didn't answer but spurred his horse to move farther out in front of the tight little group. The mounted man behind him followed—he had no choice, for the ends of his reins were clutched in the sheriff's fist.

That must be the prisoner. The murderer.

The crowd and the women inside the store made a horrified murmuring sound.

Except for Maggie. The sight of him took her breath away.

He shone. His half-naked, rain-wet body glistened in the sunlight like polished copper.

His hair gleamed black. It was long, tied at the nape, but she only noticed for a moment.

It was his eyes that mesmerized her.

His eyes held her fast.

They burned, *flamed*, with a dark disdain. He looked out across the river as if he were king of the world.

He and the big iron gray looked like a centaur; he sat the horse effortlessly, with no movement at all. His body belonged to the horse and the stallion's strength to him.

He rode a fantastic, pale tan saddle covered with intricate carvings that she could see even from a distance had been done by hand and trimmed with sparkling silver. Enough silver to tempt any traveler on a lonesome road to try to take it away from him.

But who would have such courage?

The heavy muscles of his wide shoulders and deep, powerful chest rippled with invincibility.

Above his tall, black, boots that reached nearly to his knees, beneath finely woven gray cord breeches soaked to his body tight as a second skin, the long saddle muscles of his thighs flexed, bulging heavy with might. The gray danced nervously, but his rider seemed not even to notice.

Nothing about him had ever known fear.

His majestic gaze moved past the sheriff and the rabble-rouser standing up in the wagon, ignoring both. Then he turned his head, and his fiery eagle's eyes found Maggie's.

Never, ever, had she looked into so fierce a

gaze. She couldn't bear it, she could not. Yet she couldn't look away.

The look pulled the two of them out of the crowd, connected them above it, he on his horse and she in the window over the street.

I am caught, he seemed to say.

I know how you feel. I would almost rather be hanged than to stay in the trap I'm in, she responded.

Tears stung her eyes. He was the most magnificent man she had ever seen, and the most dangerous, yet he was bound.

His hot, black eyes seared her. Something contracted deep inside her.

He made Emily's words ring out in Maggie's mind: *If we ever did set out to go against Papa, we'd need the help of the Devil himself.*

Chapter 2

Maggie stopped in her tracks in the arched doorway of the parlor, her heart fluttering like a frightened bird. Fear darted up and down her spine in rhythm with the lilting strains of the Stephen Foster song the musicians were playing, and it pushed into her throat to nearly choke her. She couldn't go in to the parlor.

If she went in there, she'd be smothered. From too many people, too much music. From too little air, as every corner was filled with the heavy scents of the late roses Mama had commandeered from gardens all over town.

No. She wouldn't smother. Pierce would kill her first.

She couldn't see him in the room full of dancers, but surely he would be in a fit by now. Refusing to stand with the rest of the family in the receiving line at this levee was the most daring of all her rebellious acts so far. No telling what he would do to punish her: maybe he'd even sell her beloved Joanna, the saddle horse Grandpa had given her.

He had threatened that before, but he hadn't

done it—instead he dangled the threat over her head like a thundercloud, knowing that she'd do anything to protect that horse, her dearest treasure, her remembrance of Grandpa. The very thought that Pierce might take Joanna away sent Maggie's heart plummeting into her shoes and made her breath come short.

However there was no way on Earth she could have stood in front of the mantel with her family, greeting guests, as Pierce had decreed they should do. She would have to murmur over and over again, to every person, how pleased she was about Emily's plans. How Emily was sure to be happy. How nice it was that Emily was marrying a Van Buren man and would be building a house here on Harrington Hill near her parents as Emma and Eustacia had done.

No. She would *not* dishonor herself with such lies.

She drew in a deep breath. Perhaps she could sneak into the room and lose herself in the crowd, perhaps she wouldn't have to face Pierce until morning. She took a small step, then she stopped.

Neidell Kurtz stood beside the refreshment table, stuffing his face with one hand while he reached for the plate of peppermint tea cakes with the other. His soft, damp fingers would be sticky from the pastries. His hands were always moist, and so was his forehead.

She wanted to gag. She couldn't go in there.

If she did, he would ask her to dance. If she refused, he would make a scene. Then Pierce would truly kill her.

Neidell turned then, holding a whole fistful of tea cakes, and glanced her way. When he saw her his face lit up, and he began making his way toward her.

Maggie whirled and fled, not even knowing where to go but running anyway, glancing back over her shoulder to see whether he was still following. Fortunately, it would take a little while for him to cross the crowded parlor.

Suddenly she heard voices up ahead, just around the corner. Her blood congealed when she realized it was Pierce's voice!

She tried frantically to look for a hiding place. She grabbed and twisted the first doorknob she saw, plunging into the darkened room, pushing the door closed behind her. With a start, she realized she was in Pierce's study.

She stood stock-still in the middle of the room, thinking how furious he'd be if he knew she had entered his sacred territory. She and her sister were never allowed in this room. If he caught her here, it would be worse, much worse, than dancing with Neidell.

"I've made a decision that will solve the whole problem . . ."

Her heart stopped. Pierce! Right at the door! Heaven help her, he and whoever he was with were coming in, and there was no way she could get out, except through the window.

Frantically, she felt her way through the darkness. She found the horsehair settee across the room from the looming rolltop desk and slipped around behind it. She tried to remember whether there was more furniture between the desk and the wall, tried to picture the room as she and Emily had seen it when they peeked in through the window.

Pierce would die of apoplexy if he knew how many times they had done that, how many times they had watched him, swiveling back and forth in front of the desk, lecturing Mama as if he were a schoolmaster berating a wayward child. She and Emily had spied so they could know in advance what Mama would make them do, but they had also seen where he hid the extra key to unlock the bottom drawer that held the many account books he frowned and muttered over.

They had decided that it was what was in those account books that made him so mean. But whatever the cause, he *was* mean by nature, and he *was* intending for Mr. Neidell Pig to marry her next year—unless she died of fright right now.

Behind her, the latch clicked and she heard the music and the voices of the party—and people coming in.

". . . right in here, gentlemen," Pierce said.

Maggie reached out with both arms, and her fingertips touched the velvet draperies. Thank

God! She slipped behind them just as the door opened wide.

Terror made her legs shake badly, so she stiffened her knees and leaned back against the wall. She couldn't live like this, running from Neidell, scared spitless of Pierce. She had to start making definite plans to leave Van Buren, to go to Texas in the spring.

But how could she take over her *rancho*? If only Grandpa Macroom hadn't put in his will that she must be twenty-five to take possession of it! That was seven years from now; seven long years she couldn't wait. If Grandpa had only known his son-in-law better, he would have realized that Pierce would marry her off before she was twenty-five and her husband would take control of her property!

She heard several people shuffle across the room, and two or three voices rumbled. She recognized Judge Stone's and Sheriff Ames's.

"I'll show you the accounts, Kurtz," Pierce said. She heard the clink of glass on glass; he must have lifted the chimney and lit the lamp.

"And then you'll see we're telling you the truth, Kurtz," Judge Stone said, urgently. He was almost pleading. "None of us is making a fortune in this deal, but it's a sweet little extra income for all of us, including you."

Kurtz? Was Neidell here?

"Remember," the judge went on, "it's vital that we all stick together tight! It'll be an awful mess if the public gets a whiff of scandal."

What scandal?

Chairs creaked and drawers opened and closed. Someone lit a cigar.

"My cooperation is essential," an assured voice said, "and I only want to see how your shares are divided before Pierce and I . . ."

Neidell's father was speaking. Of course. The unctuous banker Jefferson Kurtz, and not his son, would be the one having a private meeting with the most powerful men in the county.

Pierce interrupted him.

"We came in here to make a formal agreement, gentlemen," he said in a calm voice. "After that's done, Kurtz will have no room to complain about anything."

Maggie heard paper rustling.

After a moment, a chair squeaked loudly. The portly banker was probably leaning back in one of the swivel chairs.

Maggie stared at the blackness of the velvet draperies. She strained her ears and heard Sheriff Ames's rough voice.

"All right, Kurtz, are you satisfied the books show that you haven't been cheated?"

"This is a federal crime, this paying the court vouchers at a discount . . ." Mr. Kurtz began, thoughtfully.

"Don't even *think* about blackmail," Ames interrupted. "Think about how accidents happen on dark roads and how bank robbers sometimes kill the banker."

Silence.

"Don't *you* even think about threats, Ames,"

the judge said quickly, and so firmly that Maggie was surprised. "Such as that only weakens us."

"Yes," Pierce said, "Hired villains always talk, eventually. Such a scheme could bring us all down."

Maggie's pulse beat hard and fast. A federal crime! Blackmail and threats! Good heavens, what was this whole conversation about?

Smoke drifted into her hideaway. She tried to hold her breath so she wouldn't sneeze, but she realized she needn't worry about betraying her hiding place: Terror held her frozen, inside and out.

"Here's what we've decided," Pierce said abruptly. "This will stop Kurtz cryin' that he's getting squeezed in the voucher deal, for all time."

"He's *not* getting more money," Ames rumbled sourly.

"Not money," Pierce snapped. "A wedding. My daughter, Maggie, to marry his son, Neidell, next month when Emily marries Asa. A *double* Thanksgiving wedding."

Maggie felt her blood thicken and slow to a crawl.

Pierce gave the dry chuckle that, for him, was a laugh.

"Save myself some cash, giving one wedding instead of two, and then I'll be able to borrow more any time from my new banker in-laws!"

Maggie's eyes stretched open so wide they

stung. The back of her head burned with a shimmering heat that spread like the palm of a hand over her scalp. Her beating heart went still as midnight in winter.

"Miss Maggie agrees t' that plan?" Ames asked, as all the men laughed and muttered congratulations for Pierce's cleverness. "It's hard for me to see ol' Neidell gittin' a handle on that little vixen—no offense meant, Jefferson—I don't know who could."

"The little vixen doesn't know about it yet, but her mother will make her see reason," Pierce said. "True, she's always been fractious as a cat, much more so than my other daughters, but this'll work out. You'll see."

He sounded obnoxiously, gleefully well satisfied. Nothing made Pierce Harrington happier than manipulating people, moving them around at his pleasure like playing pieces on a chessboard.

Maggie stared straight ahead into the blank darkness of the thick draperies, her mind whirling, straining and stumbling. He was selling her in a business deal. Pierce was bargaining her life away to save his money. His and Ames's and Judge Stone's.

Ill-gotten money. Illegal money. Pierce was into something that was a federal crime. All of them were.

Even Judge Stone! How in the world had he found the nerve to get into this? How could he risk Miss Cordia's wrath by betraying the family honor if the scheme ever came to light?

Miss Cordia was as mean as Pierce.

"Kurtz, do you swear that the marriage of Pierce Harrington's youngest daughter to your son will stop your bellyaching about the split?"

That was Judge Stone's voice, shaking a little, demanding a formal promise.

"Yes," Kurtz said promptly. "A family connection to the Harringtons will more than satisfy me."

"Just remember," the judge said, more forcibly. "You're in this just as deep as we are."

"Except I'm not an elected official," Mr. Kurtz said, sharply.

"Nobody wants to trust their money to a crooked banker," the judge shot back.

"It's all right," Neidell's father said, soothingly. "Don't worry, judge, don't worry about a thing. You boys go on right ahead with your scheme through the Arkansas River Bank."

Satisfied murmurs sounded all around.

"Won't be much profit in this next trial," Pierce complained, his teeth clenched on his cigar. "That Injun savage'll hang quick as greased lightning."

"True," said Judge Stone, thoughtfully. His voice had become stronger. "We won't have many witnesses and we won't make much off the jurors' vouchers—they'll not work more than half a day to hang him."

A drawer closed. Pierce's chair squeaked. When he spoke again, Maggie knew that he had stood up.

"Men," he said jovially, "we'd best get back to th' levee. You know the ladies have missed us."

The noise of footsteps floated to Maggie, then the door opened. The chimney of the lamp clinked again. More footsteps, and the door closed.

Maggie lifted her stiff arms and hugged herself, trying to hold her body together while her mind whirled.

She wouldn't stay in Pierce's house another night. She was leaving for Texas tonight, not some faraway night next spring. She no longer had a year to make her plans. She had only hours.

Through the dark, through the wisps of lingering smoke, she fumbled for the cords and jerked the drapes open. Moonlight flooded in. Luckily it was enough to see by; heaven knew she didn't dare use the lamp.

She ran across the room to Pierce's desk, pushed the chair away, and felt for the extra key in its leather case bradded to the bottom of the center drawer. Such a daring deed scared her, so much that she felt the key burn, then freeze, the tips of her fingers, making her feel as if her hands had been peeled. Setting her teeth, she drew the key out and unlocked the bottom drawer.

Grandfather Macroom's will and the deed to Las Manzanitas had to be there. If Pierce kept in this desk the accounts of a scheme that amounted to a federal crime, then her important papers must be in there, too.

Who cared if the will said she must be twenty-five to own the ranch? At this moment she would take the property away from the Mexican Army with her bare hands if necessary.

The account books were on top. She took them out, set them in her lap, and reached back in. Her fingertips touched a stiff, leather envelope tied with a frayed, silken cord; they followed the flow of the carvings in the worn leather, all the same symbol, scattered thickly over the folded case. The Running M, the Manzanitas brand.

She slid the heavy papers out and opened them, scanning quickly as she leaned toward the moonlight.

DEED OF GIFT
August 4, 1866

I, Hugh Seamus O'Connell Macroom, for a consideration of "Love and Affection" do hereby deed title to the 517,000 acres of the original Spanish land grant known as the Rancho Rincon de las Manzanitas in the County of Nueces and the 40,000 good and well-watered acres known as the Rancho San Juan del Tule in the County of Hidalgo, both in the State of Texas, to my beloved Granddaughter, Miss Margaret Lea Harrington, presently of Van Buren, Arkansas, to be solely

*hers without stricture when she shall achieve
the age of eighteen years.*

Eighteen years! Not twenty-five!

Pierce had lied to her. A terrible, stinging pain paralyzed her heart.

For four long years he had lied to her about her precious dream! And she had turned eighteen this past spring!

Her hands started shaking as if they were palsied, but she managed to replace the deed and to glance at the will. It said the same thing.

Fury rose in her: the blind, screaming fury of a daughter betrayed, a daughter who would have loved to love her father and trust her mother. She blocked out all thoughts of her mother while she tucked her papers under her arm. As she began to replace the account books, she opened the last one.

DIVISION OF PROFITS, DISCOUNTED PAYMENT VOUCHERS

Harrington	Stone	Ames

Beneath the headings were listed pages of names, each followed by the designation "Juror," "Witness," or "Marshal." Each name had a voucher number and two amounts beside it, the difference between them divided equally among the three columns.

Her hands clung to the hard covers of the book. If Pierce came after her, if he caught her and tried to bring her back to marry Neidell, this, *this* would be her key to freedom.

When the door to her room burst open, Maggie nearly jumped out of her skin. She slammed her valise shut and whirled around, trying to hide it behind her.

"Emily!" she cried. "Dear Lord, Mimi, you scared me out of my wits!"

Emily took one look at Maggie, closed the door, and threw the latch.

"Oh, Maggie, *what* are you doing in a riding dress at this time of night? Papa is furious. He sent me to tell you that he knows you aren't sick and that he'll see you at seven in the morning."

"By seven in the morning I'll be long gone."

Maggie went to her armoire and jerked it open.

"W-where are you going? W-where?"

"Las Manzanitas," Maggie said, while she pulled out an inside drawer and reached to the very back of it for her small suede bag of money and jewelry. "I'm leaving Van Buren tonight."

She tucked the stash into her open bodice, then turned to Emily, whose face had gone pale.

"He's lied to me all these years, Mimi! Las Manzanitas was mine the minute I turned eighteen."

"No! Maggie . . . you can't run away! Papa will *kill* you!"

"He wanted to keep control of the *rancho*," Maggie fumed, "until I was married and then Pierce could tell my husband how to manage it and take some of the profits, just the way he does with Eustacia and Emma's husbands!"

"H-he'll ride after you and bring you back," Emily cried, reaching for her. "Maggie! Even if he doesn't, the robbers and outlaws that roam the Texas Road will get you. Even after you reach the *rancho*, raiders from Mexico might harm you. R-remember how lawless it is down there and how many outriders we had to hire to travel safely to the ranch when Grandpa died!"

Maggie's fingers went cold as she buttoned her bodice. Both pursuit and attack had been much on her mind ever since she'd actually begun to pack.

This was real. This wasn't one of the fantasies she'd indulged in a thousand times while lying in her bed waiting for sleep to come. Of how she would go to Texas, of what she would take with her, of how she would make her escape.

Of how she would take possession of the land that was hers and live her life out-of-doors, on horseback, wild and free. Free.

This was real and she'd have to do everything exactly right, or the sky would come down on her head.

"You can't g-go that f-far by yourself," Emily persisted. "You'll h-have to h-have h-help!"

"Then come with me! Hurry, Mimi, change your clothes and let's go! You can escape from Asa and Pierce both!"

This time, not even a flicker of hope showed in Emily's teary eyes.

"No, you'd b-better stay here," she said, before she started to cry. "M-Maggie, even if you reached the *rancho* in one piece, you don't know a thing about running it. And you can't depend on Bascom—who knows if he even came back from the war?"

Bascom was real, too, and Maggie had almost forgotten about him. She let her temper flare up to warm her.

"I hope he didn't come back! Bascom was mean and jealous, and he fancied himself Grandpa's foster son. I hope he stayed gone!"

"I hope he's there!" Emily cried. "At l-least, he's someone familiar. And you're both grown up now."

Maggie ran to the bed, grabbed up the jacket to her riding dress, and stuck her arms into the sleeves. The October breeze, blowing in through the window, chilled her down to the bone. She jerked the top quilt off the bed, too, folded and rolled it tightly, and buckled the outside straps of her valise around it.

"Emily, I'll run that *rancho* even if it kills me."

Emily sniffed ostentatiously.

"Those vaqueros, white *and* Mexican, will laugh in your face," she declared. "They'll never work for a woman. And what foreman will? Who will you hire to boss them if Bascom *is* gone?"

That fundamental truth was too much for Maggie.

"*Lord*, Emily!" she cried, stomping her foot as she turned on her. "You've only been to the *rancho* once, and you hated it. How do you know so much about running it?"

But, for once, fury didn't faze her sister. It didn't even make her stutter.

"Here's what I know," she said, and fixed Maggie with a bright brown gaze while she let the tears roll down her cheeks unchecked. "I know Papa will catch you before you get out of Van Buren and make you marry somebody a whole lot worse than Neidell Kurtz."

Fear struck Maggie's heart like the slash of a sword.

"He'll have to go a long way to find that somebody!" Maggie cried. "And he won't catch me!"

"D-do you have a w-weapon?"

"The knife Grandpa gave me," Maggie said, "and in case of emergency, I took some stuff out of Bessie's sack of potions and poultices. Thank her for me, all right?"

She turned away then, grabbing up her valise and the battered cowboy hat she'd worn at the ranch long ago. She slapped it onto her head, and tightened its strings beneath her chin.

"That hat doesn't make you a *ranchero*!" Emily cried. "Maggie, you're playacting as if we were children. You've gone crazy! You'll get yourself killed!"

"I learned a lot from the stories Grandpa told and from riding the ranch with him," Maggie said firmly.

She hoisted her valise and bedroll onto her shoulder, then strode across the room to the window that opened out onto the back porch roof. Emily ran after her, caught her by the shoulders, and pulled her around into a desperate hug.

Maggie dropped her valise and held her sister close. Words of comfort flew to the tip of her tongue. She wanted to tell Emily that she had the account book, a true weapon to use against Pierce.

But she sealed her lips. Emily would be more scared than ever, thinking that Maggie would challenge their father so boldly. Moreover, Emily's conscience would drive her to tell their mother that Pierce was doing something illegal. That would be a torment to Mama, who would be torn between her strict moral code and her loyalty to her husband.

No, Emily was better off not knowing.

"I'll miss you," Maggie said instead. "Good luck in your . . . new life, Mimi."

"You're the one who needs the luck," Emily said, sobbing. "I'll pray for you."

She let Maggie go then and stood still, watching Maggie as she put one leg through the window, bent, and stepped out onto the roof. Maggie moved slowly, testing the slick soles of her riding boots on the shingles, looking ahead to the huge branches of the overhanging oak.

She had almost reached the cover of the tree when Emily's call made her look back. Mimi had thrust the whole upper half of her body out the window.

"*Think*, Maggie! *Think* how Papa is!" she called, sobbing pitifully. "You need someone to help you."

Her words stopped Maggie so quickly that she slid on the roof, making the account book and the leather envelope from Las Manzanitas in her pocket slap hard against her leg. Maggie caught the end of the nearest big tree branch.

Her heart halted, then started up again, knocking like a frantic messenger against her ribs.

"I'll think about it, Mimi," she promised, but her mind was whirling, grabbing bits of truth and fitting them faster and faster into a wild, foolhardy plan.

She did not hear another word from Emily.

Instead she tumbled headlong into the darkness of the tree, scooting in among the thick leaves and along the stout branch to its huge, solid trunk. Her arms fell gratefully around it, and she slid downward, slipping toward the ground as smoothly as the shocking scheme was falling together in her mind.

Her breath caught in her throat and wouldn't come down into her chest. Did she dare? She had to.

To get out of Van Buren without Pierce's knowledge would take a miracle. To ride safely, alone, eight hundred miles into the wilds of Texas would take another, even bigger, one. And once she arrived at Las Manzanitas, giving orders to the hard men who worked there, much less knowing what orders to give, would take a veritable act of God.

If she could use the account book against Pierce, then she could use it as blackmail against the judge and the sheriff, to buy freedom for the Choctaw prisoner. *He* was the man, the only man, who could do what she needed to be done.

Even if he *was* a dangerous murderer.

She had to risk it. She had no choice.

The walls of the jail cell closed around Cade like a giant's fist. It squeezed him full length, tightened his lungs so that he could take only the shallowest of breaths.

Cade stood rigid, as he had done ever since the jailer had locked his cell, and stared out into the dark through the bars. The branches of the huge sycamore tree brushed the window, rustled and whispered to him, as if to comfort him. But not even that tree held enough power to calm him.

The leaves moved in the crisp night wind, turning black and then silver in the moonlight, beckoning him to come out. But he would never ride into the sensuous arms of a sweet-tart autumn again.

He would never ride Smoke again. Nor any other horse.

He would never be free again. They were going to hang him.

His heart started beating so hard and fast that he thought it would burst. It sent his blood stampeding into his head. He clenched his fists, hit them hard against his thighs.

He would do anything, *anything* to get out of here!

Panic clawed at him. He turned away from the enticing moonlit wind and began to pace back and forth across the small cell. He needed to be free.

He would do anything.

What if *the feeling* came over him and he was caught in a cell, unable to step onto his horse and ride away? Would he die of its prickling unease?

It would serve him right, for letting his restlessness rule him all those years when he was free. He'd been a worthless rambler, a roustabout, a man so selfish, so irresponsible that he had neglected his family and let a tragedy almost happen to them.

If he could get out, if he could get free, he would take care of his people, he would live in the Nation, he would make a family for Cotannah with Aunt Ancie and Uncle Jumper. They needed him.

No telling what would happen to them in the years to come if they were left on their own. They had no idea how to cope with the white world—sending Cotannah to the academy had proved that. They needed him, and they had needed him all this long time that he had been gone.

But he couldn't stay in one place. It would kill him.

Guilt, fear, and hot regret washed over him in a wave as he hit the stone wall and turned on his heel to pace the other way. If he could, he would make it up to them. Some way.

He would do *anything* to get out of here.

He measured his steps to the rhythm of those words marching through his head.

If only he had stayed in the Nation where he belonged, and grown up in the Choctaw way, if only he had become a shape-changer— then he could get out of here!

But if he had stayed with his Choctaw roots, he wouldn't be in this fix. The thought stopped his restless feet in their tracks.

He hadn't stayed in the Nation because of the tragedies foretold by the red sky burning—his father's death and his mother's. Had it also meant that he, too, would die young, even younger than they?

Was this unjust hanging by white men another experience with an ironic message?

He wouldn't think about it. He would be a real Choctaw and put his mind to the here and now. Somehow, pray God, he would find a way to get out of here.

He turned and paced the other way, back toward the window, lifting his face to catch the tantalizing, traitorous strumpet of a breeze tempting him to go with her and then blowing away without him.

Oh, dear God, he would do anything to get out of here! *Anything*.

Suddenly, a door banged against a wall somewhere, and the wind swept in carrying with it the sound of a woman's voice, a voice as tart and lightly sweet as the night itself.

"The Choctaw prisoner," she said. "I must see him this instant. Don't argue with me. I have no time to lose!"

Chapter 3

The blood in Cade's veins froze. She had to mean him—he was the only prisoner. Who was she?

"Nobody's allowed to talk to th' prisoner," one jailer said. "We got orders to keep the lanterns burning and everybody out of here. You gotta wait for Sheriff Ames to git back, miss."

"The judge is right behind me," she said. "He'll tell you it's all right. Now, step aside."

She sounded young. And spirited.

Cade heard the voices of both deputies raised in protest, and then the noise of rapid, light footsteps striking the wooden floor. He stepped to the bars and stared down the narrow hallway.

The girl rounded the corner, both deputies at her heels. She turned toward them and stopped.

"This is a private matter," she said. "Leave us, please."

Three lanterns hung at intervals along the wall, but Cade couldn't see her face beneath the wide brim of her hat. "*Leave* you!" one of the appalled lawmen gasped. "Why no! He's a murderin' savage! He's liable t' grab you through them bars an' . . ."

The outside door banged shut.

"Garrison! Branscum!"

"There's Judge Stone," the girl said. "Go."

The deputies hurried away.

She ran the last few steps toward Cade's cell, then stopped when she saw him. Her eyes flashed, but her face was still in shadow.

"I've come to get you out of here," she said, her voice suddenly breathless. "If you'll do what I ask, I can save you from hanging."

Cade's heart stopped.

She was crazy. Deranged.

Or else he was. He must have conjured her out of thin air—he was so desperate to get free that surely he was imagining her, intriguing voice and all.

"Who are you?"

"Maggie Harrington. I saw you in the street when they brought you in."

She pushed off her hat, a cowboy's hat that dangled down her back from strings tied at her throat. She took a step toward him, into the light.

"I don't know if you remember," she said, "but you saw me, too."

The lantern's glow outlined the perfect heart shape of her pale face and caught the blaze of her big blue eyes. She was a pretty little thing, with her hair spilling in curls from a rakish knot at the crown of her head.

"Yes," Cade said. "You were standing in the window."

He stared down at her, hard, determined to see the truth.

A young lady, judging from her manner and her speech. And a rich one, judging from the cut of her clothes. Yet she'd met his gaze in the street, bold as an adventuress, and she had come alone into the jail to play with his life. Spoiled, rich white girls were becoming more daring every day.

"What are you doing here, Miss Harrington?"

The words burst out of him harsh as a slap, pushing her a half-step backward. She recovered and stood her ground.

"I'm blackmailing the judge into letting you go," she said. "*If* you'll promise to take me safely to Texas and stay for a year to help me establish myself on the *rancho* I've inherited there."

"Where in Texas?"

She came another step closer.

"The Nueces Strip," she whispered. "But don't mention Texas out loud. My father will guess where I've gone, but there's no sense shouting it."

He tried to laugh, but the sound came out as more of a bark.

"You're a great actress," he said. "You seem entirely sincere."

"I *am* sincere!" she cried. "Why else would I be here?"

"On a dare," he snapped. Grasping the bars of his cell with both hands, he rattled them in her face. "To get a thrill for you and your friends. To play a little game of 'tease the wild Indian.'"

This time she set her delicate jaw and refused to move back a single inch.

"You're the one playing games," she said, keeping her voice level, "which is a stupid waste of time for a man about to hang."

"The Nueces Strip is a stupid destination for a woman," he said. "It's nothing but hell right now."

"Don't you think I know that? Why else would I be asking you to act as my escort?"

"Why me? You have the money to hire a bodyguard."

Her straight gaze never wavered.

"It has to be you because you're the only man I ever saw who's meaner than my father."

Her naive bluntness brought a harsh chuckle up from his knotted belly.

"If that's true, then aren't you afraid of me?"

"No. I'm betting you're a man of honor and you'll owe me for saving your life. If you promise to help me, then you won't hurt me."

"You're risking your life on an assumption."

That truth didn't make her back away, either.

"I'd rather risk it with you than lose it on

the certainty of the marriage my father's arranging for me."

"Hurry, Miss Maggie!" the judge's voice called angrily from the other room. "I've already sent a man to get the prisoner's horse. You two need to be gone."

The words brought Cade's heart thundering into his throat. If he could get out of this cell and step up onto Smoke again, he could fight off a lynch mob or outrun a whole town full of lawmen if necessary.

"Is this a legitimate offer she's making?" Cade shouted. "You'll turn me loose so I can be her toy soldier?"

"That's about the size of it," the judge called back, his voice cracking. "Best offer you'll get—hurry up and take it."

Cade's heart leaped, his limbs screamed to run, to ride, to get the hell out of Arkansas.

Even if this were some kind of plot to shoot him while escaping . . . but it couldn't be . . . the whole town was looking forward to his hanging.

"What do you say?" Maggie Harrington demanded, abruptly. "Have we struck a deal or not?"

"We have a deal."

"Deputy," she called, in her bright, brisk voice. "Please come open this door."

The judge barked an order, and a moment later a deputy bustled into the narrow hallway, keys in hand.

Relief flooded Cade like a river. He was getting out of here! He would be free—he'd be riding out into the night wind, leaving Van Buren forever!

"Hurry," the judge called again. "I have the marriage certificate ready, witnesses already signed."

The words took a minute to cut through Cade's elation and hit his brain. He stared at the girl.

"What marriage certificate?"

"Yours and mine," she said crisply, stepping to one side so the lawman could get to Cade's lock. "My father can't force me into a wedding if I'm already married."

Cade glared at her, but he hid the deep, strange feelings assaulting him, the bitter resentment crawling through him. God help the world, wasn't this just like the white-eyes? Give an innocent Indian a choice between hanging and marrying a stranger?

"So," he drawled coolly, "to keep your father from forcing you into an arranged marriage, you decided to come to the jail and force *me* into one?"

She smiled. She was beautiful. Any man would look at her twice, and then a third time. But she was a spoiled, overbearing white girl, determined to get her own way, accustomed to treating other people like objects.

"It's for your good, too," she said shrewdly. "We'll be traveling hundreds of miles alone, an Indian and a white woman. People would take offense if you were not my husband."

That was true. What a clever little trickster she was!

"That shows how much you know," he snapped. "People will take offense if we *are* married."

That was true, too.

"At least, if we're married, my vaqueros and my neighbors and people we meet on the road can't fault us."

"Thank God," he said wryly. "My main concern is my reputation."

This whole situation was entirely insane.

The deputy stepped between them, fit the key into the lock, and turned it with a harsh, scraping sound.

"The deal we struck was for one year," Cade said.

As if he were capable of staying in one place for a year! He physically could not do it. But he'd try. He'd do anything to get out of here.

He held his voice calm in spite of the wild feelings of resentment and relief roaring in his ears. He wasn't going to hang.

"Yes, *one year*," she said quickly, glancing at the deputy and putting a gloved finger to her full lips to remind him not to say "Texas."

If he had a scrap of integrity left in him, he would let them hang him instead of permitting them to break his pride, to force him to dishonor his word in false vows. Yet, that line of thinking was, in a practical way, as silly as this audacious girl.

He was a practical Choctaw, wasn't he? He

wanted to live, didn't he? He could certainly manage this impulsive, spoiled girl for a year. He would try his best to stay with her for a year.

After that, he could return from Texas and slip back into the Nation to take care of his family. A year from now would certainly be better than never seeing them again at all, better than leaving them forever to cope in the white world with no knowledge of how to survive in it.

What was he thinking? This pretty little piece of fluff standing in front of him would never make it to the Nueces. After a hard day or two on the trail, long before they reached Red River, she would turn tail and run back to her father and whoever he intended for her to marry.

There was no sense in going through a farce of a wedding tonight.

"Think about this," he warned her, "under your law, you'll be married to an Indian."

"It won't be *real*!" she cried.

In other words, she was too good to *really* be married to a loathsome savage. Her eyes flashed, and her delicate features, limned by the moonlight streaming in between the bars, hardened. She was horrified at the thought, even though the pretend marriage was all her idea.

His insides churned, and his head whirled as he fought the contradictory emotions catching at him. He didn't want to marry her, he wouldn't have her on a bet, yet he was seething inside because she would never, ever marry him for real. For the simple fact of his race.

And for that same fact, she was willing to *use* him in any way she saw fit.

"Hurry up," she demanded. "Are you going back on our bargain or do you agree to marry me and help me for one year?"

He made her wait for another long minute.

"It's better than hanging," he said finally, and then he stepped through the door and walked past her.

"Well, thank you very much!"

She was piqued, proving she was spoiled, he thought with a little surge of satisfaction. She was accustomed to suitors kneeling at her feet, spouting poetry about her charms. *Time to grow up, Miss Maggie.*

"Surely you don't expect a declaration of undying love?" he said, tossing the words at her over his shoulder without slowing his stride. "I won't be your lapdog."

"I'm not asking you to be!"

But she was, Maggie thought, as she hurried along behind him, followed by the curious deputy rushing up on her heels so as not to miss a single word of their exchange. Her stomach sank.

She had taken him out of his cage, this fierce panther. This smart, quick, wary stranger, this Indian who had killed a white man. Now what would she do with him? She certainly couldn't put him on a leash and lead him around.

Oh, merciful heavens, what had she done?

He moved like a panther, too, graceful and swift, around the end of the flimsy wall and into the room where the judge was pacing back and forth in front of a desk. His muscles gleamed as he passed through pools of light, great bulges on his arms and shoulders that could pick up the judge or the deputy—or her—and break them in half with no effort at all.

He filled the room with his half-naked presence.

His hard eyes scanned every corner, then came back to rest on the judge. He took a step toward him.

"My possessions are in that desk," he said. "I'll take them now."

Her heart turned over. He was the hardest man she'd ever seen. *How* was she going to control him?

Judge Stone gave him his things. He hesitated over the pistol, but one impatient gesture from the Choctaw horseman, and he handed that over, too.

The outer door burst open and a gust of wind blew Maggie's skirts hard against her legs. She whirled, glimpsing her own horse and the big gray one in the alley. The other deputy's bulk filled the opening.

"The prisoner's horse is outside, judge," he said, "but I still don't understand . . ."

"All you need to understand," the judge

barked, creasing the folded paper he held in both hands, "is that it's to all of our best interests to get this business over with quietly, and *now!*"

He moved away from the desk as the Choctaw began strapping his holster around his slim hips.

"Remember," Judge Stone said, looking from one lawman to the other. "You never saw Miss Maggie with the prisoner. They are two separate runaways."

The Indian ignored them. He tossed his long, loose hair back from his face to throw a glance at Maggie. The deputies must have taken the thong that had bound it earlier.

"Did you bring an extra horse? Food?"

She drew herself up straight and lifted her chin before she spoke, just so he'd know that he didn't intimidate her one bit.

"No," she said, "we'll buy some."

"Buying takes other people and time. We'll be riding ahead of pursuit."

"Maybe not," Maggie said, and looked at Judge Stone, who had stopped pacing and was now fidgeting nervously.

"If anyone follows me," she told him, "those letters I mentioned to you, which I already have written, will be mailed by an unknown party. Be sure to tell my father I warned you of that."

She tried to hold his shifty gaze.

"I wish Pierce could know about this wedding, too," she said. "Maybe he would declare me dead and wouldn't even *want* to bring me back."

"I'm not telling Pierce Harrington *that!*" the judge cried. "He'd kill me if he knew I married you to an Indian. I don't want to do this, Margaret."

"Do it," she said. "A married woman can't be forced to marry again."

Cornered, the judge returned her straight look with one of pure, impotent fury.

"I'll make sure there'll be no pursuit."

"How you aim to stop a posse?" one deputy demanded hoarsely. "Come morning, the whole town'll see the Injun killer's gone. They'll be yellin' for blood and me and Toby are the ones on duty to catch the blame!"

"Tell 'em the Indian killed himself," the judge said in a high, tight voice, slapping the heavy paper against his leg for emphasis. "We'll dig up that Cherokee gunslinger shot a few days ago, cover his head, and pass him off as the Choctaw. They're about the same size."

He jerked his gaze from the deputy and fixed it on Maggie while he pulled a small, black book from his coat pocket.

"Margaret Harrington," he blurted, before he'd even opened the little tome. "Do you take this man, Cade Chisk-Ko, to be your lawfully wedded husband?"

Startled by his abruptness, she said, "Y-yes."

Cade. His name was Cade.

"Cade Chisk-Ko, do you take this woman, Margaret Harrington, to be your lawfully wedded wife?"

The huge Choctaw came out from behind the desk and stood an arm's length from her. He looked at the deputies behind the judge, at Judge Stone, and then at Maggie.

"At a shotgun wedding," he drawled, "how can the groom say 'no'?"

Only then did Maggie notice that both deputies had drawn their guns. They were afraid of him. Good. Everyone else would be, too.

"No offense," Toby said to Cade. "But you're armed now."

"And I'm riding out," Cade said, ostentatiously moving his right hand away from his pistol. "No need to worry."

He could probably still draw faster than Toby could fire, Maggie thought.

"Let's get this done!" the judge cried. "Chisk-Ko. Do you promise to care for this woman in sickness and health, for better or worse, for richer or poorer, so long as you both shall live?"

"Yes."

"Miss Maggie."

He repeated the vows and she took them, her heart raging like a storm in her breast at saying the solemn words for such unholy reasons. But saving her own life and sanity was holy. And the wedding wasn't real, she kept telling herself. It wasn't real.

"That'll do," the judge snapped. "I pronounce you man and wife. Miss Maggie, here's the certificate you wanted."

"Just a moment," Cade Chisk-Ko said, in a voice that rang with unimpeachable authority.

He took a step toward her and in that one, sure movement took control of the room and everyone in it.

"Isn't there a vow in that book about a ring?"

A moment of surprised silence fell.

She didn't want a ring. If he put a ring on her finger it would say she belonged to him, and she didn't.

"I don't need to wear a ring," Maggie cried. "I just want this marriage to be a legal fact."

She just wanted to grab the certificate and run to her horse. But Judge Stone was several steps away from her and somehow, she couldn't move from where she stood. Cade Chisk-Ko had taken charge of the proceedings.

"You have a ring for her?" Judge Stone asked, incredulously.

Cade Chisk-Ko stepped to her side in a majestic gesture that was doubly striking, considering he was long-haired, half-naked, and looking savage as a storm.

"Yes."

He spoke that single word with such assurance that the judge immediately dropped his gaze to his little book.

"As a token of the sincerity of your intentions," he read, "you may present a ring to your bride."

Maggie watched, mesmerized, while her groom stuck two fingers into the front pocket of his tight pants, pulled out a tiny leather pouch, and shook a ring out into his huge palm. She stood very still as he reached for her left hand, lifted it, and began peeling off her kidskin glove, finger by finger.

His touch shocked her, benumbed her. But at the same time, as each rough, callused finger brushed against one of hers, it sensitized her. It made her whole body thrill, made her feel as if she were wearing only her skin. It made her blood race, but it stopped her breath.

He slid the ring onto her finger.

A sapphire. A beautiful, hot blue stone that flashed in the lamplight, on a silver band, surrounded by a web of delicate silver filigree.

She stared at it.

He had no right to put a ring on her! This marriage wasn't *real*! Hadn't she told him that already?

She moved to pull it off, but, swift as lightning, he squeezed her hand and captured it inside his bigger fist.

"Remember our reputations," he drawled, smiling down into her eyes with a glint of victory in his own. "We can't ride along all day holding our certificate out for everyone to read, now, can we?"

The ring burned a circle of fire around her finger. If he thought he was going to take over this whole situation, he had another think coming.

"I'm *not* wearing . . ."

He tightened his huge hand even more securely around hers and squeezed it. Gently.

"We'll be going now," he said to the room at large, his narrowed gaze on the lawmen's guns.

He tucked her arm beneath his muscled one and stepped forward to lift the marriage certificate from the judge's shaking hand.

"Remember, no pursuit," he said, with a dangerous edge to his voice. "I would hate for someone else to be killed."

Then he was whirling on the heel of his boot, pressing Maggie's arm against his hard, naked side, taking her with him toward the outer door. She could feel the heat of his body through her clothes.

She could feel the *strength* of his body—and the strength of his will—in the core of her soul as he forced her to take two steps to every one of his long strides, as he whisked her out into the wild, windy night. She'd do well to be careful of him even though he'd agreed to her bargain tonight. It was a long way to Texas.

"I'll take the marriage certificate," she said as they reached the horses. She tried to pull loose from his grasp but he wouldn't let her. "I . . . I'll carry it with my other documents."

"Fine," he said.

He pressed her arm closer and bent down to put his lips close to her ear. His breath was cedar-scented and hot, but feeling it on the side of her neck made her shiver.

"We'll have to ride quiet and stay to the shadows so the good folks of Van Buren who haven't heard about 'no pursuit' won't be jumping out of their beds and baying on our trail."

With her feet barely brushing the ground, he whisked her around to Joanna's left side. The mare was moving restlessly up and down the hitching rail opposite the gray.

"Here's your piece of paper," Cade said, then he finally let go of her.

Maggie took the certificate, shoved it deep into her pocket with her other documents, and turned to face him.

"And here's your ring," she said, starting to pull it off.

"No. We've gone this far in your little charade. Wear it."

His huge hands, hot and powerful enough to crush her, suddenly spanned her waist. Her breath lodged in her throat. He picked her up, set her unerringly into the high-cantled side-saddle on the fretful Joanna's back, and stepped away to untie the mare.

"But I don't *care* to wear a ring," Maggie said tightly, mustering all her dignity to try to counter his natural authority. "All I wanted was the certificate to show my father if he follows me."

Cade Chisk-Ko came close again, holding the reins up to her as he gave Joanna a calming pat on the neck and a muttered, "Easy, now, easy."

He glanced up at Maggie, but he ignored her words.

"Follow me, at a walk so we don't raise an alarm," he commanded, "and without another sound."

He turned away.

"I'm not ignorant," she called to him in an angry half-whisper. "I *know* why we can't gallop out of town!"

Before she even finished the sentence, he was mounted and moving. Joanna fell into step, her nose at the haunches of the gray. She was such a good little girl, doing what she was told. Restless, rebellious Joanna, who usually had to be held back every minute, walked along like an old horse pulling a dray.

Cade Chisk-Ko had gotten his way with her with only one gesture, just as he had with the judge when he had asked for his gun. Maggie stiffened her spine and sat more deeply into the saddle. She must be aware of that and not let him do the same to her. She could still feel the heat of his body against her arm and his hands spanning her waist!

Behind them, somebody, or else the wind, slammed the jailhouse door. Ahead of her, Cade Chisk-Ko moved like a shadow in the night, keeping to the dark places, riding so that the horses put their feet down silent as ghosts. The town lay quiet except for the music coming from a saloon way back up the hill on Main Street.

Above them, long buttermilk clouds scudded across the moonlit autumn sky. Maggie watched them and prayed that nobody would see her leaving Van Buren, and that Mama and Mimi would be all right.

Quickly, she looked at Cade Chisk-Ko again and tried not to think about home anymore. After all, she had plenty to think about. She was on her way to freedom, she hoped, and she had someone to protect her on the trail. Someday soon she'd be on the soil of Las Manzanitas!

Cade signaled a stop in a crescent of huge, rustling trees when they had ridden a little way downstream along the bank of the river. She rode up beside him and tried again.

"Mr. Chisk-Ko, I want you to take back this ring," she said. "It's valuable and I'd be devastated if I should lose it. I don't know how you could feel that it's so necessary for me to wear it."

He twisted around in his saddle, not to look at her as she first thought, but to open one of his saddlebags. The moonlight gleamed on his coppery skin, it caressed the muscles rippling on his huge upper arms. Watching them stirred a strange sensation inside her.

"If you don't trust my judgment," he said, his voice a low rumble between high calls of the wind, "we're in trouble before we get started. You trusted me enough to get me out of jail. Do you trust me not to leave you when we cross into the Nation?"

Fear brushed her heart.

"But you won't," she said, stoutly.

"What makes you so sure?"

"I told you at the jail. You gave me your word. I've heard that Indians always keep their word and that Indian killers have even come back to be hanged whenever they promised they would."

He slanted a look at her, a hot, sharp glance that focused her awareness on him alone. Her gaze followed the shape of his broad shoulders against the sky and clung to the dark profile of his handsome face.

"So you know all about Indians," he drawled, as he reached into the leather bag.

Her heart began to beat at the same slow rhythm of his words. Her hands tightened on the reins.

She watched him pull out a jacket and throw it across one powerful thigh while he rebuckled the soft pouch.

"I know about *you*," Maggie said. "I knew the minute I saw you that you were a man of honor."

He shook out the garment, made of the same light-colored fabric as his breeches, and slipped his arms into its sleeves. He shrugged it onto his huge shoulders and turned toward her again. The jacket hung open in a V on his dark, naked chest.

"Well," he said, "I just gave my warrior's word of honor that I'd take care of you, and I'm telling you to wear the ring."

His warrior's word of honor.

Her heart clutched in her chest. He looked so wild, so dark and dangerous with his eyes glinting bright in the moonlight and his hair blowing back from his face in the windswept night. If she didn't need him so much for protection on the trail, she'd turn Joanna and race away from him.

Soon she'd be alone with him, and a long way from home. Maybe she should have listened to Emily.

"You stop trying to control me! I saved your life and you can just do as I say," she cried.

"Not a chance," he said in an amused tone. "You'll have to do more to earn my respect than bribe a judge."

This was hopeless. He thought he could boss her all the way to Texas.

"You *are* the Devil! My sister said that if we stood up to our father we'd need the Devil himself to help us, and I also thought of that when I first saw you."

He gave a low, bitter laugh and kept on looking at her.

"So the minute you saw me you knew I was both a Devil and a man of honor?" he drawled. "Why not admit you saw a tool, an Indian pawn you could use? Think again, Miss Harrington. *I'll* make the decisions from now on."

He turned his horse and rode away toward the river.

Trembling with frustration and fear, choking on the words that wouldn't form into sentences on her tongue, Maggie slapped her heels to her horse and chased him into the chill waters of the Arkansas. She didn't realize where she was until, underneath her, Joanna lost her footing and began to swim.

Chapter 4

The cold water instantly soaked Maggie through to midthigh on her stirrup leg. It froze her all over, all the way to the bone. The shock took her breath away and stopped the blood from pounding in her ears. Fear stopped it from even flowing in her veins, fear worse than what she'd felt when she'd waited in the shadows to blackmail Judge Stone as he left Emily's levee.

She and Jo both could be washed away, carried downriver and drowned! She squeezed her leg around the high horn of the sidesaddle until it cut into the inside flesh of her knee; she held onto the reins as if they were lifelines.

Dear Lord in Heaven, what was this man *doing* by crossing here? And why had she been so stupid as to follow him in?

The current seemed to grow stronger with every stroke Jo swam. It sucked harder and harder at Maggie's foot and leg, pulling like a hungry dog at a bone. Then the water slammed them back again with a terrible force.

Maggie bent forward and grabbed for the horse's mane. She drove her fingers in deep enough to clutch the crest of Joanna's neck, gritted her teeth, and held on, fighting tears. Was Cade trying to get her killed so he wouldn't have to take her to Texas? Or was he trying to ride off and leave her? Was this some kind of test for that trust he'd been talking about?

She turned her head slightly, trying not to move much for fear of unbalancing herself and her horse in the water. From the corner of her eye she saw that the gray horse was treading water, waiting for her to catch up, staying as a barrier between Joanna and the worst force of the current. Cade Chisk-Ko was watching to see that she was all right. That made her relax just the tiniest bit.

The moonlight glimmered off Cade's pale cord jacket, making his shoulders look axe-handle wide. They were level and steady, he was floating along as if he were sitting in a chair. She blinked and looked again.

He was sitting with his ankles crossed on the horse's withers in front of his saddle! The idea made her gasp with dismay at her own lack of foresight, but then she'd never gone into a river on horseback before. He could have warned her.

She saw the river pull the gray horse side-ways, and for a minute the anguished fear that he would be carried away from her made her forget about being cold and wet. Cade moved with the current, but he stayed where he could break its force before it hit her. At last, he straightened out again and the gray swam strongly beside her. She wanted to say something to Cade, though she wasn't quite sure what. Besides the shock of the cold water had taken not only her breath but her voice as well.

Even with the gray horse protecting Joanna, the current felt strong enough to suck them all under. Maggie gasped in terror. She had to get out of this river!

"Come on, Jo," she said, looking straight ahead to the precious land looming on the other side. She let go of her hold on the mare to lean forward and pat the dry part of her neck. "Go, girl!"

Finally, after a seemingly endless struggle through that awful water, the gray reached the land on the Choctaw Nation bank. Jo slipped as she came out. When she got her footing again, she started climbing up the slanting bank, a task made difficult with the water sluicing off the other horse's body. Maggie pulled Joanna to the right, into a drier path, and urged her to come up even with Cade.

"Thank goodness we're out of that!" she called across the space between them. "But, in the interest of the trust between us that you mentioned, Mr. Chisk-Ko, the least you could've done was warn me to keep my boot dry!"

This was one time she was glad to be using a sidesaddle, she thought wryly. Uncomfortable as it was, it had saved one of her feet from being cold and wet.

He was in shadow, but she glimpsed the flash of his eyes as he turned to her.

"Didn't you see the river had water in it?"

Maggie sucked in a shocked breath.

"You surprised me," she said defensively. "I had no idea you would take it into your head to cross right there!"

"Did you expect us fugitives to take the ferry?"

Truth was, she had. She'd never thought about getting across the river any other way.

"No! I expected us to ride down the bank to the sandbars where it's not so wide," she lied, with as much dignity as she could muster.

She shivered when they came over the top of the bank and the wind hit her wet skirts.

"I didn't even know we were going into the river until we were *in* it!" she said through chattering teeth.

"Then I suggest you pay closer attention to your whereabouts, Miss Harrington. A week from now, if you last that long, we'll be riding the same roads as a lot of shady characters who will make it their business to know exactly where you are."

He lifted the stallion into a long trot and pulled a little ahead of her.

"If I last that long!" she said, smooching to Joanna to keep up. "What's that supposed to mean?"

"A day or two on a hard trail, and you'll likely be ready to go back home. You're accustomed to soft living."

"And just how do you know that?"

"By the cut of your clothes."

"Humph," Maggie shot back. "Haven't you heard you can't judge a book by its cover?"

"I can read every page of your life without ever opening the cover. You never swam a horse across a river before tonight."

His flat, superior tone stung her pride.

"You sound as if that's a scandal," she said haughtily, pushing Joanna to keep the pace. "I may be inexperienced, but I'm not stupid. I know you crossed the river right there to try to make me quit, go home, and leave you alone with your freedom, which *I* got for you."

"I crossed the river right there to get us out of Arkansas."

He smooched to the gray and took off at a long lope. In the dark!

To make her have to keep up, no doubt. He thought she'd be too scared.

Maggie set her jaw firmly and sent Joanna cantering after the gray, hurrying across the grassy river-bottom land, which looked fairly flat in the moonlit places, though it could be full of holes. The wind filled her ears and blew her hat off to bounce on her back. It loosened her hair from its bindings and slapped it, stinging, across her face. Her wet foot squished in her boot, and her boot slid in the stirrup. But she wouldn't slow down, not if it killed her.

He kept moving, faster and faster into the darkness ahead, and Maggie kept Joanna right on the tail of the gray. It was an effort; she had to struggle for breath against the wind while she worked to keep her balance. She gave up trying to see the ground ahead of them.

At last they made a sharp turn to the right, and she could tell by the feel of Joanna, and by the sound of the hooves, that they had ridden onto a beaten trail of some kind.

"Where are we?" she called. "Is this a road?"

"Quiet!"

The next minute he was slowing his horse. Maggie pulled back on Joanna, who, as usual, didn't want to slow down.

"Whoa! Whoa!" Maggie murmured to her. "You can't run all the way to Texas."

The moonlight flashed from the silver trim on Cade's saddle, and the trees seemed to reach out from the darkness and pull him deeper into the night. When Maggie lost sight of him for a moment her heart lurched, but Joanna kept following the gray. Thick-leaved branches, arching from both sides of the path, rustled in the wind over their heads. They dropped to a walk.

"Here," he said, finally.

Maggie squinted to see where "here" was, but all she could see was the gleam of the gray's haunches. It wasn't until she rode up beside him that she saw a barn looming dark against the sky at the end of the lane between the trees. They had stopped a stone's throw from it.

"Wait here," he said, and stepped down.

Dimly she could see him, silent as a shadow, going away from her.

Gratefully, she slumped in her saddle. It felt wonderful to be out of the direct force of the wind and to be still. And *free!*

A great wave of happiness swept through her. Her plan was going to work! In only a few, short hours she had escaped from Pierce's house, obtained a bodyguard and guide, and gotten out of Arkansas.

Her heart leaped in her breast. At last, at long last, her dreams would come true, the ranch would be hers if she could just hold onto her courage. She *was* tough enough to ride all the way to Texas and she *would* get the upper hand and start making the decisions as soon as she had rested a bit!

"We'll stay here until first light."

His rich voice came from the right of Joanna's side. He was close enough to touch her.

"I didn't hear you come back!"

His spicy, masculine scent drifted to her on the night air. He chuckled.

"You'd better open your ears."

"Well, you *might* give me some warning."

"A bushwhacker on the trail won't."

"Then I'll stab him!"

He chuckled again.

"If you have a knife hidden somewhere in all those skirts, you couldn't find it, much less use it, before you were trussed up like a bird on a roasting spit."

"*If?*" she repeated. "Don't you believe me?"

His only answer was a noncommittal grunt.

"I *do* have a knife, and you'd better watch out!"

He laughed, a low, lazy sound that sent an unexpected thrill down her spine.

"I'm scared," he said sarcastically.

He wasn't taunting her, just teasing her. And somehow that made some of the tension drain from her body.

"Well, I do know a bushwhacker had better be scared of the two of us!" she said. "Look what we've done tonight: You're not hanged and I'm not drowned. We're out of Arkansas and we're free!"

She threw her arms into the air in celebration.

He laughed again, and she did, too, reveling in the warm, contagious sound.

"Right," he said. "We may have half the lawmen of the federal court riding after me and your father's henchmen coming after you, but there's no cage around us tonight!"

"And we can get warm and rested," she added, realizing suddenly how very tired she was, how wrought up she had been. "Swimming a cold river takes a lot out of a person!"

With a grin on his face, he moved past her, touched Joanna's shoulder, and reached beneath her neck for the reins of the gray.

"Ride on into the barn," he said, "so the horses will be hidden."

"Nobody's after us," she said, determined to prove that she *was* a competent person, deserving of some authority on this trip. "You saw how nervous Judge Stone was. He won't say anything tonight, and my father won't miss me until seven tomorrow morning."

Cade Chisk-Ko half turned to look at her.

"You can't be sure of that."

"Yes, I can."

"How?"

"Judge Stone doesn't want Pierce to bring me back. He'd die before he'd let word of the scandal he's involved in reach his mother, and it would—I'd throw stones with notes wrapped around them out my window to any passersby if I had to."

He stopped still and stared at her.

"You blackmailed him with the threat of telling his *mother?*"

"Yes. His mother was waiting on the veranda for him to bring the carriage around to take her home from my sister Emily's levee. I waylaid him at the stable. I threatened to run and show her my proof that he, my father, and the sheriff have a plot to discount court vouchers for profit."

"What! The judge let me out of jail and cheated the whole town of a hanging to keep something from his *mother?*"

"You don't know Miss Cordia. She lives for

the honor of her family, and she's ruled him from the minute he was born."

"How did he ever become a judge?"

"He took his father's place when he died. Everybody in town agreed that that was the way it should be."

Cade shook his head.

"But if his mother rules him, then he wouldn't have enough sand in his craw to get involved in an illegal scheme."

"I wondered about that while I waited for him to come out of the levee," Maggie said. "I decided he did it because it was his one chance in his whole life to rebel."

"Like you," he said.

"Yes," she said. "And no matter what happens now, I'm glad I didn't wait until I was as old as Judge Stone to do it."

"So am I," Cade said dryly, and led his horse across in front of her. "You'd have been even more bullheaded by then."

She laughed and turned Joanna to follow them.

"The judge is also scared of Sheriff Ames, who threatened accidents on dark roads if the truth comes out," she said. "I believe he'll do just as I told him: wait until morning, go to my father, tell him that I overheard their plot and have proof of their guilt, and that the only way to keep me from getting letters to the governor and the president is not to come after me."

"Don't believe it too much," Cade said over

his shoulder. "*Never* assume you have no pursuit."

"Assuming we *do* have pursuit, why aren't we trying to ride on as fast as we can?" she demanded, stung by his lack of admiration for her plan.

"That's what a posse or your father would expect. If they come tonight, they'll ride past us."

"What about the farmer who owns this barn? Wouldn't he notice two people and two horses when he does his morning chores?"

"This is a hay barn," he said. "It's nowhere near a house."

The sweet smell of hay hit her. It grew stronger as Cade took Joanna's bit and turned her to walk along the wall inside. Maggie felt rough wood brush her arm. Then, as her eyes adjusted to the light laid out in streaks by the moon hovering at the wide opening at the barn's other end, she saw the tall stacks of hay that threw long, deep shadows. Cade moved among them as confidently as if he lived there: He took over the big barn just as he had the jail office.

Panic scraped her mind. He took over everything he touched. *He* had made the decision to stop for the rest of the night. *He* had decided where to cross the river. Maybe, as her guide and bodyguard, he should do those things, but she had to watch that he didn't try to control everything, including her.

He stopped suddenly. Maggie sank lower in

the saddle as Joanna stopped, too, and watched as he walked around his horse and started to unbuckle the cinch.

"It'll be a long trail, and you'll have to learn how to do chores," he said.

For a minute she didn't know what he meant. She was so tired she only wanted to sit there and not think at all. Then his words sank in, and she stood up in her squishy boot and climbed down off Joanna. Her feet were so numb they couldn't feel the dirt floor of the barn and her legs shook, but she stood on them anyway and started unbuckling her cinch.

"We'll hobble them here in this hallway and let them eat hay," he said.

"And have stealing added to our list of sins?"

"The owner won't care, he's a friend of mine. When he hears I've escaped, he'll guess I was the one here."

"Then what are we doing lurking in the hay barn?" she said. "Why don't we stay at his house like civilized people?"

"I don't want him to have to lie or put himself in jeopardy if a lawman comes by asking questions."

"Oh, you have all the answers," she grumbled tiredly. "Most likely you don't even know him."

That brought another chuckle from him.

"What happened to your opinion of me as a man of honor?"

She thought about that as she pulled her saddle off, relieving poor Joanna of the wet, sweaty blanket.

"I still think you're a man of honor," she said. "But you're no gentleman. You let me get my boot wet in the river and made me gallop through the dark to keep up with you."

He laughed, actually, truly laughed. It was a low, charming sound rolling out of the darkness.

"I'm gentleman enough to give a lady a chance to change her mind," he said in a pleasant tone. "Another reason for stopping tonight is to decide which direction to take at daylight."

A chill colder than the water in the river came over her.

"What do you mean?" she cried. "We're going *south*, you know that!"

"You said yourself that your father will guess you've gone to the Texas ranch," he said smoothly. "Surely you have friends somewhere else . . ."

"I'm afraid of my father, yes. But I have you and this marriage certificate to protect me from him. I'm not *going* somewhere else!"

". . . or we could drift for awhile, toward New Orleans or St. Louis."

"No!" she cried. "I got you out of jail to take me to my *rancho*!"

He didn't answer. He was moving around the gray, brushing his back, slipping the bridle from his head. The bit made a small jingling noise.

"Mr. Chisk-Ko," she said, her heart pounding hard and slow as a blacksmith's hammer. "You cannot charm me into changing my mind. Are you going to try to *force* me onto another road?"

He didn't answer her, only slapped his horse on the rump and pushed him around so he could squat to hobble him. The moonlight shone against his black hair. Finally, he finished with the horse and stood up to face her.

"If I were the man of honor you take me to be," he said, solemnly, "I would do just that."

Maggie stood paralyzed.

"What are you talking about?"

"I needed to be out of that cage so badly that I agreed to a bargain that trades my hanging for your death. Listen to me. You can't survive alone on the Nueces."

Panic touched her heart with the tip of one cold finger. Would he leave her here? Go back on his word?

"Alone? You're going *with* me! That's why I saved your life, *remember*?"

She took a deep breath, then another. She made her racing blood slow down and tried to force her voice to stay steady.

He didn't answer the question. Instead, in that smooth, rich voice he tried again to charm her over to his way of thinking.

"Just the names for the Nueces country tell you it's no place even for a man to try to ranch," he said in a calm, reasonable manner that made her want to scream. "The Border Country, the Nueces Strip, the Wild Horse Desert. Mexicans still dispute it's in Texas, bandits roam there because there's no law, it's too dry and hot for hell."

"I don't need a geography lesson, Mr. Chisk-Ko," she said, trying to keep her panic out of her voice. "All I want to know is whether you are willing to keep our bargain or not."

Her voice shook in spite of her best efforts.

He stared down at her with hard, dark eyes. He could reach out and grab her, take her anyplace he wanted.

This very day he had killed a man.

Fear rolled in her stomach. He had brought her to this secluded place and no one would hear her, no one would help her if she screamed.

"I saved your *life*! You are supposed to do what I say."

"Don't play that card every time we disagree," he snapped. "I don't want to hear it— you're a spoiled child, *that's* why you think you can control me."

She set her jaw.

"Well, you are an overbearing, rude man, *that's* why you think you can control me and you *can't*! All I'm asking of you is that you keep our bargain."

"I can save your *rancho* for a year, but when that time's up, I'm gone."

The flat rawness of his tone made chill goose bumps stand up on her arms even as relief flooded warmly through her.

"Fine!" she cried.

"But why should we both go through the hell that year will be if you can't hold on after that?"

"I can hold on. I *can* and I will."

"You can't."

The finality in his voice was like a slap to her face.

"How do *you* know so much about it?" she demanded. "My grandfather ranched there! Have you ever even been there?"

"I was there during the war and I've drifted through there twice since," he said, still with that infuriating sureness. "The Texas Rangers are disbanded, and the Mexican authorities are condoning full-scale plundering, hide-peeling, rustling, murdering, and thievery."

"Well, I've been there more times than you," she said, contradictory words tumbling fast off her tongue to drown out his discouraging ones. "Right before my grandfather died, my mother and Emily and I traveled from Van Buren to the *rancho* with no trouble at all."

"Horseback?"

"No. In a coach."

"How many outriders?"

"Ten. Or twelve."

"How long ago was that?"

"Four years."

"It has steadily gotten worse."

"I can survive it."

"No woman can."

"I'm different from most women."

His bark of a laugh stuck a barb into her heart.

"Yeah. You're more impulsive. More foolish." He turned away from her and reached for his bedroll. "And you're married to an Indian."

Maggie drew back, startled.

"My wearing this ring doesn't mean we're really married!" she protested. "You had no business with such a thing in your pocket, anyway! Where'd you get it?"

"Won it in a card game," he drawled, as he walked toward the stacked hay. "It's good to find a way to put it to use."

"Well, I'm glad that makes you happy," she retorted, fighting to keep her tone as offhand as his. "Now it won't go to waste."

She turned back to Joanna and began to rub her down. He wasn't going to go back on his bargain, they were going to Texas. She had to remember that that was the important thing, not his opinion of her.

"Practicality is a Choctaw trait, did you know that?" he said conversationally.

Maggie glanced over her shoulder and saw him spreading out his bedroll on a low platform of hay bales.

"How could I know that?"

"As an Indian ethnologist, studying Indians'

honor, you might have run across that fact."

He sounded as if he was *teasing* her! Honestly! The gall of that man to tease right after he'd just insulted her! She did not understand him at all.

"Mr. Chisk-Ko," she said. "You might understand my confusion. One minute you're threatening to take me to New Orleans, the next you're insisting we're married, the next you're insulting me, and the next you're giving me ethnology lessons."

He went on talking as if he hadn't heard her.

"My father always said that the Choctaws' natural interest in the immediate and the practical was what made us different from the other four Civilized Tribes."

He got his bags and placed them at the foot of his bed.

"Seems to me you fall short of the Choctaw ideal," she said, tartly. "At the moment, you can't think about the immediate for worrying about a year from now in a place where you won't even be."

He laughed.

"Very good!" he said. "I like women with wit."

Goodness, he was enough to exasperate the very *life* out of her! Who was he, anyway?

"I don't care what you like," she snapped, stepping around Joanna to brush her other side.

He ignored that, too.

"Papa also believed that the Choctaw practicality was the reason we were the most economically advanced of the Civilized Tribes when the white man came."

"Well, you do seem to be a true Choctaw in that way," she said. "Your horse and saddle, your clothes and boots are the finest quality. As an impulsive woman I must ask, how do you make your money?"

The question didn't offend him as she had hoped it might.

"Gambling and trading, catching wild horses and buying renegade stocks."

"You could try working for a change."

"I've tried it, but I've never made any money at it."

He began unrolling his bed on top of the hay platform.

"Besides, I never stay in one place as long as a year."

Maggie didn't respond to that. As things stood, he would stay a year at Las Manzanitas, and she didn't want to risk his changing his mind. Silently, she put the brush away, hobbled Joanna, and knelt beside her saddle to untie her quilt.

"Come to bed," he said.

She froze.

Did he mean that she come to his bed? Was this yet another reason he had stopped here? She'd never been alone in the parlor with a man before, much less in a hay barn. And certainly not with a man like this one.

"I'll make my own bed."

He gave a low, slow chuckle.

Her heart flipped over. She was going to be alone with him on a lonely trail for many nights to come. She couldn't let him know he scared her.

Hugging her quilt, she forced her shaky legs to walk the few steps to the platform of hay. Cade Chisk-Ko, sitting on the opposite side of it, chose that moment to strip off his jacket and leave his naked shoulders and V-shaped back gleaming in the moonlight. Looking at him sent a shock through her.

How stupid, she told herself. Hadn't he been shirtless all the day before? But she couldn't tear her eyes from his rippling muscles as he crossed one leg over the other and pulled off his boot.

She turned her back to him only to realize that there was nowhere else to spread out her pallet except the dirt floor, where snakes and spiders and scorpions could get on her. She hated crawly things.

So she whirled and spread out the quilt on the hay, moving silently as if she could do it without his noticing.

"Take off your riding boots and your clothes," he said, without turning around.

Maggie gasped.

"I'll keep them on, thank you!"

"Want me to help with that wet boot? Or maybe with your bodice hooks?"

"No!" she cried. "What do you know

about . . . ladies' . . . undergarments, anyway?"

"Enough," he said, twisting around to grin at her over his shoulder, "to be of assistance . . ."

"I am *not* removing my clothes!"

"Suit yourself," he said, and turned back to his task. "Your body will be sore and sick of wearing them after a whole night and twelve hours in the saddle tomorrow."

He dropped his other boot.

He was right, she thought. He'd had her so wrought up that she'd forgotten about her soggy foot.

"But shouldn't we be ready to run if somebody did, by chance, follow our trail?" she asked.

"I'd hear them coming long before they got close enough to chase us away without our clothes."

His unassailable confidence in his powers irritated her almost as much as her attraction to his sensual voice. She had never felt so many strange, contradictory feelings. She didn't know *herself*, either, and that nearly scared her worse than not knowing him. What would she do with her freedom?

"Why don't you just brag on yourself?" she snapped.

"That's not a brag. It's the simple truth, meant to reassure you."

"Well, I'm reassured, so you can hush now!"

She dropped down on her bed and untied

her boot, fighting the wet leather laces with both hands. Finally she stripped it off, then her other boot and both stockings.

She loosened her belt and the waist of her riding dress. She took a deep, shaky breath. He was right, she already felt better. She threw her quilt over her shoulders and, beneath it, wiggled out of her dress. Then she put her bare feet up and wrapped herself in the quilt.

She turned to see if he was looking at her. He wasn't—he was sitting with his back to her as if she didn't exist. But right then, as she watched, he rolled up his jacket and thrust it beneath his head for a pillow, swung his legs around, and stretched out on his back. All in one, fluid motion as primal and as potentially dangerous as the panther she compared him to.

He turned his head and looked at her through the glinting moonlight.

"Want to come over here and get your money's worth?"

A new shiver ran through her.

"What . . . money's worth?"

"You bought me," he drawled. "I'm yours. I assume you want full service, especially after you arranged a wedding and all."

Her blood leaped and began racing. A heat like the sun's filled her veins.

"Mr. Chisk-Ko," she said, in the most dignified voice she could form from the wisp of breath she had left, "I cannot imagine what you might be talking about."

He smiled.

"All the more reason to come on over here and let me show you."

Something deep inside her, something at her very center, contracted again, as it had when she'd seen him in the street. It caressed her like a hand moving over her skin.

She couldn't move. She could barely speak.

"Don't think you can control me!"

He laughed, but this time it was a bitter sound.

"And don't you waste your sweet breath ordering me around in your snobbish, high-handed way," he said, "nor telling me that I'm not *really* your husband. That's another thing I don't ever want to hear again."

Then he turned over, away from her, onto his side, and pulled his blanket up around him.

Maggie stretched out on her bed and turned away from him, too. What had he meant by that last remark? The marriage wasn't real and he knew it. And she wasn't snobbish . . . or high-handed, not really.

She squeezed her eyes shut. She'd forget about him, forget all her worries and just *sleep*.

But, hard as she tried, she still saw him, King of the World, sitting the dancing stallion in the street in Van Buren. And there he was, the chief of the Choctaws in the sheriff's office, fresh out of his cell, ordering Judge Stone to give him his gun.

This man was accustomed to doing exactly

what he wanted, *when* he wanted. What if he decided he really wanted her?

Tonight, there was no way of knowing.

No more than there was a way of knowing how to stop herself from wanting to look at him, no way to stop her body from remembering the feel of his hands at her waist, lifting her into her saddle. No way to forget the power of his hand curled around hers to hold his ring on her hand, even if she was scared of him.

She touched the sapphire with the fingertips of her right hand. Where had the ring come from? Had he really won it—maybe from some scarlet woman who would think nothing at all of gaming with men in some gambling den? Or had he bought it for a woman he knew?

He never stayed anywhere as long as a year, he had said. Where had he been just before he went to the academy and killed Mr. Haynes?

Cade Chisk-Ko was a killer.

A little frisson of fear made her tremble.

He was meaner and stronger than Pierce, though, and the very thought of her father scared her even more, scared her into total stillness. She froze, clutching the quilt to her breast with both hands, thinking of Pierce's anger when she wouldn't be there at seven o'clock tomorrow morning.

And when he found the documents missing.

Cade Chisk-Ko was more than a match for Pierce Harrington, even if her father sent a dozen men riding hard to hunt for her. *That* was what she knew, what she must remember.

Cade fell asleep within seconds. Maggie lay awake, listening to his even breathing, until the moon had moved so far up into the sky that its light didn't come in through the door anymore.

Chapter 5

Cade woke at first light with a sudden, gut-wrenching clutch of his heart. The jail—he had dreamed he was still locked up in jail.

But the sweet-smelling hay crackling beneath his blanket mingled with the scent of horses and fresh, frosty air. He opened his eyes and looked up at the high, soaring rafters of a barn. Tandy LeFlore's barn.

He lay still, listening carefully, as the events of the previous day and night came flooding back through his mind. He didn't hear any voices or horses outside, no scraping of boots on the ground telling him that lawmen crept closer. He heard nothing but the shufflings of the hobbled horses inside the barn and the light, slow sound of someone's breathing coming from an arm's length away.

His jaw clenched. In a way he *was* still in jail, the foolish white girl's jail. Despite what she said, she had no concept of real life on the Nueces.

Slowly, he turned his head. Sure enough, there she was—a small, curled-up lump huddled so deep into her quilt that all he could see were a few stray tendrils of curly black hair. She'd probably want to spend an hour combing and dressing herself before they rode out this morning, and she would expect her servant of a savage "husband" to wait patiently.

Resentment poured through him as he thought of her vehement insistence that their marriage wasn't real. He would be responsible for her every morning and all day long, *every* day for a whole, endless year, bound to stay in one place and to fight at the risk of his life to hold the *rancho* for her. God in heaven help him, how could he put up with it? What if *the feeling* came over him, the hot, prickling misery with life, the dissatisfaction that seared his soul and drove him to ride out into new country to try to find some peace?

You're not looking at a hangman's noose, though, Chisk-Ko. Show a little gratitude to the Powers that Be.

If he got out of reach of the Van Buren law before that crooked judge worked up the nerve to send a posse after him, he'd never hang for killing Headmaster Haynes. He glanced down at his hands as he sat up. Too bad he had hit the scum so hard—killing was too good for the perverted son of a bitch.

"Wake up, Miss Harrington," he said, as he reached out to nudge her. "Time to go."

He picked up his boots and started pulling them on. Today was the day that young Miss

Harrington would learn what it really meant to run away from home.

Simple fairness forced him to admit, though, that she had already proved tougher than he would ever have thought. He had to admire her a little in spite of himself: she had stuck with her mount like a trooper when they swam the Arkansas, and she had ridden at a good, fast clip through the dark without falling off or crying out. She had spunk. She was funny, too.

And she hadn't panicked when he'd teased her about coming to his bed. *That* was a small wonder, prejudiced little snob that she was!

Bitterness twisted his gut again.

You're the only man I've ever seen who's meaner than my father.

She wanted him because she thought he was some sort of a wild savage.

No matter how much grit she showed or how much wit she had, she looked down on him. She could ask him to say farcical wedding vows, to risk his life for her and her *rancho*, but she would never want him for a *real* husband because he wasn't good enough for her.

She had saved his life, though, he had to remember that. And to stay alive, he had better get on the trail.

"Miss Harrington! Get up!" he called. "We need to get going."

She didn't stir.

Cade stood up and looked down at her. She

had scooted considerably closer to him during the night, drawn, no doubt, by the heat of his body. He shook his head. What a silly twit! This was October. Soon the nights would be downright cold, and she had brought only the one quilt.

Well, she'd learn to survive or she wouldn't live to tell of it. He wasn't going to carry her around on a pillow.

He leaned over and jerked the quilt off her.

She sat up, blindly grabbing for it with both hands while she kept her eyes squeezed shut.

"Mimi, you stop it! I'm cold!" she said, her words slurred with sleep. "*Give me my quilt!*"

When she couldn't find it, her eyes opened, heavy-lashed eyes that, for an instant, didn't see him. Then they focused and flashed blue sparks. What a beauty she was with her black hair curling wild around her face!

He stepped back and held the quilt out of her reach as she came scrambling off the hay.

"Time to ride," he said.

She looked like a creamy-skinned doll, all arms and legs and delicate lace underclothes. She took a step toward him, then stopped, glanced down at herself and tried to cover her full breasts with her hands. Her pale face turned a deep pink.

"Mr. Chisk-Ko!"

She used one hand to reach for the quilt as he stepped behind her and laid it like a shawl around her shoulders, thinking briefly what a shame it was to cover her. For one fleeting second, his arm tangled with hers and the warm-silk sensation of her bare skin filled his senses.

Instinctively, his arm tightened around her and he felt the alluring full curve of her breast and the swell of her hips against his thighs. Time stopped for the space of one long heartbeat, for one shining, crystal moment, there in the middle of Tandy LeFlore's barn with the hay smelling like honey. The sun coming up threw sparkles of light all over the frosty morning.

He was free. He was alive. He had never been more alive.

She jerked the edge of the quilt from his nerveless fingers, and he let her go. He had to, or he would have held her all day.

She stepped away from him and whirled to face him.

"You have an incredible amount of gall, Mr. Chisk-Ko," she said breathlessly, her cheeks full of high color and her eyes full of fire. "As I said last night, you are no gentleman."

"I called your name to wake you," he said, "but you wouldn't budge."

Stiffly she drew herself up to her full height and wrapped the quilt more tightly around her.

"I still cannot believe that you ripped off my covers when I'm in my . . . unmentionables!"

"You wouldn't wake up. We need to get on the trail. What was I supposed to do?"

"Anything but strip me naked and throw your arm around me and embarrass me half to death!" she scolded, blushing harder. "That was a totally uncivilized thing to do!"

Cade's breath froze in the middle of his chest.

He looked down into her heart-shaped face filled with disdain.

"You're the one begging to go to an uncivilized country," he said, roughly. "Get ready to ride."

Riding the trail made hours seem like days and still it seemed that night would never come. Not even when she had spent long stints in the saddle riding over Las Manzanitas with Grandpa had she ridden so hard, been so tired, or felt so beaten to a pulp by the constant, jolting movement.

But Cade Chisk-Ko wouldn't stop. He kept to the darker places, picking difficult paths, galloping when the ground was soft, pushing constantly. He didn't abuse the horses, though, she had to admit. He slowed them to a trot on the hard ground and they walked some, but he rode without stopping, away from the roads, putting miles and miles between them and Van Buren.

And she followed. She had no idea where she was, but she knew by the sun's position that they *were* going south. He was keeping their bargain.

She knew she had offended him, though it had taken her a while to figure it out. While she'd dressed and they'd saddled the horses, through the meager breakfast of tiny ham-and-biscuits she'd stolen from Emily's levee, a forbidding silence had hung between them. As if he had the right to be offended about *any-thing* after the way he had behaved that morning!

That thought roused her temper so much that she'd refused to even try to apologize for calling him uncivilized. He was. That was all there was to it, and no matter what conclusion he had jumped to, it had nothing to do with the color of his skin.

Good Lord, he was a strange man. He'd known she wasn't dressed when he ripped away her quilt. She would never forgive him for that. He was the one who ought to apologize!

And he also ought to apologize for throwing his arm around her and holding her against him so familiarly!

Remembering that made her arms tremble and her hand loosen on the reins. She still hadn't recovered from having her body pressed against his.

If she admitted the truth to herself, it was the strange, aching sensations that he made her feel which she couldn't forgive.

But he wasn't apologizing. He wasn't even speaking to her. He rarely even looked back to see how she was faring, and he never offered to stop so she could rest.

Maggie set her jaw and took a deeper seat in the saddle. She could ride as long as he could—he'd be surprised to see that! And he would be surprised to see that no matter what he put her through, she would not turn back. By the time they reached the *rancho*, he would admit that she was tough enough to survive in the Nueces.

The thick hills closed in behind them, and they kept on riding. They never glimpsed another person, or road, or human habitation the whole day, and they stopped only twice to water the horses. Finally, as the sun flirted with the top of the purple line of hills to the west, they rode at a quick trot into a stand of black-jack trees. Maggie could see no trail at all, but the big Choctaw urged his horse faster without hesitation. She kept right on his heels, fighting off low tree limbs, leaning back to help as her horse started downhill.

Once they passed the trees and the long hillside was behind them, a narrow valley with pale grass and a big creek opened to take them in. Cade Chisk-Ko led her into it at a lope, riding fast down a grassy strip that ran between the rushing water and the steep rock wall that formed one side of the valley.

"This is the best place around here for us to stay the night," Cade called back over his shoulder, his voice hoarse.

Thank goodness. They could rest now.

Halfway down the valley, in a patch of deep grass that was beginning to turn brown, he reined in his horse. Of her own accord, Joanna walked up beside his gray stallion and stopped, too.

Numb with fatigue, dizzy from the constant motion, Maggie swayed in the saddle and had to wait for strength to flow back into her legs before she could get down. In spite of her exhaustion, a great wave of exhilaration washed over her. She had done it! She had kept up with him! She had ridden for a whole day, which he had never thought she could do.

"Well," she said, with great satisfaction, "I guess you see now that I can make it to Texas."

He pushed his hat back on his head and shot her a quick, sidelong glance.

"Not quite," he said dryly. "Your Wild Horse Desert is a world on the other side of Red River and we're not even halfway to the Red."

Every cell in her body flared up in anger.

"That's not *fair!*" she cried. "You can't give me credit for a hard day's ride because you can't admit that you're wrong about me being soft and spoiled and helpless!"

He made no response. He simply sat his horse and looked slowly up and down the valley. Then he stood in his stirrup and dismounted.

"That's all right," she snapped. "You can't make me turn back. I'll ride right on your heels across all of Texas."

He stepped closer to her horse and looked up into her face. She thought he looked almost surprised, maybe a bit admiring, although it was hard to read his face.

Tentatively, she straightened out her right leg along Joanna's neck—her knee had been bent so long she truly thought it might break. Her other leg trembled from the hours of keeping herself balanced in the stirrup.

"Not in that sidesaddle, you can't."

Disappointment stabbed her. He wasn't admiring her, he was just as arrogant as ever.

He started loosening the cinch on the gray. "The stupid contraption's going to ruin your legs," he said. "I never understood why women put up with them."

"My legs are none of your business," she said. "And you have no inkling of what women put up with."

He threw her a quick, slanting glance, one black eyebrow raised.

"I've known a lot of women."

"I'm sure you have," she retorted, "at least in the biblical sense. But that doesn't mean you know a thing about me."

He shrugged as if to say he didn't care, either.

"Miss Harrington, if you'll get down and gather wood for a fire, I'll scout out the best place to build one."

Suddenly, she didn't care about anything but eating hot food, enough to fill her empty stomach. The thought made her eyes sting with tears. She had never been this tired or this hungry in her whole life.

"All right," she said, and threw her aching leg over Jo's withers, "I brought a spider-skillet and some sausage balls. I'll heat them up."

"Sausage balls," he said. "Along the same order of those dainty little sandwiches we ate this morning? That ladies' teatime fare wouldn't fill up a mouse."

"I haven't seen *you* providing anything!" she cried. "You have a nerve to complain!"

She kicked her left foot out of her stirrup and let herself slide off her mount. The instant her feet hit the ground, her knees buckled.

Thank goodness, he hadn't seen her.

She grabbed her stirrup leather, clutched it with both hands, and pressed her forehead to Jo's sweaty side while the blood rushed painfully into her legs and her feet. She couldn't walk. She was sure she would never be able to walk again.

And she'd never be able to climb back onto Joanna.

She hung there for a moment, looking down at the unfamiliar ground, staring at the bright colors of the leaves, blown by the wind into the tall grass. Then she made her fingers turn the leather loose and forced her feet to move.

Cade Chisk-Ko left his horse saddled and walked west toward the rocky wall of the hill. He climbed its sloping foot and took another long look, all up and down the valley, his narrowed eyes moving slowly in a careful, sweeping circle. Maggie managed, by leaning on

Joanna now and again, to take several steps. Finally, she got her balance and walked stiffly away from the mare to start her search for fire-wood.

"Bring the wood to the mouth of this little cave," he called, gesturing toward the wall at his back. "You can sleep in there tonight."

"Where will you be?" Maggie called back.

"Gone to get provisions. I'll be back by morning."

Maggie's breath whooshed from her lungs. She whirled in her tracks and ran back toward him.

"You . . . you aren't going to leave me here . . . *alone?*" Terror gripped her. What if some outlaws came?

What if Pierce came? What if he found her when Cade was gone?

"You promised to take me safely to Texas!" she cried. "Not to leave me alone in the mid-dle of nowhere!"

"I can't take you anywhere if you've starved to death."

"You can hunt, you can kill us something to eat! Where can you go get provisions way out here, anyhow? There surely aren't any stores for miles around!"

"Hunting takes time," he said, "and we don't have it. Now, gather me up some wood while I see if there's an animal denned up in your cave."

"An animal! What? A wolf? A bear? A . . ."

"Probably nothing," he said, unsympathetically. "You'll be perfectly safe."

He strode into the mouth of the cave.

"You *are* a barbarian!" she yelled after him. "And a sadistic one, at that! You can't leave me alone, in the middle of nowhere, *in a cave*, in the dark. All night! Why, I've never spent a night by myself in my whole life!"

He kept on walking. Then, as if he considered her fear, he half-turned back toward her.

"Then it's high time you did. It'll prepare you for the barbarous, masochistic pursuit of ranching alone in the Wild Horse Desert."

She dropped her outstretched, pleading hand to her side and turned away from the sight of him. Her jaw set and she forced her tear-stung eyes to search the grass for sticks of dry wood. This was another of his cruel tests. Another of his attempts to get her to cry "uncle" and turn back.

Perhaps, deep in his heart, he was determined not to go to the Nueces Strip, but to honor his word he would just try to make the journey so horrendous that she would give it up. She was certain that was how he was thinking.

Well, he would see what kind of "mud she was made of," as Grandpa Macroom used to say. She would die right here in the hills of the Choctaw Nation before she'd quit now.

When she reached the cave with an armful of wood, he had already searched it, declared it empty, gathered some wood himself, and built a fire. Now he showed her how to keep it going.

"Gather some more wood before dark falls completely," he said. "Get enough to last you all night."

"I will," she said. Despite her fury and fright, she managed to keep her voice calm and steady. She wouldn't let him see her fear again, no matter what. She added her firewood to his pile, then she moved and spoke nonchalantly when he showed her the inside of the cave.

But she couldn't resist following him down to the horses when he started to leave.

"You'll be all right here," he said, as he tightened the cinch and stepped up onto Smoke. "No wild animal will approach the fire and nobody will be likely to ride through this valley tonight."

His hand went to his waist. He unbuckled his gunbelt.

"Wear this," he said, holding it down to her. "If you need it, don't worry about aiming— just point it and fire."

"I can aim and hit what I target," she snapped. "Grandpa taught me to use a pistol *and* a rifle."

She took the gun, wishing she could slap his face with it, but wanting the protection it offered. If she'd had more time to plan her departure, she would have brought her own weapon.

"I left my bedroll in the cave," he said.

"With it and your quilt and the fire, you'll stay warm."

She straightened her spine.

"I'll be fine," she said haughtily. "Thank you for your concern."

He touched his heels to the gray and they were gone. He and the horse grew smaller and smaller as they loped down the valley into the gathering dusk. Maggie watched until she couldn't see them any more.

Had she made a terrible mistake? Had she run away from home only to be abandoned in a wilderness where she'd die, her bones never to be found?

No! She would show that obnoxious Cade Chisk-Ko a thing or two. If he did come back, he would see she didn't even need him. If he didn't come back, she would survive. And if he didn't come back, she would find him wherever he was and take him back to that jail and stuff him into his cell with her own two hands!

From the corner of her eye she caught a movement and whirled to face it, her heart thundering wildly in her throat. A leaf, caught in a swirl of wind!

Shakily, she buckled the holster around her waist, walked to Joanna, and hugged her. She led her up to the mouth of the cave and began to remove the saddle and pad.

"It's just us now, Sweetie," she said, her voice so scratchy in her dry throat that it sounded like a stranger's. "But we'll be all right."

She forced her fast, shallow breathing to slow down and deepen. She would face each moment, each problem as it came. For now, for tonight, she wouldn't let herself think about Cade again. She would behave like a practical Choctaw and put her mind onto the immediate.

This night was something to celebrate. She was out of Pierce's house and she had come a long way out of his clutches. Her dream was coming true! She was on her way to the *rancho* at last!

She hung Joanna's bridle on a bush, then walked out of the shadow of the mountain, threw up her head, and held her face to catch the last warm, slanting rays of the sun. The air smelled like cedar and drying wildflowers, their cinnamon-honey scents scattered on the wind.

Soon it would be full of dust and the sweet fragrance of mesquite fires and, from far away, the tang of the Gulf waters in Corpus Christi Bay. Soon—in two or three weeks—she would ride onto Las Manzanitas! She would be home at last. Free at last.

Joanna stomped a forefoot and made a doubtful snuffling sound.

"It's true, Jo," Maggie told her, as she slipped a soft halter onto her and used a handkerchief to scrub at the sweat on her face. "We'll be home soon."

She tied Jo to the bush on a loose rope so she could graze, and set her skillet on the fire. Once she'd spilled the sausage balls into it, she walked away from the cave again. She didn't like it. If she slept inside it at all, it would have to be right in the mouth, by the edge of the fire.

But for now she wouldn't think about night. She'd enjoy the last of the day.

The trees flamed orange, yellow, and red in the dying sunlight as she walked slowly toward the hard-running creek. It was going to be all right. Everything was going to be all right.

The wind gusted hard around the end of the hill, carrying the chill of the coming night. It whipped her skirts against her legs and tore her hair loose from its bindings, making her stop still and hug herself hard, as if to hold herself together. The cold spread through her and brought back her fears.

She had no idea where she was—all she knew was that she was somewhere in the Choctaw Nation. It would take days for her to reach Red River and Texas, even if she could find the way. She probably couldn't get back to Van Buren if she wanted to.

She didn't know where she was, and neither did anyone who loved her. Emily had probably lain awake all night and gone through hell today while Pierce tried to make her tell what she knew of Maggie's plans.

Oh, if only Mimi were here! And Mama!

But she was alone, which she had never been before. And she might never see any of her family, ever again. A terrible heaviness overwhelmed her.

She had gone away forever without telling her Mama good-bye. She had gotten Cade out of jail and out of hanging by blackmail, which ultimately might ruin Pierce and bring disgrace onto her whole family. She had put herself and her safety into the hands of a murderer.

The blood in her veins turned to bitter water. This madness was all her own doing. Then she heard Grandpa Macroom's voice as clearly as if he were standing next to her instead of being four years dead.

You're the tough one, Maggie, me love. And you're the one who loves this wild land. Aye, you're the one to have me rancho.

Las Manzanitas was the reason she'd done what she'd done. Las Manzanitas was all she had now. Her life and Las Manzanitas. If she wanted to keep them both, she'd better get her backbone up and get busy.

She'd better get Joanna watered, now that she had cooled.

Before that chore was done, dusk started coming down fast. Maggie hurried the mare back to her tethering place and with her empty stomach growling, went to her supper. She used the tails of her skirt to protect her hands, pulled the spider pan from the fire, and ate, tossing the little balls of sausage, cheese, and spicy dough back and forth between her palms to cool them fast.

Mama would be horrified if she could see that, but Maggie had never been so hungry, and she had to hurry and eat so she could concentrate on keeping her fire going. When she'd finished, she laid another stick on so the flames wouldn't go out, and went to her saddlebags piled to one side of the cave's opening. The provisions she had left consisted of exactly three lemon tea cakes wrapped in a napkin and a small tin of sugared pecans.

She lifted the pistol from the holster that hung below her hip on a belt that was hopelessly too big for her, and hefted its weight. She stood up and aimed it, looking at it in the glow of the fire.

"I don't know," she muttered to Joanna. "Can I shoot fast enough to kill something to eat if I have to?"

The answer came in a sudden fluttering noise, one that stopped her heart.

It was a bird of some kind.

She whirled around and looked up. Suddenly they came swooping down at her through the column of dancing firelight, a black blanket of them, chittering and crying, slapping hundreds, no, *thousands* of wings.

Not birds. Bats!

Maggie's mind froze solid, while her body went into fast, crazy action. She screamed and fired the pistol once, then twice, and threw her hands over her head, the awful weight of the gun dragging at the end of her shaking arm. She fired again. Then she dropped to the floor beside the fire and huddled there in a heap, clutching the firearm in her sweating hand, pulling the trigger once more, only by a miracle keeping the muzzle pointed up.

Somewhere on the other side of the terrifying curtain of repulsive black bodies swarming between her and her horse, Joanna bellowed and screamed. But Maggie couldn't go to her.

She couldn't move.

She couldn't survive. This fright would kill her.

Then they were gone.

Maggie lay still, trying to stop trembling. Never, ever before in all her life, not even with Pierce on a rampage, had she known such fear. Even now, she thought her heart was going to tear its way out of her chest.

Finally, she managed to draw her legs up beneath her and sit cross-legged in front of the fire. An eon later, she used both sweaty hands to slip the heavy pistol back into the holster.

The bats would be gone until dawn. Somehow she knew that, she'd read it somewhere. They came and went from their caves at dusk and at dawn. At dawn, she would not be in this cave.

But for tonight she couldn't make herself leave her fire. She huddled beside it, holding her trembling hands out to its warmth as if the air were freezing cold. When she stopped shaking, she got to her feet and walked toward the darkness to see about Joanna.

No matter how black the night, she would be able to see the mare's white spots.

The bush was there. Maggie reached out into the blackness and felt it. She caught the rope in her palm and followed it, hand over hand, to its short, ragged end.

Joanna was gone.

For a long time Maggie stood still, staring out into the dark night. She *had* made a terrible mistake, she knew that now, but it wasn't running away from home. It was not fighting hard enough to keep Cade Chisk-Ko from taking control—she should never have let him leave her here like this.

He could have gotten provisions along the trail, day by day. Of course he could have, he could do anything.

But he could not take control of her and manipulate her into letting him out of their bargain. That was the real reason he'd gone off and left her to be frightened within an inch of her life: He was playing a game in which he made all the rules, a game meant to make her beg to go home again and leave him with his freedom.

She clenched both hands into fists.

It was a game he wasn't going to win.

Chapter 6

Cade slid Cotannah's arms from around his neck for the third time and put them down by her sides. Her clinging drove him crazy and made him feel guilty. He had to get out of there.

"You know I must go," he said.

Her eyes filled with hurt, and he brushed back a stray lock of her hair.

It smelled of fried bacon. Poor child. She'd been up half the night helping Aunt Ancie cook and pack provisions for him, in spite of the pain and terror Haynes had put her through and her hard, wild ride home after that.

It had taken Cade and Maggie twelve hours of hard riding from Tandy's barn to the cave where he'd left Maggie; he'd ridden another hour from there to reach his family's cabin. Cotannah had made it all the way from the boarding school near Van Buren to home in ten hours. The poor child had been fleeing through the dark night alone, anguished that he was caught and about to be hanged, while he'd slept those few hours in the barn. Thank goodness he had slept most of this night past—now maybe he'd have the strength to tell Cotannah good-bye and then deal with Miss Maggie.

But Cotannah was the one he needed to protect. She was a brave, tough one, this little sister of his; and though he didn't know her well, he knew this.

She looked up at him.

"Cade, we could hide you in the hills," she whispered, grabbing his arm and holding onto it desperately.

His wanderlust grew. It wasn't *the feeling*, really, but his chest tightened, and he wanted, with a sudden, wild burning in his belly, to be gone. He couldn't stay here for any length of time, he'd never been able to since his childhood. And he didn't need this responsibility, didn't want it.

Yet he wanted to keep her safe. After all, she *was* his little sister, and he hadn't done much for her during her short life, except send her money.

"I have to go now," he said again. "You don't want a posse to catch me, do you?"

"No, but if you went back into the hills, I'd bring you food every day." Her eyes shone with unshed tears. "You could live in a cave."

There *was* a cave he had to get back to, with another girl he had to protect. Damn it all, he was besieged!

"Thanks for the offer, 'Tannah," he said, forcing a lightness he didn't feel, "but I'd better put a few more miles between me and Van Buren. Don't worry, my sweet *itibapishi*, I'll get a message to you later."

He patted her cheek and turned away, toward his horse. Cotannah stepped back with a sudden hopelessness that fed his guilt.

He strode across the yard to Smoke. Uncle Jumper was fiddling with the packs Cade had balanced behind the saddle. Cade had to bite his tongue to keep from telling the old man to get away from his horse.

"Don't take any unnecessary chances, Cade," Aunt Ancie said, as she came around the corner of the cabin with a battered basket of the last of the fall tomatoes.

She tied the basket to his saddle strings. This irritated Cade, but he said nothing. She'd only argue, and that would delay his departure.

"We'll be praying for you, praying hard," she said, then patted his arm as she stepped back from Smoke.

Uncle Jumper agreed. "Yes, and we're sorry you're on the run. We know that, at bottom, it's our fault."

It sure as hell is. I told you not to send her to that school. But Cade didn't say the words. They would only cause more hurt.

"Don't be mad at them, Cade," Cotannah said quickly, running to him. "They were only trying to prepare me to live in a white world when they sent me to the academy."

Guilt slapped Cade again. The child couldn't bear for him to be angry with the only parents she knew. A happy family, all living together, was all she'd ever wanted. Hopefully she'd have one of her own one day.

"That horse is tired. I wish you'd take one of the mules," Uncle Jumper said, in his light, dry voice.

"You need your mules to haul wood," Cade said. "Smoke's fine."

He stepped up onto the stallion.

"Thanks for the supplies," he said. "Mostly I just wanted to see that Cotannah made it home safely—and to let you know I'm out of jail and I won't hang."

Out of jail, but not free.

"You all be careful," he said before he took off at a long lope.

Cotannah called after him, "Cade! Ride safe!"

He didn't look back, but he lifted one hand in acknowledgment. At that moment he could have sworn that her voice was his mother's. That was exactly the same thing Mama always said each time he left home.

Cotannah didn't know that. She'd never known her father or her mother—she deserved a little time with her brother before she was completely grown up. He had never been able to give that to her.

And now he couldn't, either. He was bound to do whatever Miss Maggie Harrington wanted.

His jaw tightened. She *was* spoiled, she had no idea what she would find in Texas, and she didn't have enough brains to see that she might not survive that savage place. The very fact that she was so determined to take over that *rancho* proved that she expected to get what she wanted no matter how impossible.

And to get it, she would sacrifice an Indian in a heartbeat.

You are a barbarian, and a sadistic one, at that!

His lips formed a grim smile, and he wondered how the superior, civilized Miss Maggie had enjoyed spending the first night, *ever, in her whole life,* alone. She was probably hysterical by now. Well, it served her right. She ought to have stayed home with her mother.

An hour later, he stopped at the top of the wooded hill and looked down the length of the narrow valley where he had left Maggie. Immediately he searched the mouth of the cave. It was empty. No girl, no fire, no horse, no scattered bedroll.

Had somebody actually ridden through here during the night, some renegade who had taken her? Had she tried to follow Cade, or maybe even tried to find her way back home?

His fists clenched. Now she was lost in the woods, God only knew where, and he'd have to go looking for her!

It couldn't be that her father had found her. Even if the judge had talked, no posse could have followed them—Cade had been too careful to hide the trail.

He put his heels to Smoke and started him moving. The horse went down off the hill in a purposeful trot that carried Cade past a long line of pines. As soon as those trees were out of his way, he saw smoke curling up from a spot of woods in a curve of the creek.

He kneed the stallion in that direction, his mind immediately racing. Somebody *must* have come through here during the night, unlikely as it was, because Maggie couldn't have made her own fire.

He left Smoke behind a scraggly cedar tree and moved silently on foot toward the creek's bend. Once he slipped into the little stand of woods, he heard nothing: no voices and no horses, just the sound of the water running between its banks and the birds chittering high overhead in the mulberry trees. Finally, he was close enough to hear the fire popping and the hiss of food frying over it. He stood behind a tree trunk and looked.

Maggie was facing away from him, bent over the fire with her small, round backside pointing up into the air. The skirt of her riding habit was pulled up between her legs and tightly tucked somehow, leaving her legs, beautifully curvaceous ones with delicate ankles, bare from the knee down. She was barefooted, too, in the cold morning.

Her mass of black hair spilled all the way down to her waist, curls flying wild in every direction. Her clothing looked utterly disheveled, and water-splattered, too.

"I'll be right there, Jo darling," she called.

"Just let me put the other one in the pan before I run out of grease."

Joe! Cade pulled out the knife that he wore in his boot.

Joe *darling?* Damn! She certainly hadn't told him the whole story of her life! But how could she have rendezvoused with someone here when she hadn't known which way Cade would take her or where they would camp?

He flicked his gaze quickly around the small clearing, looking for movement in the surrounding brush. Nothing. No one answered her.

"I know you're hurting," Maggie said, busily turning whatever was frying in the skillet. "And it's all my fault, but if you hadn't run off from me, you wouldn't have gashed your leg."

His eyes, carefully circling her new campsite, found no other living creature except for her paint mare. Then he saw it. A bleeding cut about a hand's width long slashed the white of the horse's foreleg. The mare stood tied short, very short, with her nose high against the trunk of a post oak tree. Maggie had used a leather belt, which barely reached around the base of a limb and through the side of the halter. The leadrope dangled, broken.

He dropped the knife back into its sheath, slowly letting out his breath. Of course, what an idiot he was! When she'd called her mount "Joanna" yesterday, he'd thought it was a hell

of a name to give a horse. Typical of a fluffy
girl like Maggie.

He gave another sigh of relief. Thanks be to
the Great Spirit, she was safe.

Not only was she safe but she was also
cooking breakfast on a fire she had built for
herself, and whatever she was cooking she
had supplied herself. She said the horse had
run away, and obviously the mare had been
hurt and, therefore, frightened, but somehow
Maggie had caught and tied her.

He grinned and shook his head. Now
wasn't she something? As an experienced
gambler, he would have bet that she'd never
stay on the trail even this far. He'd been
wrong to think she was all fluff—he owed her
an apology. Seeing her like this surprised him
as much as hearing that Cotannah had made
that long ride in ten hours.

He thought about that. Surprising as it was,
Maggie and Cotannah were much alike—they
both had grit to spare. True, Maggie was
funny and Cotannah was serious, and Maggie
was spoiled and Cotannah was not. But in
their souls, where it mattered, they were alike.

As he looked at Maggie, bent over her fire,
a new idea blew into his heart and stuck there
like a tuft of white hairs from a cottonwood
tree: maybe, just maybe, if he took very good
care of Maggie, and did it ungrudgingly, he
could atone to the Great Spirit for not taking
care of Cotannah. Maybe that would somehow

make amends in his own heart, too, for neglecting his family.

He owed Maggie more than an apology. He owed her the fulfillment of their bargain, his time given with a free heart, if for no other reason than to honor her strength of spirit. From now on he would give her credit for what she did, and he would willingly teach her the skills she would need to survive on the Nueces. He would continue to push her, yes, but for her own good.

"Miss Harrington."

He stepped out into the little clearing.

She whirled and suddenly he was facing his own pistol, which she was holding in both her hands with the muzzle pointed at his chest. He stopped in his tracks.

"Here, now, there's no need for that," he blurted, raising his hands.

"Mr. Chisk-Ko," she cried. "You didn't have to sneak up on me that way!"

Her voice shook. Her eyes blazed into his with surprise and fear and anger, and then with relief. Her hands trembled so that the gun wobbled crazily, up and then down, threatening just about every inch of him.

His gut tightened.

"Give me the gun," he said, his hand held out.

She shook her head. Her eyes glazed with tears.

"You scared me half to death!"

Her anger began taking over. Her cheeks

flushed pink with it and she blinked the tears away.

"I couldn't very well come galloping in shouting my name," he said lightly. "With the fire in a new location, I thought somebody was with you."

He took a step toward her, still holding out his hand.

She ignored it.

"Oh!" she said sarcastically, "I understand. You thought somebody else was here because you didn't think I was capable of building a fire by myself!"

The gun wavered back and forth, still pointed at his chest.

He took another step.

"Give me that."

"Stop right there. Don't come any closer."

She held him in her bright blue glare and steadied the gun as if she'd really like to shoot him.

"Your opinion of me as a helpless tenderfoot is as unfair as your going off and leaving me. If you'd been here last night, as you had *promised* to be, you'd have been surprised to see all I can do!"

"What would I have seen?" he said in a calm voice, hoping to dissipate her anger so he could get the gun from her.

"I caught Joanna when she was hurt and crazy with fear."

Her voice broke suddenly.

"And I managed not to go crazy myself

when thousands of nasty, horrible *bats* swooped down on me—didn't you *see* them in that cave before you left me there?''

For one moment, for the space of one heartbeat, her fear won over her anger and filled her face. She had been terrified.

His heart twisted with remorse. He was a cad. He shouldn't have left her alone, no matter how much he needed to see Cotannah safe or how much Maggie needed a lesson in the realities of the trail.

''Lots of caves have bats,'' he said. ''I wasn't even looking for them—they wouldn't have hurt you.''

''But they nearly made me hurt myself.''

Her blazing eyes narrowed until he had a wild, quick fear that she might actually, deliberately, pull the trigger.

''They scared me so bad that I fired off this gun and spooked Joanna into running away and cutting her leg. It's a bad cut.''

''How many times did you fire the pistol?''

She gave him a swift smile, not a friendly one.

''Less than six.''

He stretched his hand out a little farther.

''I'll take it now,'' he said.

She shook it at him and he dropped his hand.

''Not yet, you won't. If we're going to ride eight hundred miles together, we're going to be equal partners, open and honest with each other. And you'll stay with me and protect me

as you promised in exchange for your freedom—or I'll shoot you here and go on alone."

Her blue eyes hardened.

"I see you're wearing denims and a fresh
white shirt. Where'd you get them?"

A flash of anger darted through him at the
fact that she would keep on holding the gun
on him this way, but so did the urge to laugh.
She had a lot of guts. She deserved his en-
couragement and his protection.

"They're mine," he said. "I had left them at
my family's cabin. That's where I went to get
provisions."

Surprise flicked into her eyes.

"You have a family?"

"Did you think I sprang full grown from the
antlers of a deer?"

"No-o-o. But you . . . you're so . . . well, you
don't seem to belong to anybody."

That truth pierced his heart. He stood there
and realized it, stood there and looked at her
while her words ran through him. It hurt as
badly as if she had shot him. He had never
known it before, but it was true.

He didn't belong to anyone.

How could she see into him that way? No
one else, *no one*, ever had before.

"I don't," he said.

She frowned, staring at him, blue eyes blazing.

"Why couldn't I have gone with you to see
your family?"

Anger boiled up in him again. Damn it all,

he didn't have to submit to an inquisition. She might be able to see into his heart, but she didn't have to know *everything* about him.

"I didn't want to expose them to insult," he snapped. "You might've told them that they were downright barbarous and uncivilized."

Her face changed in an instant.

"I'm sorry about that," she said sincerely. "Not sorry about what I said, but that you took it as a comment on your race. I would've said it to a white man just as fast."

That surprised him as much as her wheeling on him with the gun in her hands. He had been wrong about her again.

Then he surprised himself even more.

"And I'm sorry I left you here alone," he said. "I shouldn't have done that."

"But you couldn't resist trying to teach me just how tough the trail to Texas can be," she said. "Well, give it up, Cade Chisk-Ko. I'm not turning back even if you push me into a pit full of rattlesnakes."

She took a step toward him, steadied the muzzle of the pistol, and trained it on his chest again. This time it didn't waver. Neither did her gaze.

"I have lived my life with my father plotting and scheming and my mother keeping secrets," she said fiercely. "I never knew what was really going on and I refuse to live that way another minute. Do you understand me?"

He could take the gun from her in one swift lunge. But he wouldn't. She needed to feel she had some control. Last night's events had made her vulnerable to the core.

"Yes, I do," he said.

He opened his hands, then closed them again, wishing he had the power to take away the hurt he had caused her.

"Well, then, what'll it be? Shall I shoot you, or are we partners—talking, making decisions together, letting me know exactly what's going on all the time?"

Cade looked straight into her determined blue eyes.

"Partners. And I would say the same even if you weren't facing me down with my own gun."

She didn't smile when he did, only searched his eyes to make sure that he was serious. Evidently, his expression satisfied her.

"So," she said, just as he had in the jail, "we have struck a deal."

"Yes," he said, "we have struck a deal."

She was close enough to touch. A long, red scratch ran down one side of her neck, her clothes were torn worse than he had thought, and her hair held bits of twigs and leaves. The mare must've given her a merry chase, but she had caught her. Last night had been hellacious for her, but she had everything under control this morning. Including him.

He grinned. Wasn't that just the way of life's crooks and turns? Now that he'd decided to give her his protection, she didn't want it anymore.

With a sudden motion, she threw the gun at him, turned on her heel, and marched away, her back held ramrod straight, her bare feet and legs gleaming in the morning sunlight.

He stuck the pistol into the belt of his pants and followed her.

"Where are your boots?"

"I took them off to go fishing," she said, as they rounded the trunk of a big sycamore tree growing close to the stream.

"Is it fish you're frying . . ."

He stared past her, too amazed to finish the thought. She was headed for a long limb hanging out into the water, where a bundle of some kind dangled. Dangled and jumped.

"Miss . . . Harrington?"

As she untied it and pulled it out, Cade realized that the strange contraption was her stocking. A stocking full of water. With a fish as big as Cade's two hands leaping around in it.

She turned and came back to him, holding out the fish.

"Would you clean this while I take the other one out of the skillet, please?" she asked. "I honestly hated killing the first one and I never could have done it if I hadn't been starving."

"It's easier if you ask the fish's permission," he said, as he took it. "Say a blessing like, 'Brother Fish, we need the strength you'll give us. Thank you for the food.' "

"I will," she said. "Thank you, Mr. Chisk-Ko."

"Call me Cade," he said. "We're on a long trail."

"Call me Maggie."

Without another word, she turned and marched back to the fire, her backbone straight as a poker. Cade watched her until she bent over her skillet and began forking pieces of fish onto a big sycamore leaf. Then he went downstream a bit, found a flat rock, blessed the fish, and gutted and cleaned it.

His mind kept returning to Maggie, imagining her out in the middle of the rushing water, her bare feet planted determinedly well apart in the rocks of the creek's bed. She had stayed in that freezing water until she'd caught two fish in a net with a mouth no bigger than the fish's head!

Yes. Miss Maggie Harrington was a woman to be reckoned with.

He was almost back at the fire, with pieces of fish ready to cook, before the thought hit him. Her name was Maggie Chisk-Ko.

"Here's the next course of your meal," he said. "I'll fry it for you while you eat."

She was sitting cross-legged beside the fire now, ravenously consuming her breakfast.

"No," she mumbled. "That one's yours."

"I ate at Aunt Ancie's," he said. "I have coffee and biscuits and even tomatoes in my packs. Slow down and I'll get you some."

He squatted beside the fire and dropped the pieces of fish in the spider skillet.

"Where did you get this grease?"

"Cooked it out of the last of the sausage balls."

"Not bad!" he said, and glanced up to catch her eye. "You're not quite so fluffy as I thought."

Her hand stopped halfway to her mouth. Her shiny, lush lips curved into a stunning smile.

"If I were as fluffy as you thought," she said, flashing her blue eyes at him, "you'd still be waiting for your hanging in the Van Buren jail."

"Fair enough," he said, grinning back at her. "Hold on and I'll make us some coffee so we can drink to our freedom."

They did that, and Maggie ate her fill of fish and tomatoes and fry bread, while they looked at each other as if for the first time.

"I never thought you'd say you were sorry that you went off and left me," she said as she sipped her third cup of the potent coffee he'd brewed. "I appreciate that, Cade."

"I said that at gunpoint, you may recall."

She laughed and brushed at the debris from the trees and brush still clinging to her hair.

"Maggie," he said, "would you really have shot me?"

"That's for me to know and you to find out if you ever run off and leave me again."

He laughed as he set down his cup and got to his feet.

"We need to be riding. Let me take a look at your mare."

"It's a deep cut, but it may be all right to ride her," Maggie said. "I put ointment on her leg from a tin I brought in my pack."

He strode toward the tethered mare, silently berating himself for taking so long to get around to looking at her. They only had two horses, after all, and he was forty kinds of a fool for wasting so much time.

The instant he came up to the horse, he saw she was not well enough to ride. The cut was actually more of a puncture wound; it looked as if she had run into the stub of a broken limb sticking out from a tree trunk. The skin gaped, and blood welled slowly on each side of the salve Maggie had applied. A rider on her back would only cause it to bleed more.

Now, damn it all, they'd have to find another horse somewhere.

Briefly, as he spun on his heel and strode toward Smoke to get his own medicine, he considered going back home for one of the mules or for Cotannah's horse. But that would take a big chunk out of the daylight for traveling, and a second round of good-byes would take too much emotion. A posse could be riding behind them if the judge or one of the deputies had crumbled. He and Maggie needed to get to Red River as soon as possible.

"Do you think she's cut bad?" Maggie called.

She was pulling dry stockings from her bag, and she modestly turned her back to him to put them on, as if he hadn't already seen her naked legs and feet. And her round arms and beautiful shoulders when he'd jerked the quilt off her the morning before in the barn.

"The mare can't be ridden," he called to her. "If you're at all attached to that sidesaddle, take it up to the cave and leave it inside."

"What!"

"She'll be better off with nothing at all to carry. We'll be luckier than a handful of aces if she can keep up."

"Well, we're not leaving Joanna in the cave or anyplace else!" she cried, twisting around to look at him with blue eyes blazing. "We'll slow down if she can't keep up!"

"And let your father catch us."

"Let him try," she said grimly.

Then she stood up and turned to him, her boots in her hand. "I know! Let her rest a bit more while I clean up a little. I need to wash up and dig some different clothes out of my pack."

"No time," he said. "Think about it, Maggie. We're only a long day's ride from Arkansas. A posse could be riding hard to intercept us at Red River. You need to pack up the camp while I poultice this wound."

To his surprise, she didn't argue.

"What do you have for medicine?" she asked, while she sat down again to put on her boots.

"Dried red elm bark."

She was already cleaning the plates with sand and putting out the fire when he went to

the creek for water to mix with the red elm
dust. Her father must be a scoundrel, he
thought, if Maggie was so afraid of him.

Cade spread his concoction liberally on
Joanna's wound and tied Maggie's one small
bag, her bridle, and her rolled quilt and saddle
pad onto the supply packs that Smoke carried.
Maggie brought him the skillet and other gear.
Cade secured them, then picked up the last of
the medicinal paste he had mixed on a piece
of stiff bark. He turned to throw it away.

Maggie was still standing there, and his
gaze fell on the long scratch on her neck. It
was growing redder by the minute.

"Be still," he said. "Let me put the rest of
this on that scratch."

"*What?*"

"It's good for two-footed animals as well as
for four-footed ones," he said, laughing.
"Hold still for me, now."

He took some of the salve onto his fingertip
and spread it on the wound, stroking fast and
gentle down the length of it so as not to hurt
her more. He realized immediately that it was
a grievous mistake to have touched her, for
her skin felt like warm honey in the sun.

And as if she had sensed his reaction, her
heart-shaped face flushed pinker, making him
ache to cup it in his two hands.

She gasped at the pain, even careful as he
was, so, as he finished, he slipped his palm
around the nape of her neck to comfort her.
The pulse at the base of her throat beat like a

butterfly's wing beneath his thumb.

"Thanks, partner," she murmured.

Her full lips trembled with emotion; they pulled his gaze to her mouth and held it there.

Desire hit him like a wall falling. His whole body remembered how she'd felt in his arms the other morning. How, small as she was, she had fit there exactly. He wanted to lean over and taste her mouth. A hard, painful knot formed in his groin.

But he had promised himself and the Great Spirit to take care of her and to do what was best for her. And he was a man of honor. Maggie had seen that, too.

He pulled his hand away from her neck and tossed the piece of bark away. Then he reached for his leadrope, now attached to the mare's halter, to keep from reaching for Maggie. He held it out to her.

"You ride in front of me on Smoke and lead her," he said. "Give her enough slack to stay out of Smoke's way but not enough to get her tangled in the brush."

"I think I can handle it," she said, breathlessly, and stuck her toe into the stirrup.

She mounted in a flurry of skirts. He helped her, then forced his hand away from the tantalizing curve of her hip. He got up behind her, reached around her, and picked up the split reins from Smoke's withers.

He tried not to touch her, but even as slender as she was, it was well nigh impossible. He sat back away from her. He had to get a grip on himself, had to get his mind on something else.

"Are you going to leave that saddle there?"

"My father traded the Western saddle Grandpa gave me for a *more ladylike* sidesaddle," she said levelly, as he swung the stallion around to head south. "I can't imagine why I haven't left it somewhere before now."

He laughed at the dry irony in her voice.

"Good for you."

She smelled of woodsmoke and creek water, morning air and lilacs.

Her curly hair blew against his cheek, then brushed his chin. That must be the same sensation as feeling a cloud. He picked a leaf from the tangles of her curls and let it float away on the breeze.

"You have so many leaves on you that you can hide in the woods without even standing behind a tree," he teased her.

"Then I won't comb my hair the whole trip," she said, glancing back over her shoulder, past Cade, "in case my father comes up behind us."

The fear was clear in her voice. She was truly afraid of the man.

"When we get out onto the plains you'll have to find another disguise," he said.

"How about a set of Levi Strauss denims like yours? Then everyone who sees us will think I'm a man."

He chuckled.

"Maybe everyone who needs spectacles," he said.

He let himself move a little closer to her. The wind lifted her skirts and blew them back to embrace his legs. What a perfect armful she was!

What an idiot *he* was! He sat up straighter, dropped his left arm to his side, and held the reins with his right—without touching her. He wouldn't touch her again.

But soon afterward, exhausted by the trials of her harrowing night, she slumped back against him, sound asleep. He slipped the mare's lead out of her hand, took it into his own, and shifted in the saddle so he could hold Maggie cradled in the crook of his arm.

Chapter 7

Maggie sighed and tried to snuggle more deeply into sleep, tried to fall far and fast back into her dream. She was in her bed in her room at Las Manzanitas, listening to the jingling of spurs and bits, the creaking of leather, and the early morning snorts of the horses as the vaqueros gathered in the yard beneath the big tree outside her window. Later, she and Grandpa would ride out together to see them at their work.

But something pulled her into wakefulness. A heartbeat, deep and steady, beneath her ear. Her drowsy breaths were coming exactly matched to its vibrating rhythm. She opened her eyes.

Cade Chisk-Ko! She was in the middle of the Choctaw Nation instead of at her *rancho;* in his saddle instead of her bed. Why, she had been sleeping in his arms!

"Wake up," he said, quietly. "We're about to meet some people."

Her heart leaped into her throat.

"Pierce? Has he found us?"

Fear of her father paralyzed her for an instant. Then she grabbed the saddle horn, pulled herself up straight, and looked around.

Cade was here, he hadn't abandoned her. Cade was still with her and surely he wouldn't let Pierce take her back to Arkansas.

Joanna was still here, too, right beside Smoke. But they weren't moving. They were on top of a hill covered with pine and juniper trees. The afternoon light threw shadows from the west as the sun slipped toward the top of the highest purple mountain.

"We can hide," she said softly, "or travel on a ways . . ."

"It's not your father," he said. "It's our chance to get a horse."

Cade was looking down into the valley between their hill and the western ones. Maggie leaned forward to look, too. A dozen or more people were moving around a blazing fire, making camp where two faint trails crossed. She heaved a sigh of relief.

"They have wagons and children and pigs and milch cows," she said. "Pierce would have sent men only, on horseback, after me."

"Hmmm," Cade ignored her, his attention on the scene below.

Maggie turned to look at him, shivering. Her whole body had chilled since she'd moved away from him, and, without thinking, she leaned back, seeking the warmth of his arms.

He closed them around her and smooched to the horses to go forward. When they'd gone a short way, the breeze carried music up from the camp—a lively melody played on a fiddle.

"Who do you suppose they are?" she said.

"Settlers. Most likely headed for Texas. They're trailing plenty of stock, so it's also likely they'll trade horses with us."

That destroyed the last vestiges of sleep.

"I'll not trade Joanna!"

She sat up away from him, looking around frantically for the leadrope behind her, and snatched it up when she found it lying across his lap.

"Think!" he said impatiently, as he started Smoke moving a little faster. "She's slowing us down."

"I'm not *ever* getting rid of this mare!" she cried, clutching the lead in both hands. "Grandpa gave her to me."

"He gave you a *rancho,* too. If you want to reach it alive you have to have a horse that can travel."

"Then I'll *buy* one of their horses!" she cried. "I'll ride it and lead Joanna."

"She'll still slow us down. We'll have to rest more often."

"*I don't care!* I'm not leaving her!"

"So," he drawled, "the spoiled little girl replaces the woman who conquered the night."

A shiver raced through her. Would he really try to trade her horse? She fought back.

"And the selfish dictator replaces the partner who agreed to make decisions together."

"Be reasonable!" he said.

He smooched to Smoke again and they moved even faster down the hill.

"How much money do you have?" he said.

She gasped. "None of your business!"

"Then how are we to make decisions together, *partner?*"

"You don't know what the word means!" she snapped back, shivering again because she'd lost the warmth of his embrace.

"Look, Maggie, if you hadn't panicked and shot up the world last night we wouldn't be in this fix," he said in an infuriatingly calm tone. "You can't hope to run a ranch on your own if you make such sentimental decisions."

"She's my friend! You'd be sentimental if it was your precious Smoke up for trading!" she cried.

"How much money?" he said impatiently. "I'm not plotting to steal it, all I'm trying to do is set my bargaining limits."

Maggie whipped her head around to look him straight in the eye.

"If it's *my* money, then it's *my* bargain," she said. "I'll do the talking."

"Use your head," he said flatly. "Those men won't do business with a woman whose husband is with her."

She faced front again, fast. Husband! Goodness, he *was* her husband! Legally, Joanna was his, Maggie's money was his, and he could do as he pleased in any trade.

"You aren't really my husband! Remember that!"

She leaned back for balance to help Smoke go down the steepest part near the bottom of the hill, and though she tried, she didn't succeed in keeping her shoulders from touching Cade. The next instant his cheek was against hers, his lips and his cedary breath warm against her ear.

"If you want to get to that *rancho* of yours before winter, you'd better start seeing me as your husband," he murmured. "You'd better make these people believe it, too. Just keep remembering we want to trade horses with them."

"We do not! We want to buy a horse from them."

She twisted around to look at him.

"Just this very morning," she said firmly, "you promised to treat me as an equal."

His eyes were fixed on the people below.

"You were holding me at gunpoint. What choice did I have?"

"Gun or not, you meant what you said," she told him. "I saw it in your eyes."

He turned to look at her.

"We need another horse in the worst way. Those white people down there own the only spare horses to cross our path, and you're white and I'm Indian," he said. "We have to behave like any loving, married couple where the husband is the head of the house."

The figures of the people were growing larger and larger as Smoke carried her and Cade closer. Some of the men had heard the hoofbeats and were turning to look up the hill.

"What was all that malarkey you gave me back at the jail about people not approving of our being married?"

"They won't approve," he said. "But they'll be much more bent out of shape if they think I've kidnapped you or that we're unmarried lovers."

She gasped.

"But we're *not*!"

"I know," he said, with the most infuriating smoothness. "We're married."

"I mean we're not lovers!" she said, pounding the horn with her fist.

"Hello, the camp!" Cade called, lifting his hand in an amicable wave. "We're friends, coming in!"

With his lips hot against her ear, he said, "We must act like lovers. Maggie, do you understand me?"

"Yes," she said reluctantly. "But if you trade Joanna off, I'll never forgive you."

Cade chuckled and his breath tickled her neck.

"Trust me a little," he murmured. "I came back to get you this morning, didn't I, when I could have disappeared into the hills?"

"Y-yes."

"And I won't trade Joanna," he said, "unless they say they have no use for money."

Relief ran through Maggie like a warm river.

"Then we *can* be partners!" she cried, turning to smile up at him. "We can both work at charming them into taking money instead of Jo."

"Good idea," he said. "But let me do the talking at first."

He held her more tightly in the half-circle of his arm, her hip against his thigh. The closer they got to the strangers, the tighter his muscles coiled for action. Feeling the leashed power in his body stirred her senses mightily.

They came off the last, low ledge of the hill and down onto the flat road. Abruptly, the music stopped. Cade's muscles tensed even more. Maggie's breath caught in her chest.

"Hello," one of the men in the camp called to them in the suddenly eerie silence. "If you're friendly, come on in!"

He was an older man, holding a shotgun down low. He motioned with it for another man to come stand beside him. Two others came, too.

Several children tried to run to see the strangers only to have their mothers pull them back. Women and children peered around the wagons with curious eyes.

"They've got no real high-dollar horseflesh here," Cade muttered thoughtfully. "But I'll give thirty dollars or maybe more for that big bay mare over there."

"I have some jewelry, too," she whispered, just as he reined up. "Maybe they'd rather have it than money."

"Howdy, strangers," the man with the shotgun said, flicking his wary gaze from Cade's long hair to his bronze features to his starched, neat clothing.

He looked at Cade's arm around Maggie. Then he looked up into her eyes. His weathered face showed that he had seen a lifetime of hard living.

"Ever'thing all right with you, ma'am?"

"Yes . . . yes, except that my horse is hurt."

Maggie smiled at him but he didn't smile back.

He began edging to the opposite side of Smoke, away from his friends who were inching up on the near side of the stallion to put Cade between two sets of guns. Cade half-turned to glance at them, then he stiffened in surprise.

"Cade Chisk-Ko!" one of the men blurted. "You old son of a gun! Seth, it's all right—I know him."

"Greenwood Youngfox! What are you doing here?" Cade cried.

"Git down," the old man said. "Git down. If'n Greenwood knows you, you're welcome in this camp."

Cade dismounted, and he and Greenwood hugged and slapped each other on the back. Cade shook hands with the men as Greenwood introduced him to all of them, then turned back to Maggie. Behind Greenwood, the women and children were coming out of hiding to see the strangers who had turned out to be friends, after all.

"Maggie, this is an old friend I grew up with," Cade said. "Greenwood Youngfox. Greenwood, this is my wife, Maggie."

"Your *wife*!" Greenwood exclaimed, smiling at her. "Hello, ma'am."

He gave Cade a sly look.

"Well, now, Chisk-Ko, this is a surprise," he said, his irrepressible grin widening. "Lydie Doak will be mighty sorry to hear you've finally gone off and got married. She asked me about you not two moons ago."

Maggie stiffened.

"Who is Lydie Doak?" she blurted, as a sharp, unnamed emotion stabbed her unexpectedly.

Some of it must have seeped into her voice, for Cade looked at her quickly. He caught her eye and held it for a long, amused moment. Then he flashed her a teasing smile that made her bite her tongue.

Greenwood grinned at her.

"Ma'am, you'd better watch out for Lydie," he said, with a mischievous twinkle in his eye. "She was Cade's childhood sweetheart."

"Don't worry, darling," Cade said, flashing her a sweet smile, "Lydie's married."

"Not anymore," Greenwood said. "Husband ran off to California and that's why she was asking for you."

"She'll find somebody else soon," Cade said, then leaned toward Greenwood and, speaking in a stage whisper loud enough for everyone to hear, said, "Maggie's the jealous kind. She's crazy about me and she'll get all stirred up if we keep talking about Lydie."

Maggie felt the heat rising to her cheeks.

"Why, I am not . . ."

She bit her tongue as she remembered they must act like lovers. Then she laughed with the others. That devilish Cade had better watch out—two could play at this game.

"Wal, I reckon it's all right, boys!" the old man with the shotgun cried gleefully. "This fierce-lookin' Injun here's a friend of Greenwood's."

He took a step toward the two men.

"So, Mr. Chisk-Ko," he said, "I take it we don't need to hunt up a rope and hang you for carrying off a white woman?"

He turned his head and spat a blob of tobacco juice onto the ground as he chuckled at his own wit.

"No, Maggie's the one who carried me off," Cade joked in return. "She just snatched me right up and married me before I knew what hit me."

The jest was so unexpected—and so true— that Maggie laughed out loud. So did everyone else.

"That's happened to more than one old son of a buck, I reckon," the old man said, when he could catch his breath. "Myself included. Dolly, there, why she had me tying the knot as soon as I come to from where she knocked me over the head!"

When the laughter died down, one of the

women called out from the back of the group,
"You know better than that, Seth Sedgewick!
You know it was *you* wouldn't let me alone."

"Yeah, Grandpa!" one of the children cried.
"Remember what you said—you done married her for her biscuits and gravy!"

So in the midst of laughter, instead of the
hostility they'd expected, Cade lifted Maggie
down to the warm welcome of new friends.
As the boys led their horses away to be
tended, the older people escorted them
through the growing dusk to their fire.

"Welcome, friends of Greenwood Youngfox," Seth said, with a smile that made the
word cordially sincere. "Our dearest neighbors in Mississippi was the Youngfoxes. That
would be thirty-odd years ago, before the Indians was sent west and before Greenwood
was born. Me and his daddy used to hunt together."

Greenwood gave an abrupt nod to confirm
that. "The Sedgewicks came across into the
Nation to see my folks on their way to settle
in Texas," he said. "I'm riding with them as
far as Red River."

"Maggie has inherited a *rancho* on the Nueces," Cade said. "We're on our way there."

"We hear that's rough country," Seth said.
"We're aimin' for East Texas, ourselves."

The Sedgewick clan was gathering close
around the fire to see the newcomers and hear
what they said.

"Last night my wife's mare was spooked by

some bats, tore off through the woods, and stuck a stob in her leg," Cade said. "I need to go see to her."

So the men and boys went with him to examine Joanna's wound, and the women surrounded Maggie, who was staggering a little because her legs were so wobbly after all that riding. The oldest woman of the group put an arm around her for support.

"I'm Dolly Sedgewick," she said. "Is that Indian really your husband, honey?"

Maggie leaned on her, though she tried not to.

"I'm Maggie . . ." she said, but she couldn't quite bring herself to say "Chisk-Ko." "Maggie. And, yes. Yes, he is."

The woman's sharp eyes caught the fine ring on Maggie's left hand. "Is he good to you?" she asked.

"Yes," Maggie said, trying again and finally succeeding in making her numb legs hold her. "Except for continually bossing me within an inch of my life."

"Lord, Lord, don't they all?" Dolly said. "Well, he's the best-looking thing in breeches that I ever seen, Maggie dear, and I'm fifty-four years old." Then she paused and stepped sideways for a clearer view of Cade. "You just enjoy looking at that man," she said cheerfully. "Remember, sugar, he *could* have been bossy and ugly as sin, to boot."

All the women laughed, and Maggie joined in.

She could stand right here and look at him all day, too, she thought, as she watched his strong, lithe movements while he tested the mare's painful wound. Remembering how it had felt to be cradled in the curve of his body, recalling his rich voice murmuring in her ear made a sweet ache pool in her stomach.

Suddenly Maggie realized how *she* must look to *him*, how completely disheveled she was.

"Could I go somewhere and freshen up?" she asked. "I'm a mess from chasing that mare through the woods last night in the dark."

"Of course!" Dolly cried. "Come on down to the creek. Sally, run to the wagon for soap and a towel. And the ointment."

A little girl started running, calling, "Yes, ma'am, Granny."

"I don't want to trouble you," Maggie said. "I have my own things. I need to get my other clothes . . ."

"Jasper!" Dolly bellowed, and a boy turned from looking at Joanna's wound. "Bring Maggie's clothes!"

"Yes, ma'am!"

Cade untied the bag and handed it to the boy, who then gave it to Maggie.

"You git cleaned up and we'll have a good supper," she said, in a tone that warmed Maggie. "You need some meat on your bones."

But before Maggie turned away, Dolly reached out and caught her arm.

"You all must share our camp tonight,"

Dolly said. "That man of yours will be another protection for us on this wild, lonesome road, but mostly it'll just be a treat to visit with a new woman friend."

Her eyes crinkled at the corners, and Maggie thought she saw the sheen of sudden tears.

"It's a wonder," Dolly said, "what lies ahead of us all down there in Texas."

"That's true, but then it's a miracle what we've managed to leave behind," Maggie said. "At least, it is for me."

Dolly stared at her for a moment, then threw back her head and laughed. She folded Maggie into a generous hug.

"That's right, honey," she said. "You're young, but you see beyond your years."

Maggie let her face rest for a moment on Dolly's shoulder. Her tired muscles began to relax.

"Thank you for the invitation, Dolly. I'd love to stay, and I'm sure Cade wants to visit with Greenwood."

Impulsively, she reached into her bag and took out a brooch set with small rubies.

"I want you to have this," she said. "And not only because I appreciate your hospitality. Wear it when you have hard times in your new home, and think of me making my ranch down there on the Nueces. We can stick, Dolly. We can stick on our places in Texas."

Dolly took the brooch in her work-worn hand and held it to catch the light from the fire. Her face went bright with pleasure.

"Thank you, Maggie, dear."

She reached out and patted her cheek.

"You so young and cheerin' me up—why, I'm ashamed of myself. Now you go on and change your dress and I'll go find us some of my homemade wine to celebrate havin' company!"

So a while later, when they all sat around the fire drinking coffee and eating biscuits and rabbit stew, with Maggie clean at last and in her prettiest blue dress, she began to forget her troubles for the first time in a long while. Her father might be coming after her and she might be playacting the happy bride to a man she hardly knew, but that man was fascinating and handsome, the setting sun was brilliant, and the air was crisp with autumn. Instead of being under Pierce's thumb or alone in a cave, she was safe in good company.

And she was a new woman. She had been able to shore up Dolly's spirits because she knew her own strength now. And she knew it because of Cade.

The realization had come to her early that morning while she'd caught the fish and doctored Jo's wound. She had proved herself at last.

Oh, Maggie, you're so independent! Oh, Maggie, you're so brave!

Mimi and the others had always told her that, but she had never believed it. Last night she had proved she was independent—which she would never have been able to do if Cade hadn't pushed her. Really, he had done her a tremendous service by leaving her alone at the cave.

She would never tell him that though, she thought with a little smile, looking at him over the rim of her cup. He smiled back and her breath caught a little.

His eyes lingered on her for a moment before he returned to his conversation with Greenwood and the Sedgewicks. She loved watching his pleasure at being with his old friend, loved seeing him and hearing him talk without his usual wariness. But she wanted more of his attention on her—she wanted him to tell her how good she looked in her clean, blue dress.

No, what she really wanted was his arms around her as they had been when they were riding Smoke. Or to dance with him! That was it! Dancing with him would put her back into his arms!

Seth's brother, who'd been introduced as Lon, had finished his meal and was picking up his fiddle again. Maybe they could have a dance.

Everyone was spellbound, though, listening to Cade and Greenwood recalling old escapades and to Cade answering question after question about life in Texas. Maggie watched the firelight play on the high, chiseled cheekbones of Cade's face. Dolly had been right. He was indeed the handsomest man in the world.

But he was ignoring her. Oh, he met her eyes from time to time and smiled at her, but that was all. She drank the wine and started on a second cup while she sat beside Dolly and listened to the men. Cade had forgotten all about her and Joanna, too. The next thing she knew, the men would go off by themselves and make the deal without her.

Finally, a moment of silence fell.

"Sweetheart," she said, with a coquettish smile, "have you mentioned that bay mare to Mr. Sedgewick yet?"

Cade looked up in surprise and his eyes locked with hers. At least she'd gotten his attention.

"Not yet."

"What about the mare?" Seth said, but he spoke to Cade, not to Maggie.

"We need another mount," Maggie said. "And we need to buy because I want to keep my horse. What price would you put on your bay?"

A shocked silence fell. Seth half-turned toward her and then back to Cade again, looking embarrassed.

"Uh, well, that mare ain't exactly on the market," he said, settling his eyes on Cade. "She's one of our seed stock and I'm afraid we'll need every head."

Maggie felt the heat rise into her cheeks. Cade had been right. Seth was *not* going to do business with a woman whose husband sat right there.

"Maggie's like you," Cade said, with an indulgent smile. "She's in a hurry to get to Texas."

He shot Maggie a quick, warning glance.

"Seth, Maggie's done give me a brooch worth twice what that mare would bring at home or in Texas," Dolly said. "Seems to me we could trade it for the mare."

"No!" Maggie cried. "I didn't give it to you as a trade for a horse. That's a gift for you, Dolly!"

Cade set his bowl down in front of him and flashed her an irritated look.

"We could give money for the mare," he said reluctantly. "If you could spare her."

He made it clear that he was embarrassed that Maggie had ruined the evening with inappropriate talk of business.

Maggie smiled at him.

He frowned back.

Dolly glared at Seth, who stubbornly shook his head.

"That mare's Kentucky stock. I aim to start a running line with her."

"For shame!" clucked Dolly. "To deny help to some wayfaring strangers!"

"*I* know!" Maggie cried. "Mr. Sedgewick, my address is Rancho Las Manzanitas, Nueces County. Send me word of where you settle and I'll replace your mare with two from my grandpa's Kentucky line. They're Eclipse bred, the line goes all the way back to the Darley Arabian, as you know. My vaqueros will be

on the road to East Texas the day after I get
your letter."

Seth threw up his head and looked straight
at her. The whole family stared at him, waiting
for his response. The slanted, shocked look
Cade shot at her made laughter bubble to life
inside her, but she held it back and held her
breath.

"Two Eclipse bred, hmmn?"

"Yes!" she cried. "And I'll return your mare
into the bargain."

Seth looked at Greenwood and then at Cade
as if asking whether this bold young woman
could be trusted. Both men, in turn, gave him
a curt nod.

"Done!" he cried, and his grandchildren
cheered.

"Ain't that Eclipse stock got the best mus-
cling on them?" Seth asked Cade.

"I don't recall ever seeing any of that line,"
Cade said.

He threw Maggie another look. He was
changing his assessment of her again.

She gave him her most brilliant smile.

"Ain't you seen Maggie's horses?" Seth demanded.

"No. I've never been to her ranch."

"Well, how long have you two been married?" Greenwood asked.

"Seems like all my life," Cade drawled,
keeping her gaze captive with his. The corners
of his mouth twitched. He was trying not to
grin.

Maggie threw him a flirtatious look and took another sip of her wine.

"You all have found out our secret," she said, smiling happily. "We're newlyweds."

One of the girls in the family let out a scream at that exciting news, and the boys whooped and yelled.

"No *wonder* Miss Maggie is jealous of his old sweethearts!" Dolly shouted lustily. "She ain't had him very long for herself."

The whole camp erupted in cheers, and Dolly threw her arms around Maggie in a great bear hug. Children shrieked and men stomped their feet.

"Lon, git that fiddle to playin' some dance music! Denny, where's your banjo?" Seth shouted.

"We'll give you our wagon tonight so's you'll have a real bed all to yourselves!" Dolly called out over the noise. "It'll be nice and private!"

Maggie's warm blood leaped in her veins and roared in her head. Alone, in the wagon, nice and private! Her pulse raced. Oh, what had she done?

Cade was surrounded by men shaking his hand and slapping him on the back, but he caught her eye and gave her such a look that she laughed out loud.

Everyone began crowding around, pulling the two of them together.

"Let's have a dance!"

"No, by cracky, let's have us a chivaree!"

"Newlyweds! A chivaree! A dance *and* a chivaree!"

"Hot licks, Lonnie Joe, how's about a chorus or two of "The Eighth of January"?

A full-throated cry arose.

"Newlyweds lead out! Newlyweds lead the dance!"

Lonnie jumped up to get out of the way, already changing his sweet song for a fast one. Several other instruments appeared as if by magic, while the bigger boys paired off and ran to all four of the wagons. They removed the wooden tailgates in a few quick motions and laid them down side by side near the fire to make a dance floor.

Everyone else swarmed around Maggie and Cade, pushing them ever closer and closer together.

He laughed down at her, his teeth and eyes glinting in his handsome, dark face. As he stepped nimbly toward her across the open circle the Sedgewicks were making to hold them, he was already moving to the rhythm of Lonnie's music, while he came nearer and nearer.

He was smiling at her with a definite dangerous glint in his eyes.

Her heart pounded hard and fast with the rhythm of the wild mountain music. What had she gotten into? Soon they'd be alone in that wagon!

The many voices died away as everyone watched them come together. Lonnie softened the music so everyone could hear them, too.

"Mrs. Chisk-Ko?" Cade said, as he made a graceful, gallant bow. "May I have this dance to celebrate our marriage?"

She opened her mouth to accept, then heard the rest of the sentence. What did he mean by that?

Oh, Lord, what had she done?

A frisson of fear and hot excitement ran through her as she remembered the seduction in his voice as he'd invited her to come to him that night they'd slept on the hay. His dark eyes gleamed with an inner flame that set the core of her on fire.

"I'm glad you've arranged this," he drawled. "A nice, private bed is exactly what we need."

Everyone cheered again, and Maggie felt herself turn crimson while his brilliantly white, slightly crooked, entirely tantalizing grin struck her right in the heart. His eyes were dark and glinting with purpose, daring her, tempting her, mocking her, and beckoning her. To come to him and do much more than dance.

He had no mercy.

"You *devil!*"

"Ah, Maggie," he said, his voice dropping to a profoundly sensuous richness. "Come on—dance with the devil."

He held out one huge, bronze hand.

His palm would feel wonderful, all hard and callused and strong as the sun against her skin. And his arms . . . oh, she knew exactly how they would feel!

Whatever she had done, she was in for it now.

She lifted her hand and slipped it into his.

Chapter 8

H e set his hand on her waist and drew her into the circle of his arm. His boot heels struck the boards with a tantalizing rhythm that immediately attuned her pulse to its sensuous flow. As the dance brought them swinging closer to each other, she could feel his hand grow hot on her skin, the heat seeping through her dress. Her heart took flight.

For this moment, for once in her life, everything was perfect. For this moment, she was happy.

Cade's touch and the wine warmed the blood in her veins, roused her senses to exhilaration. The melody, the beat of the rollicking tune, made her jubilant.

Her father was far behind her, and her *rancho* lay ahead. They could reach it sooner because she—*she*—had actually traded horses with Seth without sacrificing Joanna!

Cade spun her away from him into the hands of one of Sedgewick's men and was gone before she knew it. She looked at him over her shoulder, followed him with her glance as they whirled in opposite directions

on the wooden boards. The music grew live-
lier and louder. By the time the dance brought
Cade back to her, her blood was fairly singing!

He smiled down at her.

The stars were out, scattered white and
bright all over a black satin sky, and the moon
was rising huge and yellow over the mountain. Sweet woodsy smoke from the fire rose
into the night like a banner of victory, and the
air smelled like pines and pungent autumn.

He gave her that devilish grin before whirling her out of his arms, then bringing her back
into them. Maggie's heart swelled with happiness until she thought she would burst.

An intoxicating thrill ran through her. What
would it be like, to be alone with him in the
wagon?

Finally, the music rolled and spun downward to a lilting stop. The Sedgewicks surrounded them.

"Let's put these here newlyweds to bed!"
Seth yelled. "Now it's time for th' chivaree!"

"I won't let 'em come inside the wagon,
honey," Dolly said, elbowing her way through
her family to Maggie's side. "I'm givin' 'em
the refreshments out here. You just let 'em
whoop and holler and then they'll leave you
all alone."

She looked from Maggie to Cade and back
again, beaming.

"Why, soon's you two get inside that wagon
and drop the doorflap, you won't even know
there's anybody else for miles around!"

"Dolly . . ."

Maggie stopped. She had no idea what she wanted to say. All she knew was that *she was going to spend the night in the wagon with Cade*.

"Your pack is in my wagon, Maggie dear, and I just put out the featherbed with clean sheets. There's a basin of fresh water, too, and some more of my homemade wine. Go on in there and enjoy yore handsome husband and get away from this bunch o' heathens!"

With whoops and hollers, the younger Sedgewick men gathered around Cade and began escorting him to the steps of the wagon. A moment later, Maggie felt her feet leave the ground as the women swept her up and delivered her to him. He reached down for her, and, to the great delight of their audience, picked her up in his arms.

A deep thrill roared through Maggie's blood, and her body immediately melted against his. She didn't even struggle. She didn't want to be free.

"Since we married, the best shelter we've had is a barn," Cade announced jovially, as if he were making a speech. "We want to thank the Sedgewicks of Tennessee for our first real bed!"

"You're welcome!"

"Git on in there, now, and git right to it!"

"Enough talk, time for some action, now!"

"Make him holler, Maggie!"

That was Dolly's voice. Heat rushed into

Maggie's cheeks as the girls screamed gleefully at that.

One of the boys yelled, "Make her beg for
more, Cade!"

Cade raised his hand in acknowledgment as
he smiled down into her eyes.

The noise of cowbells and pots and pans
clanging together grew to deafening levels.
Cade waved once more, turned, stepped over
the seat, and carried her into the privacy of the
wagon. He dropped the flap closed behind
them.

He nuzzled his face against the crook of her
neck and cradled her closer, put his lips
against her ear.

"Maggie," he said, "you're the devil. You're
the one got us into this."

His breath on her skin, the faint brush of his
warm mouth made her speechless, made her
shiver with pleasure. He kissed her on the
neck, quickly, lightly, and took a step deeper
into the wagon. When he made a move as if
to set her down, she reached up and slipped
her arm around his neck, pulling his head
down to hers.

The noise outside, if anything, was growing.

"Got us into what?" she asked, flirtatiously.
She tightened her arms around his neck.

He laughed, and another thrill raced
through her blood.

"Into temptation."

His mouth was so close to hers. In the
golden lantern light filtering in through the

wagon cover his eyes shone dark and intense. "Cade . . ."

His lips brushed her ear again, barely touched her cheek. Then, with a groan, he kissed her mouth.

Maggie wrapped her arms tighter around his neck and clung to him desperately, her body instantly coming alive. More alive, much more alive than she had ever felt before. Alive in a whole new world where she was the only inhabitant and Cade was the sun.

The sweet shock of the kiss sent tingling, unfamiliar sensations running along every nerve, over every inch of her skin. The heat of his mouth made her whole body open like a flower in the summer heat.

Her blood set to burning, and a deep, voluptuous beating started in her heart. The slow, sensuous rhythm, the pull of his mouth on all her senses overcame the raucous noise outside and made it fade away.

His mouth held the wanton, deep sweetness of wild honey. She would never get enough of it. She knew, in that instant, she could never get enough.

The searching tip of his tongue called to her then. The shock of such an intimate thing stilled her for an instant, then she met it joyfully and kissed him back in the same way. Dimly, in the back of her mind, she thought it seemed shameless, but she couldn't help it, she couldn't do anything else.

He finally broke the kiss, even while her

throbbing lips tried to keep his mouth on hers.

He took a couple of steps farther into the wagon, dropped to his knees, and laid her down.

She sank into the fresh-smelling featherbed while he loomed over her.

"You amaze me," she whispered, running her hands along the tops of his shoulders, then over his chest. "How can your body be so hard and so warm at the same time?"

Her lips felt new and different. She could hardly move them. She could still taste his honey.

He made an incoherent sound deep in his throat.

"How can yours be so *soft* and warm?" he whispered.

He stroked her arms from her shoulders to her wrists, then cupped her shoulders hard and shook her a little.

"Damn it, Maggie, I didn't know until I came back this morning and saw you cooking over your fire how much I'm attracted to you, how much I have been attracted to you since the minute I saw you standing in the window of that store, like a picture in a frame . . ."

"I'm not, though," she whispered. "I'm alive. Cade, I've never been this alive before."

He took a deep, shuddering breath.

"Listen to me. I want your attention."

You have it. You have the complete attention of every inch of my body.

"Maggie," he said, his voice low and rich

and knowing. "You wanted me to kiss you. And you kissed me back. You wanted us to be married and now you've gotten us into this honeymoon. If you don't want this marriage to be a real one, you'd better learn not to provoke a man."

Her breath was coming in short spasms. She couldn't speak.

I want to provoke you to kiss me again.

Her head felt dizzy from the kiss, but she sat up anyway. His hands stayed on her shoulders.

She wanted . . . she needed . . .

Kiss me, Cade. Kiss me again.

"Why not?" she said with a toss of her hair, which had come loose from its ribbons during the dancing. "Men provoke me all the time."

He groaned.

"That's not the kind of provocation I mean and you know it."

"No, I don't," she said archly. "What kind do you mean?"

He swallowed, hard.

"Jumping into men's conversations to try to start a horse trade out of the blue, after I told you I'd take care of it . . ."

"But you had talked for hours and you weren't saying a word about buying a horse," she said. "Your 'men's conversation' was provoking *me*." She smiled at him in the dimness. "So, Cade, that *is* the same kind of provocation, now, isn't it?"

He laughed, shaking his head as if to say

this conversation was hopeless. His fingertips grew warmer; she could feel their shape through the fabric of her dress.

Her blood raced even faster—it leaped—as his touch changed and gentled. Slowly, he reached out and brushed his fingertips to the sensitive skin at the base of her throat.

She gasped.

Oh, Cade.

His callused finger followed the shape of her scooped neckline, then trailed down the line of tiny buttons. His hand brushed the curve of her breast, the one that covered her thundering heart, setting a trail of fire.

How can you do that? she wondered. *I never knew such sensations existed.*

"Do we agree not to provoke each other?" she said.

She barely knew what she was saying. Her flesh smoldered everywhere his hand had been.

"If you'll stop, I will," he murmured, his low voice rich and seductive, openly lying.

"I will if you will . . ." she said, fighting for air.

His hand stopped just below her breast and spread out to grip her rib cage. One squeeze, she thought, and he could stop her heart.

She reached up to brush back her unruly hair, then forced a deep breath of air all the way to the bottom of her lungs. Cade's hand tightened on her instead of letting go.

His hot fingers were melting her.

"So," he said, his voice rumbling deep in his chest, "you're throwing down the gauntlet."

"Yes," she murmured, "I am."

She took a quick, ragged breath and leaned toward him. But she forgot what else she was going to say.

"Cade?" she whispered, as if he could tell her what it was. She touched his face.

"Ah, Maggie!"

He drove her down beneath him into a featherbed smelling of sunshine. She fell all the way through it, sinking down and down into the wondrous world of his kiss until she floated, mindless, clinging to Cade with both arms around his neck. Forever. She wanted to do this, only this, forever.

His hard hand moved up to surround her breast. He caressed it, then drew his thumb back and forth across its aching, standing peak.

No. *This*. This was what she wanted forever, this *and* his kiss.

Wanton pleasure shimmered through her like a heat wave rolling down a summer road; it instantaneously sent her raging to a fever pitch. This was ecstasy. How could such ecstasy exist?

She cried out when he broke the kiss.

"You kiss like a little vixen," he whispered, his breath warm against her skin as he pressed his burning lips to her throat. "That's another provocation."

She ran both palms recklessly over his back,

soaking in the breadth and the power of him through her skin, aching to tear away the shirt that covered his magical muscles. The yearning became unbearable; she had to feel his bare skin against her hands while his hot lips kissed her or she would die.

She pulled the shirttail loose and thrust both her hands beneath it, slid them across his rippling muscles, then trailed her fingertips up and down the cunning tunnel of his spine. He buried his face in the valley between her breasts.

"So," she said, and she gave a desperate gasp as he turned his head and pressed his open mouth to her breast. "You are criticizing my kissing."

He lifted his head.

"Not criticizing," he murmured. Without hesitation he started undoing her buttons.

"I wasn't sure how to do it," she said trembling, "because I've never kissed a man before."

He went completely still.

She slid her hands away from his naked back to reach for his shirt buttons and to urge him to go on with what he'd been doing. But she was too late.

"You've never *kissed* a man before?"

He was propped on both elbows, hovering over her. She caught a glimpse of his fierce eyes.

"You say that like I'm ... backward or something," she cried. "I know I'm eighteen and nearly an old maid, but Pierce never let me have any beaux!"

She drew in a deep, shaky breath.

"Lester Perdue pecked me on the lips one time," she confessed, "but he was a boy, not a man. And now I know that wasn't really a kiss."

"*Damn* it," Cade said. "Damn it all right straight to hell."

"What's *wrong*?"

"Pull your knife, Maggie, and make me get away from you."

Her whole body chilled.

"I don't want you to get away!"

She tried to throw her arms around him again, but he rolled onto his side, onto one elbow, and caught both her wrists with his other hand. He held them in a burning grip.

She hurt, she actually hurt all over because she lost his arms from around her, his mouth on her breast, and his sleek, silky back from beneath her hands!

"I thought you . . . had more experience," he said, the words rasping out of his throat. "I should never have kissed you . . ."

"You *said* the minute you saw me I was a fluffy, overprotected, helpless, rich girl! You *knew* I was raised a lady!"

"Some ladies indulge in a dalliance from time to time," he said wryly. "And you're so impulsive, such a little rebel . . . you came bursting into that jail by yourself . . ."

He shook her arms a little, as if to wake her.
And himself.

"You were bareheaded in public and bold
as brass the first time I saw you, looking me
right in the eye!"

She jerked her arms free.

"So? What difference does that make?" she
cried.

"I'm sorry," he said. "I should never have
touched you."

"I touched you, too!"

She reached out and touched his face, traced
the shape of his high cheekbone, trailed her
fingertips down his jawline to his lips.

"I *wanted* you to kiss me, Cade, and I
wanted to kiss you, I wanted you to touch me
and I wanted to touch you." She swallowed
hard and whispered, "I still do."

He caught her wrist and held her arm down
by his side.

"Don't mess with me," he growled. "Don't
tempt me, Maggie. You're playing with fire."

"I'm a big girl now."

"No," he snapped. "You're an innocent girl,
ten years younger than I am, away from home
for the first time, listening to your body instead of your good sense, if you have any."

Outside, the noise was changing again, from
chivaree to music. Cade dropped onto his
back, threw his arm over his forehead and lay
still.

She leaned over him. "I'll have you know,

Cade Chisk-Ko, that I have plenty of good sense!"

She smelled of lilacs.

A song filled with yearning floated from the fiddle strings outside the wagon. Its melody rose and fell with the rhythm of their tense breathing.

Maggie stayed still, waiting for his answer.

He gave none. He kept his arm where it was and his eyes on the dim cloth overhead. If he looked at her, he would grab her and pull her down across him and lose himself in her lush mouth. He would rip that dress away and free her soft, perfect, breasts, which fit his hands exactly.

"I'm here to do a job," he said roughly. "I'm your man-jack-of-all-trades for one year. If we became lovers, with you in this vulnerable state that you're in, you'd . . ."

"I'd *what*?" she demanded, sitting flat down, her hands on her hips. "Beg you to stay once the year's up? You have harped on that since the minute we met!"

He sat up, too.

"More than one young lady has mistaken a roll in the hay for a declaration of love."

"Cade Chisk-Ko! Are you saying that I would fall in love with you—that you could break my heart? I have never seen anyone with such a high opinion of himself!"

"I know women," he said.

"You don't know me! You think you do, but you don't!"

The sweet melody from the fiddle changed into a faster one. A dozen feet clattered on the makeshift dance floor. She leaned toward him, so close to his ear that her breath blew warm on his cheek.

"Make no mistake," she said. "My love is Las Manzanitas and it always will be. I'm not falling in love with any man and giving him any power over me!"

Cade clenched his fists to keep from reaching for her.

"You flatter yourself," she cried, her eyes flashing in the flickering shadows. "I'd rather be in *jail* than be here with you! I can't stand another minute of this!"

She scrambled to her feet and started toward the back canvas flap.

"I know how you feel," he said, forcing a soothing note into his tone.

And he did. He wanted out, too. He would give every dollar he had to jump off this wagon, onto Smoke, and be gone from this whole stupid, noisy mess.

But the mess would be a whole lot worse if she ran outside yelling that she couldn't stay with him another minute, that he'd trapped her into the wagon. In spite of all Greenwood could do, old prejudices would be aroused and would cause a fight here or a visit from the law somewhere down the line.

He couldn't tell her to stay put, though. She'd do just the opposite.

"I would surely appreciate it if you'd go on

out there and stop that racket," he drawled, "but I doubt you'd enjoy explaining all night to Dolly and the girls why you've left your poor groom to pine away alone."

She whirled around to face him.

"That's right!" she cried, over the shouting and laughing and music outside. "Ooh, I can't stand it! I simply cannot bear this! I wish I'd never thought of bringing you along and made Emily come with me instead!"

She dropped down onto the bed and buried her head in her hands.

"Who's Emily?"

"My sister, one year older than me."

"You think you're trapped," he said, gruffly. "All my life I've been running and now I have to run to *your* rhythm when I ought to be taking care of my sister Cotannah."

He swallowed hard.

"Cotannah would give anything to live in a family like yours," he said. "But our parents are dead. Instead of asking her to run away with you, you should've stayed there with Emily. Both of you belong with your mother and father."

She lifted her face and sat up straight to stare at him.

"Don't give advice unless you know what you're talking about," she said fiercely. "You don't know anything. Pierce can't be called a father."

"Why not? You may think he's dictating to

you when he's only trying to act for your own good."

"Hardly," she said icily. "Slowly drowning a litter of kittens in a tub and forcing us to stand and watch as he placed the small, dead bodies in a neat row on the grass can hardly be called acting for our own good. That's what he did as punishment when we didn't behave properly while there were guests over at the house."

Pity stabbed him, she sounded so bleak, and protectiveness surged up in him like flood-waters rising. He would never let anyone hurt her again.

But she had survived all that cruelty with her strength and her spirit intact. She had such guts! And he would help her, he would make her *ready* for that *rancho*.

The corners of his mouth turned up in a smile as the irony of their situation struck him. They were much more alike than he had orig-inally thought—they were both survivors. She was white, but she'd had someone try to break her spirit just as Headmaster Haynes had tried to break his.

"Now I've gone off and left Emily at his mercy," she said. "That breaks my heart."

She sounded so forlorn that Cade ached to gather her up in his arms and hold her close. Instead, he sat back, away from her, and leaned against a strut of the wagon. Making love with her was not the way to take care of her as he had promised himself and the Great

Spirit. He must use only words to comfort her.

"There's an old Choctaw legend," he said, "about Deer, who grew weak and thin from lack of food one dry season. One day he crossed paths with Possum, who was fat and sleek.

" 'Possum, how do you keep so fat when I cannot find enough to eat?' Deer asked.

"Possum said, 'I live on persimmons and they are especially big this year. I have all I want to eat.'

" 'But persimmons grow high above the ground. How could I get some?'

" 'Do what I do,' said Possum. 'Go to the top of a high hill, run down very fast, and strike a persimmon tree with your head so hard that all the ripe fruit falls to the ground.'

" 'I can do that,' said Deer. 'Watch me.'

"So Possum waited near the tree while Deer went to the top of the hill, turned and ran down quickly. He hit the tree with such force that all his bones were broken and he was killed.

"When Possum saw what Deer had done, he laughed so hard he stretched his mouth, which is still very large today."

Maggie looked at him. He looked at her. Outside, the fiddles played.

"Cade," she said. "Why did you tell me that?"

"I don't know."

She laughed. Truly laughed. Warmth spread through him, and he had to fold his hands behind his head to keep from reaching for her. He had to clear his throat to speak.

"Maybe the story says people should make their own decisions instead of doing what others tell them."

"But I wasn't tricking Emily or telling her to do something that would harm her."

"You can't know that. Maybe she's better off staying there than riding this trail."

"I don't see how that could be," Maggie said soberly. "Pierce is making her marry grouchy old Asa Cunningham at Thanksgiving."

Then, to Cade's delight, she laughed her silver laugh again. "Or maybe the legend means that if you make fun of other people's troubles, you'll always have a big, ugly mouth."

"Maybe," Cade said. "Or maybe it means that each one's fate is destined. Even with the power Deer has, he's fated for men's dinner tables."

"True," Maggie said thoughtfully. "But I can *not* believe that Emily's destiny is to be wife to Asa."

"Is she resisting the marriage at all?"

"No. I'm the only one she even talks to about how much she hates the whole idea."

"So Emily's older than you but not as brave?"

"I don't know if brave is the word. She's not as . . . desperate, somehow. If I had married Neidell I think I would have literally died. And if I'd had to stay another night in Pierce's house, I would've died. Or killed someone."

She gave a little gasp.

"I . . . forgot," she murmured. "I didn't mean to bring that to your mind."

"Maggie," he said, because suddenly he had to say her name.

He tasted it on his tongue.

He said it again.

"Maggie. I killed Haynes, yes. He needed killing. But I only meant to hit him as punishment."

"Punishment for what?"

"For cutting my sister with a whip because she resisted his attempt to violate her. For abusing a girl I loved so that she killed herself from the shame. For all the beautiful innocents whom he terrified and ruined."

The light from the lanterns flared stronger. He could see the pale set of her face. Her eyes were huge and dark.

"Dear Lord," she said, with a catch in her voice. "Another supposedly respectable man like Pierce and the marshal and the judge!"

"He was worse," Cade said, old bitterness rising with his memories. "I've seen a lot of bad men, but he was the most despicable."

"Is your sister badly hurt?"

"She'll be scarred, inside and out, but she's strong, like you, and she'll overcome it."

"Was she at your family's house when you got the supplies?"

"Yes."

Suddenly he felt Cotannah's pleading arms

around his neck, and he blurted, "She begged me not to leave."

"So did Emily. I felt like a heartless deserter to leave her."

"So did I."

"I can't save Emily," she said, quietly. "*That's* what the legend means. She has to save herself."

They fell silent, remembering, listening to the sweet, mournful melody of the mountain ballad the Sedgewicks were singing. Slowly, with a long sigh, Maggie lay down again across the featherbed. She drifted off to sleep wrapped in the emotional closeness that had leaped to life between them, remembering the little smile she'd seen on his face before he'd told her the legend. The stone face had cracked, finally. He had shared his deep feelings.

When the song was done at last, Cade heard the slow, even rhythm of her sleeping breath. Poor thing, she was worn out. No wonder. He reached for the sheet and pulled it up over her, careful not to touch her at all. He could still taste her and still feel her satin skin, but he must never touch her again.

She was an innocent girl. But she also was a woman grown.

A woman he wanted with all of his being, like none he had ever known.

Why would that be?

He leaned back again, tilted his head, and

stared up at the shadows the moonlight made on the top of the wagon.

For one thing, he liked her. Despite the fact that she was a spoiled, fluffy white girl, he admired her spirit. But that was no reason, really. He liked and admired most women. Almost all of them. Women were the real heroes of the world. They bore the brunt of marriages and families, which was what life was all about.

And what he would never have.

Because of *the feeling*. Because it would never let him stay with any one person in any one place for very long. That thought made his heart stop.

Never, in all the years since riding onto the academy's fenced-in grounds for the very first time, had he lived through a whole day and night, much less two days and nights, without once fearing *the feeling*.

Never.

Until now.

Chapter 9

⟨◦◦⟩

They rode out of camp the next morning as they would ride for the next three weeks: armed and watchful of strangers, teasing and laughing, keeping everything lighthearted with each other. They couldn't deal with the emotional tie that the night had forged between them in any other way.

At least, *he* couldn't because he was damned scared, Cade thought. And Maggie was scared, too. He could tell, because when he'd helped her saddle and bridle her new horse with the tack they'd bought that morning from Seth, she had been careful not to touch him, not once. When they'd gotten lined out on the trail, she'd talked about Greenwood and the Sedgewicks, about the dancing and the food, without once referring to anything that had passed between them in the wagon. No mention of her family or his, nor of marriage, real or pretend, not even a reference to Deer or Possum.

That reticence on her part made him realize how truly unafraid she usually was of her feelings, and how much he admired that in her.

Sometimes he hated being so hidebound in holding everything back.

In this case, though, it was good that he was hidebound and that she was being cautious. It was absolutely not practical at all for them to have feelings for each other. That reckless opening up and sharing of deep emotions they'd done in the wagon had tied them together almost as surely as a real wedding night would have done—if they had made love, they'd have been pulled into a morass for sure.

He clucked to Smoke.

"I'll scout to that bend around the hill up ahead," he said to her as he started to ride on ahead.

"Then I'll take Jo," she said, and stood in her stirrup to reach for the leadrope, careful not to brush fingers with him.

That was good. They would put their emotional connection and physical attraction aside and concentrate on getting to their destination instead. He would use this time to get her ready for what she had to do.

After he looked at the road ahead, he came loping back to meet her. The autumn woods blazed all over the hills behind her, and the sky glowed with the same shade of blue as her eyes. She was riding with her hat off so she could turn her face up to the sun. The sight of her made his heart turn over inside him. Her hair was coming loose and curling in every direction, and her body sat slender and straight in the saddle.

"Your face will be sunburned," he cautioned, as he reached her.

"Yours already is," she retorted, with a giggle. Then she gave him a smile to show him that she was only teasing, that she meant no harm. He had to laugh. And he had to either look away from her or pull her out of her saddle into his arms. Her trusting him enough to tease him about the color of his skin after he'd gotten so angry with her in Tandy's barn bespoke of their new intimacy as clearly as a shout in the night. It drew him to her.

Careful. He must be careful.

"That brings us to your first ranching lesson," he said lightly, fixing his gaze firmly on the tips of Smoke's ears. "If you go around making remarks such as that you might offend some of your vaqueros and end up trying to do all the work yourself."

She laughed.

"No, Bascom's the one I'll be offending, and he's white."

"Who is he?"

"If he came back from the war, he's the foreman. He wandered onto the ranch when he was twelve, and Grandpa took him in."

"You don't like him?"

"No. He used to tease me unmercifully because he fancied himself Grandpa's foster son and he was jealous that I was *really* related to him."

"Hmmm. He may give us a rough reception."

"Why do you think I wanted you to come with me?"

They laughed together, and then she began to tell him more about La Casa Grande—the division where the main house and headquarters were located—and the people who lived there. But she didn't know much about the work.

"I'm going to prepare you to run that ranch, Maggie," he said. "I'll tell you everything I learned mustanging in the Strip and cowboying in the Colorado."

"But teacher, I didn't bring my ink and pen and composition books!"

"You can't write and ride. *Remember* what I say," he said sternly. "I'll test you every evening, and if you make too many mistakes, you'll have to do all the chores."

"I'll hang on your every word!"

So, for more than a week, as they traveled south, pushing hard against possible pursuit and winter weather, they talked of managing pastures and cattle and men. Or they stuck to jesting and silliness. They stayed connected, yet kept their emotions at bay. They didn't touch, and they took turns sleeping and standing guard.

That lasted until one evening after they had crossed Red River and ridden a distance into Texas.

"Have you noticed we haven't seen a bandit

or a sign of one?" Maggie said, looking up from her cooking with a mischievous glance. "I don't think there *are* any renegades in Texas. You were only telling me that, trying to scare me."

Cade finished driving a stake into the ground and went to get a horse to tie to it.

"I need to teach you to shoot," he said, returning the look as he walked past her. "If you're on guard during an attack, you're apt to kill me and all our horses instead of the bad men."

"Well, thank you so much," she retorted. "After supper I'll show you how wrong you are!"

They hurried through the meal and the chores so there would still be time and light enough for shooting practice. Afterward, Cade dragged up a dead limb to use for a target, and Maggie carried one of his extra boxes of ammunition in both hands.

He tried not to watch her, but somehow, he had no strength to resist. She moved with a girlish grace, an eager energy that was uniquely hers. He shook his head in wonder. Nothing ever wore her down, not all the miles of hard riding or the endless chores. Soon she wouldn't be fluffy or spoiled anymore.

For a moment, when she reached him, they looked into each other's eyes. Then she held out the box to him.

He took it and began filling the loops in his belt.

"I'll wear it and hand you the rounds," he said. "It's too big for you, anyway."

That would keep him from the temptation of putting his arms around her to buckle the belt on.

"Now," he said, pulling the six-shooter, "hold the gun in both hands, one bracing the other, and sight in your target."

She took the pistol and pointed it at the dead tree limb as he stepped around behind her.

"Arms straight," he said, and reflexively reached to grasp her elbows.

He dropped his hands without touching her.

"Lock your elbows."

She did.

"I'd forgotten how heavy this thing is," she said breathlessly.

"Pretend you're shooting up a cave full of harmless little bats," he drawled.

She laughed and half-turned to hit at him.

"Here, here, careful now!" he said, laughing with her. Then he grabbed her gun hand and pointed the muzzle out ahead. She was caught in the curve of his arm, her breast against his chest.

"You don't trust me," she said, glancing up at him with her eyes blue as the October sky. "But I won't shoot you. You haven't gone off and left me again."

His breath stopped in a lump in his throat. How could he ever have left her at all? And, that night in the wagon, how could he have stopped without making love to her?

"Hey, we're trying to have a shooting lesson here," he said lightly.

"Yes, teacher."

Their eyes held for another long heartbeat, then she straightened up and took the gun in both hands, dragged in a deep breath, and sighted in on her target.

"Feet apart," he said. "Let's have a wider stance."

She did as he said, setting her feet in place with a fast, saucy precision that made the heavy riding skirt swirl around her boots and settle tightly across her small, round hips.

Then she looked up at him over her shoulder.

"How's that?"

Deliberately, he placed his hands on her hipbones.

"Just exactly right," he said, huskily.

She drew in a quick, sharp breath, but she didn't look away.

"Maggie."

She smiled at him.

He pressed his palms flat, slid them onto her belly, pulled her back against him, and buried his face in her hair. Her cloud-soft hair that smelled of lilacs.

But her lips were softer. He knew that well.

"Maggie," he said, again.

She melted into him, she couldn't help herself. She managed not to drop the gun, but that was all she could do.

His low voice sounding so mellow saying her name, his warm hardness swelling against her, his vibrant hands moving hot and hard over her belly were stirring the very core of her into a wild passion that destroyed her strength. She leaned into him harder.

The pistol dragged down on her arm, filled her hand when instead she wanted to be touching Cade. She reached back without turning around, trying to find his holster without causing him to take his hands away.

He laughed at her a little and stepped closer, shifted his hip against hers to bring the holster nearer while his palms slid in deep, languid circles on her belly. They sent a thrill trembling through her that weakened her more. The gun slipped.

Cade closed his hand over hers to take it away, and she turned into his arms. Boldly, she brushed her aching breasts against his chest, wishing with a sudden, fiercely shameless wanting that there were no clothes between them at all.

He seized her face in both hands and turned it up to his desperate kiss. She fell into the hot, honeyed world of his mouth. Its power consumed her.

Except for one small corner of her mind.

One year. He would only be with her one year.

And already, in this week past, she had

wished a thousand times that he would stay with her forever because he was her amusing companion. And her fascinating teacher. And her generous protector.

How much more would she want him to stay if he was her wonderful lover?

And he would be. This time he would not be the one who stopped them, his mouth and his hands were telling her that.

She reached deep inside for strength and loosened her arms from around his neck. She placed her palms flat against his shoulders, and although they clung there, she tore her lips free from his sweet fire.

"No," she said, gasping for a steady breath. "No, Cade."

He pressed his cheek to hers, took her chin in his hand to turn her mouth to his again.

"Maggie . . . ?" he murmured.

She stiffened her arms and made herself step back. The tears started to come.

"One year," she said, around the knot forming in her throat, "you'll only be with me *one . . . year.*"

He went completely still.

She made herself look at him so she could prove to him how strong she was, and to make herself know that she could do this.

"We have so much fun together," she said, with a sob. "Don't we, Cade? And you'll be gone from me in one year. You were right that night in the wagon. If we make love, I'll die when you go."

He stood there and looked at her with his eyes gone darker than midnight and his old stone face back in place. Then, without a word, he turned and strode away.

Every day after that, Maggie told herself that this inescapable pull, this yearning for each other's touch, would surely disappear when they reached Las Manzanitas. Of course it would. It was strong now because they were alone all the time, but with other people around constantly, plus with the ranch to run, it would vanish.

They had worked hard, both of them, to ignore it and go on the same as they had been. After some hours apart that night of the shooting lesson, they had gone back to their old, teasing ways. But now the tension was always much closer to the surface.

Nothing could ever come of it, and she certainly couldn't live like this forever. So she tried, she truly tried, not to relive his kisses over and over again, and they both made sure that they never touched each other. But still, somehow, the tormenting longings were always present.

There were days when Cade started out remote and withdrawn, other days when Maggie vowed to herself to think and plan about the ranch and forget he was there, but he was an inextricable part of Las Manzanitas now, even before he got there, and within minutes they always ended up connected again.

Somehow they were becoming even closer in spite of not touching and not talking any more about themselves or their emotions. At night they sat by the fire and explored each other's minds, they told of books they had read and of things far removed from them and in the past, Choctaw tales and stories of early Texas that Grandpa Macroom had heard or lived through.

"I almost dread going there, now," Maggie blurted on the morning they rode the wet horses out of the Nueces River and onto its west bank, the northernmost soil the old Irishman had carved out of the Wild Horse Desert to ranch.

"It's going to be awful arriving at La Casa and not seeing Grandpa, knowing he'll never be there again."

The words were already out of her mouth when she realized that she'd broken their unspoken taboo against talking about their feelings. That was what had drawn them into that instant closeness in the wagon that night and started all this. Cade's comforting her had been as seductive, as addictive, as his kiss.

But today she needn't have worried.

He threw her a sharp look.

"The Captain was dead the last time you were at the ranch, wasn't he?"

"Well, yes, if you must be so blunt about it, at the end he was. But when we arrived, a month earlier, he was alert and full of spirit even though he knew he was dying. I've never *come* here and found him gone."

"It's your place now, Maggie, and you're learning to run it," Cade said quietly, standing up in the squeaking leather of his wet stirrups to search the horizon.

"It satisfies me to say that," he said, lightly, but she knew him well enough by now to listen carefully, for he, too, was breaking the taboo against speaking his emotions.

"You've been a good student, Miss Maggie," he said. "I'm proud of you."

He sat down and looked at her then, gave her a smile that warmed her all through.

"And you've been a good teacher," she said. "You know a lot more about ranching than I'd ever have guessed."

He laughed.

"I didn't know I knew that much, either. I guess I *can* run the place until . . ." He hesitated. "For a while."

She blocked those words out of her mind. They were just getting here. She would *not* think about his leaving.

"I never knew how enjoyable it would be to pass on knowledge to someone," he said.

"That proves it *is* more blessed to give than to receive," she said.

"Oh," he said, pretending to take offense. "So you, the recipient, weren't also blessed on this trip?"

A knot came in her throat, but she made herself smile. "I had a wonderful time on this trip," she said, and watched his eyes grow warm and deep brown like autumn leaves in the sun.

The terrible desire swept through her again. She held onto her saddle horn. It would carry her away someday if she wasn't very, very careful.

She rode Joanna briskly past him, leading the bay mare.

He laughed with the pleasure those few words had given him. He caught up with her effortlessly, just as she turned to throw him a glance.

The sight of him took her breath away. The morning light limned his face in copper, reached in beneath the brim of his hat to caress his high cheekbones, his aristocratic nose, his strong jaw. The look of him, the handsome, shining strength of him, combined with the feelings they had just shared, reached out and twisted her heart.

Finally she gathered the strength to turn and ride on.

"Now that we're here, I'm the teacher," she teased. "What name do the raiders from Mexico call the Texas cattle?"

"*Nanita*'s cows," he said, as he rode up even with her again. "Grandma's cows. Because their ancestors belonged to the original land grantees from Spain and Mexico, who got scared and went back home."

"Well, the raiders had better learn that *we* are here, now!" Maggie said, shaking her fist in the air. "*Nanita* fled from them and left the cattle to go wild, but we won't!"

"Big talk from a little woman," Cade teased. "Talk's cheap. How far is it to your Casa Grande from here, O Mistress of Las Manzanitas?"

"Only a couple of hours. We crossed the Nueces at the spot closest to the house. We need to watch closely now for some of our vaqueros so that we can identify ourselves. Whoever's in the lookout tower might mistake us for cattle thieves."

Cade turned in his saddle to search the sprawling open prairies behind and all around them. Maggie looked, too.

The land flowed away from the river, its grass growing stirrup-high, rippling gently in the breeze out of the south. The early morning light laid a blue haze over the prairie, and lines of grayish green live oaks stood far, far away at its edges. Even farther away, to the west, a cloud of tan dust rolled and billowed, made, no doubt, by a herd of wild horses on the run.

Maggie drew in a long, trembling breath.

"Oh, I love this land," she blurted. "Don't you, Cade?"

He was drinking it in with his eyes. But he said, "I never fall in love with a place because I know I won't be there long."

He was warning her. She must take heed.

Then, he asked briskly, as if suddenly he had no use for sentimentalities, "What other defenses besides the lookout tower did the *rancho* have when you were here four years ago?"

Maggie clicked to Joanna and picked up the pace.

"The war was over," she said slowly, thinking back to those horrible weeks when her grandfather was dying. "And Bascom hadn't come back, so the head of the vaqueros, an older man called Luis, was taking his place leading the patrols. Twenty or so men patrolled the ranch all the time."

"Bascom is usually the one in charge of the patrols?"

"Yes. Grandpa used to say he wasn't workbrittle enough for anything else. He liked chasing raiders and shooting it out with hide-peelers a whole lot better than he liked branding cattle or building that fence Grandpa had started."

"You said Pierce will probably have telegraphed Bascom or whoever the foreman is, telling him that you're most likely headed this way," he said thoughtfully. "Would he order them to bushwhack you?"

The old pain of having a father who could even consider such a thing stabbed at Maggie.

"I don't think so," she said. "Pierce wants me alive and unhurt to use as a bargaining chip with the Kurtzes. He's thinking he can drag me back to Van Buren somehow, and he is *desperate* to reassert his power over me."

Cade swept the horizon ahead with his sharp, dark gaze.

"All right, so we won't be attacked by our own people. Back to the raiders. Any other defensive measures at La Casa?"

"Grandpa kept thirty stands of rifles and a lot of ammunition in the big parlor," she said, glad to leave the worrisome subjects of Bascom and Pierce. "And he'd had the brass cannon set up in the yard ever since the cow camp days. At the time he died four years ago, it still worked."

Cade grunted.

"The cannon will scare off most raiders from the area around the house," he said. "So they'll be hitting us in the pastures, hard, again and again."

Maggie's stomach knotted. They would go through more adventures, many more, than they had yet encountered. How much closer would this year bring them to each other? Oh, dear Lord, how could she keep her emotions separate, hold herself apart from him?

"Riders coming!"

He pushed his mount to get in front of Maggie. Her heart gave a leap, then began to thud in hard, hammer strokes against the wall of her chest.

"They're probably some of our men," she called to him. "Maybe I know them."

She knew Luis, she thought, and some of the others. She stiffened her back, sat up straight in the saddle, and set her hat at a firmer angle.

Luis would accept her as boss, surely. He and her grandfather had been great friends. He would want Hugh Macroom's wishes met, even if Grandpa had left the *rancho* to a woman.

But neither of the men was Luis, she saw as Joanna caught up with Smoke. They were young, and Anglo, and tough-looking. Their hard eyes showed surprise, though, as the four of them met at the base of a small knoll overlooking Manzanitas Creek and they saw Cade's Indian features and long hair.

"Who are you and where're you headed?" one of them demanded. "This is Running M-Rancho de Las Manzanitas—it ain't no public pike."

"Where I'm from," Cade drawled, "a man removes his hat when he meets a lady."

Both riders looked startled.

"I'll be damned," blurted the taller one. "Manners lessons from a . . ."

But Cade's dark eyes, impersonal and piercing as a hawk's, rested steady on him.

"Indian," Cade said. "Choctaw."

After a long, tense moment, the man's eyes shifted to Maggie.

"I'm Cade Chisk-Ko. This is my wife, Maggie Harrington Chisk-Ko, the new owner of Las Manzanitas."

Stunned silence fell as both men looked at her and removed their hats.

"I'm Ferguson, he's Dunham," the taller one finally said.

"You're the new owner ... ma'am?" Dunham asked.

"Yes. Captain Macroom was my grandfather."

"Well, hel ..., I mean, well ... well, God bless Texas!" Ferguson blurted. "So *this* is who we're looking for! We never expected ... why, we thought you'd be traveling in a coach with ... with ... a whole army of outriders, ma'am."

Maggie smiled.

White outriders, he meant, but he didn't dare say such a thing to a man as forbidding as Cade.

"My husband is all the protection I need," she said. "We've had a very safe journey."

"That's good to hear, ma'am. Let us escort you to La Casa."

Dunham wheeled his mount.

"Who's running the ranch?" Maggie asked, as they started off at a long trot.

Both *vaqueros* threw her a surprised look.

"My father has been managing the place from long distance since my grandfather died," she explained. "He ... he didn't confide in me."

Both men glanced from her to Cade.

She knew what they were thinking. She might be the new owner, but she wasn't the new boss. Her father had managed her property before she married. Now her husband would run the *rancho*.

"Bascom," Ferguson said. "Man named Bascom is the foreman that hired us on."

Maggie's stomach tied itself into a hard knot. So. She would have to fight her old nemesis for control. Since the minute Emily had mentioned his name, Maggie knew she would be confronting Bascom.

Thank God Cade was with her, for he had more natural authority than any other man she'd ever seen. Yet, that could be a problem, too, since no one would think of coming to her for orders when he was around.

And yet—they wouldn't be eager to work for an Indian either. Her hands shook on the reins, and she pulled the bay mare's leadrope more firmly against her body. Cade might have brought her safely home, but now, to keep it, they faced worse dangers than any they had encountered on the trail.

"There's La Casa Grande, if you happen to speak a little Mex," Dunham said at last as they pulled up.

"I think that's a beautiful name in Spanish," Maggie said. "You have to admit, Dunham, that it's more melodious than *The Big House*."

He only grunted in response, but Maggie didn't care. All she wanted to do was look at her home.

They were sitting in a live oak motte on top of the knoll to the west of the house. The sight of the Casa and its outbuildings below—the lookout tower on top of the old commissary, the old stockade from the cow camp days, the stables and corrals and the gracious white frame house with its porches, the hospitable house that had a wing added to the back for a big dining room—was the realization of a thousand dreams for Maggie. Small houses for the vaqueros with families were scattered everywhere, one near the big house's separate kitchen. Children played in the yards, cattle and horses moved slowly in the sun-drenched pens and pastures.

Everything was still there, still in its place, but solidly three-dimensional now and not just an image in Maggie's mind. Her heart swelled, and tears stung her eyes.

"Grandpa's first ranch house was no more than a couple of huts and a mesquite corral," she said. "He built them there on the rise by the spring in 1853, when outlaws and raiders had run all the Spanish grantees out of the whole country between the Nueces and the Rio Grande. His only neighbors were Captain King and Legs Lewis."

Ferguson cleared his throat.

"Yes, ma'am. The old hands say Captain Macroom was one tough Irishman."

"He was. He said that the marauders back then would kill for a hatband."

"Ma'am," Dunham said, as he kicked his horse and started him at a trot down toward the house, "they still will."

The sun glinted brightly off the copper cannon, and the breeze carried the faint sounds of a hammer striking an anvil in the black-smith shop. Some of the vaqueros' children ran to see the newcomers, waving gaily. The wind lifted, suddenly, and tugged playfully at Maggie's hat. Her heart pounded wild and free.

She was here, home at last, and she would stay, she thought, as they rode down the hill. Cade had helped her become a person different from the scared girl who had climbed out of her bedroom window in Van Buren. She could ride all day now, hard, and still take care of her own mount and make camp. She could cook over an open fire and catch her own fish, live through a night alone in the woods and catch her terrified horse. She could shoot a pistol and a rifle and hit at what she aimed.

Bascom had better watch his step.

As if the thought conjured him to life, Bascom stepped out the front door as they rode into the yard.

"My dear Maggie!" he said, and made her a sweeping bow before he came down the steps toward her. "It's been a long, long time. You've changed from a pretty girl into a beautiful woman. Now you're all grown up."

She stared at him over her shoulder as she dismounted, turned when she had her feet on the ground, and looked again. This man was a far cry from the gangly fifteen-year-old she had known. He was what Emily would call "a fine figure of a man."

"So are you, Robert," she said. "Eight years

has made a lot of difference—in appearance, at least."

He laughed, holding her gaze as if they were the only two people in the world.

"Eight years and a lot of miles," he said, coming to meet her with both hands outstretched. "I promise, Maggie, I haven't caught a single scorpion to scare you with."

Reluctantly, she gave her hands, intending to let him barely touch her gloved fingers, but he caught and held them in a warm, firm grip. A welcoming grip.

Amazement ran through her.

"Ever since your father telegraphed that you might be coming this way, I've had our vaqueros on the lookout for you, hoping that bandits wouldn't get you before I could see your pretty face."

"God help us all, Bascom," she said, tartly. "You've changed from a pestering, callow youth to a shameless flatterer."

She pulled her hands free, and he threw back his head and laughed.

"It's not flattery, Maggie," he said. "I'm glad you're here."

His smile faded and his green eyes grew sad.

"This place has been plenty lonesome ever since I came home from the war to find the Captain gone."

A warmth came over her, a feeling of shared grief.

"I know," she said. "This arrival is hard for

me. I've been dreading walking into the house with him not here."

He held her gaze for a moment.

"I know you loved him very much. I've thought about you, Maggie."

He glanced from her to the vaqueros.

"Thanks, boys," he said. "You can go back to work now."

The men touched their hat brims, wheeled their horses, and galloped out of the yard. Bascom watched them go and for the first time, he turned his head and looked curiously at Cade.

"I've arrived safely because I had a good escort," Maggie said. "My husband is with me."

Cade took a step toward her.

"Cade Chisk-Ko," she said, "this is Robert Bascom."

Bascom's thin lips fell open in surprise. He stared at Cade.

The shock, the realization that Maggie had married *an Indian!* was written all over his face. Like the vaqueros, though, he was too intimidated to say anything out loud.

"Husband!" he exclaimed, clearing his throat as he tried to recover. "Your father never mentioned a word about you marryin'."

"He doesn't know. We married after I left his house, just before starting on the journey."

She waited until Bascom looked at her again, then held his gaze.

"If you feel the need to telegraph this news

to Pierce, he might come down here and cause a lot of trouble for all of us," she said. "On the other hand, he might simply declare me dead and stay home."

Bascom nodded, his green eyes thoughtful.

"That's your call, Bascom," Cade said. "You do what you have to do. Before you decide, though, you need to know that this ranch belongs to Miss Maggie. Pierce Harrington no longer has the right to manage this place."

Bascom turned back to him. "The Captain planned for years to leave the place to Maggie," he said. "I've been running it with her in mind, knowing Pierce acted for her."

For one fleeting instant, Maggie thought she heard the echo of bitterness, of the old, jealous Bascom in his voice. But he looked at her and smiled.

"The war taught me the value of family above all else," he said simply. "I'm glad to have some family here."

That shocked Maggie. She had never thought of Robert Bascom as family, but it made sense that he thought of her that way. He had no one else.

A rush of pity filled her.

"We're glad to be here, too," she said.

They smiled at each other.

"It's been a long trip," Cade said, stepping up to take her by the elbow. "Miss Maggie's tired and dusty, and we need to let her rest a bit."

Bascom hurried around them to dash up the

steps onto the porch and hold the door open.

"Of course," he said. "Forgive me, Maggie. Come in, come in."

He ushered them into the entry hall and almost past the door to the living room with its huge stone fireplace. But then he stopped.

Maggie stepped into the arched doorway.

"Everything's just the way it always was," she said, looking from the stands of repeating rifles to the huge leather divans.

"Even the serape Luis's mother made!" she cried. "You've left it on the couch."

Then she saw the pipe stand beside the big, brown leather chair.

"And his pipes! That one looks as if he just put it down."

"Sometimes I walk by and glance in and I think I see him," Bascom said. "Other times I think I smell the smoke from his pipe tobacco. I still can't bring myself to sit in that chair."

Maggie's eyes filled with tears.

"I know," she murmured. "I can feel him here. I'm glad you've kept all his things in their places."

"I had to," Bascom said. "It comforts me to see everything looking as if the Captain has just ridden out to the pastures and will return soon."

"Where's Carrizo?" she asked, though her throat had gone tight with grief.

"He has the run of the stables and the east horse pasture. You know, sometimes early in the morning, he whinnies loud and long just like he used to do to greet the Captain."

"Does he *really*?" cried Maggie.

Tears rolled down her cheeks. Bascom made a move as if to comfort her, but Cade stood very close and put his arm around her.

"Is there a maid around to help Miss Maggie?" he said. "Could you have one of the boys out there bring in her things?"

"Of course," Bascom said, turning to go toward the back of the house. "I'll send Oleana to you, Maggie."

Cade started her moving down the hallway away from the parlor, walking quickly, not giving her time to turn and answer Bascom. A thought hit her that stopped her tears and almost made her smile. Could it possibly be that Cade was jealous of Bascom?

As soon as they were inside their room, Cade closed the door and led her toward the bed.

"Lie down and rest," he said. "Have the maid bring your supper here if you want. All that talk from Bascom is enough to wear you right into the ground."

Maggie found her handkerchief and wiped her eyes while she tried not to laugh.

"Bascom is probably lonely," she said. "He doesn't have much companionship."

Cade snorted.

"He has people all over the place and thousands of cows to talk to."

He took off his hat and threw it onto the marble-topped chest of drawers. "I thought he didn't like you. Why is he being so friendly all of a sudden?"

"He *is* a lot different from what I remembered," she admitted. "But, then, he's twenty-three now and he's been to a war and has the responsibility of running this place. He's grown up."

"Don't trust him too much," he warned. "Jealousy is a hard trait to outgrow."

A knock sounded at the door, and Cade whirled on his heel and opened it.

"*Senor*," a small, brown-skinned boy said, and peered past him to see Maggie. "Your bags. And those of the *senorita*."

"*Gracias*," Cade said and opened the door wider to let him in.

Maggie moved toward the child.

"I am called *Jorge, senorita*. Oleana is mi mama, Diego Martinez, *vaquero de los caballos*, is mi papa."

"Oh, then I know you, Jorge!" Maggie cried. "You were a very small boy the last time I came to Las Manzanitas, and I used to play with you while your mama worked in the kitchen." She smiled at him. "Do you remember me?"

"*Si, senorita*," he said shyly.

He stepped into the room, his feet bare, and deposited their bags, a load that was almost bigger than he was. Then, with a respectful tug at his forelock, he stepped out again.

"*Gracias, Jorge*."

"De nada, senorita," he said, and closed the door.

Cade turned to look at her.

"He does remember you," he said. "And he likes you. Have his parents worked here a long time?"

"They're descendants of the people who followed Grandpa across the Rio Grande in *La Entrada* when Las Manzanitas was just beginning," she said. "He went to Mexico for cattle to stock the ranch and when he bought every head that one village had, he saw that the villagers then had nothing to eat and nothing to do, so he offered them homes and jobs on Las Manzanitas. They packed up all their belongings and their other animals and came back to Texas with him in a great, long procession."

"Then we have a lot of employees who are reliably loyal," he said thoughtfully. "To the *rancho,* at least, if not to us."

Us. He was using that word again.

The strangest feelings shot through Maggie, and she once again found herself hoping that somehow he might change his mind and stay.

But that was ridiculous. She must not become any more attached to him, must not let herself have vain expectations.

Chapter 10

During the next few days, Maggie, Bascom, and Cade rode much of the La Casa Grande division of the ranch. Bascom showed them herd after herd of cattle, all of them decimated by the ferocious raiders sweeping in from Mexico. Those raiding groups had so grown in numbers and boldness during the past three years that, on some ranches, they had stolen half the cattle and more. The Strip was desperate for law and order, but none appeared to be coming.

They examined the pastures for grass and the rivers and creeks for water, made plans to move cattle around to get them through the winter, and talked about importing more purebreds to improve the mostly longhorn stock. Bascom seemed pleased to have them there—they had no trouble working with him at all.

The biggest thrill of all those days, for Maggie, was watching Cade get acquainted with the land she loved. He had been falling in love with it, too, ever since the moment he'd stopped to look it over when they rode out of the Nueces. But he didn't know that yet.

He was too busy watching Bascom, trying to catch him in some kind of chicanery. He and Maggie argued about that every night, lying apart from each other in their big bed, trying to use the disagreement to help keep them separate.

"Something's not right," Cade would say. "There's too much stock in some places, too few men in others. I don't trust Bascom."

"You are so suspicious of everyone," Maggie would say. "Get over it, Cade. Bascom has changed, that's all. Think how much you and I have changed in the last month, so why couldn't he change in eight years? I'm just glad we didn't have to confront him."

"Once a dog in the manger, always a dog in the manger."

"He's being very generous and open; he's showing us everything about the ranch."

"You *think* he's telling you everything. Who can say what he has hidden."

One night, two weeks or so after their arrival there, she plumped her pillow and settled herself on it, carefully keeping to her side of the bed.

"I'll tell you what worries me much more than Bascom," she confided. "It's whether I can ever exercise any authority around here. Do you remember how Ferguson and Dunham looked right through me even though you introduced me as the new owner?"

"Ummm."

"The other vaqueros do it, too. They don't even see me because I'm a woman! And now it's like I'm a guest, riding around looking things over with you and Bascom. When are the vaqueros going to see me as the boss?"

"When you earn their respect."

By the sound of his voice in the darkness, she could tell he had turned toward her.

"Many a man has looked right at me and not even seen me because I'm an Indian," he said, "so I know how you feel. Once they all realize we're here to stay and that Bascom's not the boss anymore, I'll have the same fight as you."

He gave a wry laugh, and his rich voice made her want to reach out and touch him. She clasped her hands together, clinging to the cotton top sheet wadded in between them.

"The trouble hasn't started yet, Maggie. Get ready for it. There'll be trouble before we truly take over this ranch."

"Because something is not quite right about Bascom," she said in a singsong voice, teasing him.

"Exactly," he said.

Soon he was asleep, but she lay awake for a long time. If only she could turn over and go into his arms! That would make everything right.

No it wouldn't. Whatever other trouble might come would be nothing compared to the havoc that loving him would cause.

The next day she and Cade and Bascom

came back to La Casa in the late afternoon and strolled around, talking a while to dear, half-deaf Casoose in the blacksmith shop and Pedro in the stables. They even dared visit Oleana in the kitchen until she hinted for them to go away so she could finish the meal.

Then they wandered out to the east pasture to visit Grandpa's favorite horse, Carrizo.

When they stopped to stand in one spot to let the old stallion come to them, Maggie stepped away from Cade. No matter what she had decided, her hands always ached to touch him and, when he walked close to her, her heart pounded uncontrollably. That was the worst. When he was close enough for her to catch the masculine scent of leather and horse and *him,* she suddenly remembered the taste of his kiss.

The nights in the same bed were growing steadily more difficult.

She had to stay away from him.

When Carrizo came straight to her and she reached up to stroke his soft nose, she realized she had to get away from both of these men. This very minute. She needed to be alone so she could think.

And she was tired of thinking about business. She needed to think about her heart and Cade. She wanted to soak in a hot bath and dream about Cade. If she imagined, over and over again, that he might stay with her forever, maybe he would—after all, she had imagined running away from home and coming to Las Manzanitas a hundred times, and she was here now, wasn't she?

"Seems pretty quiet around here for headquarters of a *rancho* this size," Cade remarked. "Where is everybody?"

"Lots of the hands are on the fencing crews I told you about," Bascom answered smoothly. "And, of course, we have our patrol out looking for possible raiders. I've got some men building a dam on Manzanitas creek and some moving cattle." He shrugged. "There just isn't all that much for them to do around here this time of year."

"You've got a good many horses to feed there in the corral," Cade said. "What's your plan for them?"

"Supposed to have a buyer from Nacogdoches come by any day now," Bascom said.

Cade nodded.

"They look like good stock," he said.

"The best on the place. All of 'em were sired by the thoroughbreds the Captain brought in to cross with his wild horses."

"The Captain knew good horses, didn't he, boy?" Maggie crooned. "And you're his very best one."

"It'll be interesting to see how Seth likes the mares you send him," Cade said.

"I know," Maggie said. "I can't wait to hear where they've settled. I'd like to go visit Dolly sometime."

She stroked Carrizo's neck. He nuzzled hers and then trotted happily away. Tears sprang to her eyes as she watched him go. The setting sun set his sleek hide on fire, made his deep sorrel color blaze against the darkening eastern sky.

Then, as he faded down the fence line into the growing shadows of the live oak trees, she turned toward the house.

"I'm going in now," she said, turning to the two men. "I asked Oleana to draw me a bath before dinner."

The two men nodded and turned toward the stables as she began walking quickly toward the house. Then she picked up her skirts and ran for her room, eager for her time alone.

The bathtub was there, in the middle of the floor, already filled with hot water. She began stripping off her clothes as she entered, throwing the garments in every direction.

The room was on the west, and it was gathering the long, slanting red rays of the sun, collecting them to warm the chill air, reflecting them off the water. Shivering a little, she ran to the bath and jumped in.

Immediately, she bent her knees and slid as far down into the hot water as she could, wadding her falling hair back up into its combs, moaning with pleasure at this incredible luxury. The luscious warm water covered her up to her neck, and she slid even farther down. She reached for the soap Oleana had left on the table beside her.

Her muscles began relaxing, and the tension of the long, exciting days began soaking out of her skin, leaching out of her bones. It would come back in force if she thought about Cade, so, for a little while, she wouldn't. She would think about something else. Her mind began to float.

She lay her head on the curving back of the tub and dozed, deep in the warm water, surrounded by the lilac scent of the soap, safe in her home. Later, she would think. Later.

Outside the house somewhere, the sharp crack of a shot tore through the air. Then, within a heartbeat, came two more. Maggie woke, her body frozen by fear.

Three quick shots used to be the signal to fort up. Was that what these shots meant?

Cade's voice came booming through the closed window before she could move.

"Stay inside!" he yelled. "Maggie, stay inside the house!"

On top of his last word a frantic banging sounded on her door.

"*Senorita* Maggie? *Senorita,* are you there?"

She swallowed hard and somehow found her voice.

"Come!" she cried. "Oleana, come in!"

The woman rushed in.

"*Mi Jorge,* he is yelling that the *bandidos* are coming!" she cried, rushing to Maggie.

Then she stopped and began hopping up and down in her fear.

"The men in the lookout tower have seen them!"

She ran toward Maggie again, reaching for her with both hands.

"Horse thiefs and *renegados*, killers and hide-peelers, they are coming straight for the Casa! Sunset *bandidos!*"

Maggie's heart leaped out of her chest as she scrambled to get out of the slick bathtub. They were *here*, already, to destroy her *rancho* and steal her stock before she'd even taken over! Horror stories whirled in her brain, true stories the neighbors had told her and Mama in that month before Grandpa died—stories of ranch houses burning, their owners killed and butchered, their hard-won stock driven south. *Nanita's* cattle.

And her horses! Those good ones in the stables and the big corral and . . . Joanna! She had seen Joanna in the corral with the good horses only moments ago!

Her breath caught at the thought. She couldn't let them get Joanna!

She tried to pull her fingers free from Oleana's numbing grip, tried to get free to go find Cade—who, damn it all, had been right as usual! Trouble, for sure, had come!

Somehow, she managed to tear free. She snatched her wrapper out of the armoire and slapped it onto her dripping body.

The window flew open and Cade thrust his head in.

"Stay inside," he ordered. "Use the Sharps. Keep the bandits from getting in close enough to burn the house."

He glared at her, his dark eyes flaming.

"Maggie, do you hear me? Do you promise to do as I say?"

"Yes!" she gasped. "Yes! I won't let the bastards burn the house."

He grinned.

"That's my Maggie."

She started to run to him, but Oleana caught her arm and clung to her, wild with fear. Cade slammed the window closed and disappeared.

Dragging Oleana across the room with her, Maggie ran to the window, opened it again, and screamed at his back.

"*Joanna!* Cade, please don't let them get Joanna."

"I won't. I'll save your mare."

He threw the words over his shoulder without slowing down, but he sounded as arrogant, as confident as he always did.

Her fear eased a little. He would. Cade could do it. Cade could drive off the bandits if she could defend the house. Her racing blood slowed enough for her to think.

"Oleana, go see about your children," she said, trying to remain calm herself. "Warn Old Casoose, since he's too deaf to hear the signal to fort up, and make sure the other vaqueros' wives are in their houses."

Oleana had already thought of her children and was turning for the door.

"But, *senorita*, you will be alone in the hacienda!"

"Whoever is in the lookout tower will help

me keep the raiders out of the yard," Maggie said, rushing with her out into the hallway. "Take a rifle with you and *go!*"

They dashed into the big room and lifted two heavy guns from their stands, then ran to the wall cabinet for ammunition.

"Many vaqueros gone building fence," Oleana said. "No men here at headquarters now."

"Bascom's here, somewhere around the stables," Maggie said.

"The bandidos may shoot him," Oleana said. "Poor man!" Then she screamed. "They may shoot *all* of us!"

The front door banged open, and Jorge flew in.

"I can shoot one of these big guns!" he cried, before taking another rifle from the stand. It was almost as big as he was, but he held it upright as he ran to get ammunition.

Oleana, her eyes filled with panic, turned to Maggie.

"I pray for you, *senorita Margarita!* Shoot straight!"

"Go to your family before the raiders get between us and them!"

Then mother and son were gone, and Maggie was alone in the house with the echoes of their running feet ringing in her ears. The back door slammed.

Cade and Bascom would be out there defending the corral and stables. The lookout would have the best view of the front yard, and he would have a Sharps—there was always one of the long-ranging guns loaded in the tower. And she would watch the back of the house.

Her hands shook so hard, and the gun was so heavy, that she had to lay it down and kneel in front of the huge leather divan to load it. Thank God Cade had been making her practice her marksmanship regularly, even though his was a much lighter rifle than this.

A whole barrage of firing began, filling the air with shots exploding one after the other, then a whole bunch together in an endlessly vicious, chattering chain. Maggie wiped her sweating palms on the serape hanging on the back of the divan, grabbed a box of shells, and ran toward the windows in the dining room, her wet, bare feet sliding on the polished plank floor.

Dusk was falling, closing in fast, filling the big rooms with shadows. And with loneliness. Oh, Lord, if only Cade could be in here with her!

How could she have been wishing so hard to be alone only a few minutes ago?

The Sharp was massive and unwieldly in her sweating hands, and she nearly dropped it twice as she ran through the house toward the back rooms. After an age, she burst into the long dining room, which had been built across the back of the original house to accommodate Grandpa's legendary hospitality.

Its wall of windows flamed red with the

blazing sunset; it showed the sky streaked and dancing with fire. Night was coming. Oh, pray God they could drive off the attackers before utter darkness came down!

Shots blazed in the twilight on the other side of the corral, then more shots, to the east of it, closer to the house. She threw herself prone beneath one of the middle windows. The floor beneath her trembled from the hoofbeats pounding the earth. All the horses were stirred up now, and those in the corral were milling, starting to gallop in a circle.

She lifted her head and peered over the windowsill. Her knees turned to water.

Cade was out in the middle of the danger, riding Smoke, tall and huge, a target big enough for a first-time shooter to hit. Except that he was moving too fast.

He was riding like a wild man, weaving in and out of the nervous horses, firing over their backs at the oncoming raiders with a pistol in one hand and a rifle in the other. Joanna's sleek spots gleamed ghost-white in the slanting red sunlight, bright as a beacon to draw every eye. He was trying to cut her out of the herd, but then what would he do with her?

That was when she saw that the corral gate was open. He was planning to take his chances on scattering the horses, or else he hoped to stampede them north and keep himself and his guns between them and the bandits. He would keep Joanna with him.

But while he was getting her, he was a clear

target, a black silhouette standing out against a wide, shining, red sky burning as if the prairie were on fire. A fire lit with flames the color of blood.

Maggie laid the rifle down and used both her shaking hands to open the window.

The sounds of hoofbeats and whinnying poured in even louder, mingled with the noises of shots and shouts. November night air rushed to surround her, cool and sharp, acrid with the smell of gunpowder. Then the roar of Cade's rifle slapped her ears, and one of the bandits who had almost reached the corral let out a scream. He dropped his gun and slapped his hand over his forearm.

Maggie's mind raced as she fought down her fear and knelt to pick up the Sharps to steady its muzzle on the wide sill. She needed to give Cade some cover.

He had his own rifle, the one with the silver-trimmed stock, but he had no saddle on his horse. Smoke wore no bridle, either. Cade was making this ride with only his legs and his voice and the love he'd instilled in his horse.

Joanna kept looking back at him. Maggie's heart went out to her. She was breaking into a run, head up, ears back, terrified eyes rolling.

Cade was riding fast and constantly faster with such consummate skill that it took her breath away. When next she saw him she would tell him that he couldn't be all Choctaw, that he must be part Comanche, for this ride would surely compare with what

Grandpa had told her of that tribe's prowess on horseback.

The red sun kept throwing its beams after him, kept chasing him with its rolling flames, glowing on his copper face like a reflection off the brilliance of Joanna's whiteness. The back of Maggie's scalp burned in terror.

Now she wanted night to fall, to have the darkness for them to hide in, the blackness to protect her brave Cade. But the sunset blazed more fiery banners across the sky, and the bandits kept on coming. Five of them.

She set her sights on one and took a deep breath to steady her hands. She pulled the hammer down and squeezed the trigger. Her target's horse, a tall palomino, reared, but the man held on as the horse came crashing down, spun around, and ran into the herd toward Cade.

And toward Joanna. The thief had his rope out, swinging in a wide loop through the air, aiming at Maggie's mare. While all of his companions were firing at Cade.

Maggie shot at the roper again, then gathered her breath to shout out the open window.

"Cade! Leave her! Save yourself. Get out of there, Cade!"

The cry sprang from her heart as a scream, but by the time it came out of her mouth it had withered to a pitiful whisper. Her heart gave a strange, wrenching twist. She squeezed the hard gun stock until her sweat-drenched palms squeaked on the wood.

He might die. A moment from now he might be dead. Cade was risking his life to save Joanna for her.

Oh, dear God, was she just going to kneel right there and watch him get killed?

Maybe not. Smoke moved like a wisp of his namesake through the bloody vermilion light, in and out among the many horses in a graceful rhythm like that of a dance.

Ah! Come on and dance with the devil.

Tears filled her eyes, seared her throat as she remembered Cade flirting with her a few weeks ago. She prayed to God to please help him, because she couldn't.

She didn't dare fire again. Every animal and every man out there was moving in a swift circle, around and around in the sunset that was bathing them in a glow like the fires of hell. She could easily hit Cade by mistake, for she wasn't used to this gun; she didn't know how to adjust its aim.

Cade got Joanna then, got in behind her and started to cut her from the herd. Smoke went to work nipping and driving her. The Sedgewicks' bay mare was beside Jo. Some of the horses between them and the far side of the corral saw that the gate was open and ran out, leading all the others. Some of them circled wide and came back toward the house.

The herd broke apart around a gimpy white mare with her colt. The two of them turned back and forth, unable to decide to go either way, then followed the other half of the herd rushing away, nearly tumbling over each other, to the southwest, away from the headquarters. The wounded bandit fell in behind them, but the others kept after Cade. Joanna had come out of the gate at last.

He glanced over his shoulder at the bandits, then threw his leg over Smoke's croup and sat on him backwards, letting him run, shooting with deadly accuracy into the knot of raiders. He hit another one, who fell forward over his saddle horn. Two of them spurred their horses forward, raised their handguns to avenge their friend, and fired at Cade at the same time.

He whipped around to face forward, but then he fell along Smoke's neck. He slid from sight off the stallion's other side.

Maggie's heart leaped out of her body. There was nothing but a hole in its place. Her whole body went hollow, her blood drained away, she became an empty, dried-up hull of herself.

"*Senorita.*"

She froze. The voice was harsh and strange. Someone was in this room with her.

Immediately, hard hands grasped her arms from behind. She brought the Sharps swinging around, but even so, she was imprisoned, helpless. Whoever had grabbed her was so much taller, so much bigger, so much stronger, that he simply ripped the gun from her numb fingers.

Her panic for Cade had so sucked the

strength out of her that she didn't even struggle.

The man lifted her and started carrying her, fast, along the windowed wall. She gathered enough force to kick at his legs, enough breath to scream, but neither slowed him one whit.

He stopped once and cocked his head to listen to the melee outside, but he didn't speak again. Then he moved even faster, carrying her easily toward the back door of the house. He was trying to take her outside, to his horse, to Mexico!

Maggie bucked and struggled in his arms, and managed to slide down and down until her feet touched the floor. She dragged them, trying to set her heels. When he loosened his hold on her to grab her legs, she reached out and caught the facing of the pantry door as they passed it.

It nearly broke her arm, but she held on until his momentum spun him around and she broke loose. As she did, she snatched at the pistol he wore holstered at his hip. By a miracle, she grabbed its handle.

But she couldn't get it out of the leather.

He spat out a string of rapid-fire Spanish that was completely unintelligible to her and slammed his hand down sideways on her wrist. A pain shot through to her bone, a pain so sharp that she thought her hand was broken. Oh, Lord, if he hurt her bad, she was helpless. She kicked upward as hard as she could.

He let out a horrible yell and grabbed his crotch with both hands. She only glimpsed him bending double as she turned and ran into the gathering dark of the house, clutching her wrist against her stomach. Fear gave her wings, and she flew down the hallway.

He was coming after her, boots thudding on the wooden floor. Each step sounded quicker and more steady than the last.

Maggie set her jaw and tried to run on tiptoe. If she could get into the living room and barricade the door, she'd have plenty of guns and ammunition, even if he brought the rest of the raiders into the house to help him.

Then she thought of Cade, trampled beneath the hooves of a hundred horses. She wanted to wither away. No. She had to stay alive even if he was dead—she couldn't give up, because he had admired her grit.

She *wouldn't* give up.

The last of the wild sunset light faded away behind her. She turned the corner and ran into the dimness of the east-facing living room, slamming the door behind her and sticking a chair beneath the knob. She winced from the pain in her arm but continued running for the door to the entry hall.

Her pursuer banged on the one she'd just barred.

She slammed the second door, ran to one of the leather armchairs, and pushed it across the room to use as a barricade. As new strength surged through her on a fresh wave of anger, the heavy chair proved no burden at all, and the pain disappeared from her arm.

She rushed back to the rifle stands and pulled out a gun. Its weight was nothing—her arm had gone numb.

The raider's pistol roared on the other side of the thick hallway door. One, two, three, four shots. He probably had a pocket full of cartridges.

Maggie threw herself prone behind the big divan and scooted on her stomach, dragging the Sharps, to reach a box of ammunition. She slid back the lid and took out some rounds.

Then, as the echoes of the pistol shots died away, she heard running footsteps toward the back of the house. A loud, raw voice shouted in Spanish, too fast for her to understand.

Her tormentor shouted back and ran in that direction.

Maggie held her breath and listened, gritting her teeth against the pain that was seeping back into her arm. A roiling anger surged into her blood. She would avenge Cade, by all the saints! Those bandits had better not be coming in here to attack her, or she would blow them to kingdom come.

But terror, the terror of losing Cade, and the sorrow of it, were rising. Rising in the very core of her, ready to wash her away. Her arms, both of them, started trembling. The bruised one ached with a fierce, pulsating pain.

Footsteps receded down the hall.

Faintly, she could hear the noises of pounding hooves and random shots outside, then a slamming door, then nothing. No other sound came from within the house. She was alone.

With two doors and four windows to watch, Maggie tried to think. The best vantage point would be the far corner of the room—she could see every opening from there. The thought of being against the wall made her feel safer somehow, yet she would actually be cornered there.

And she could see all the doors and windows from the very spot where she sat on the floor in front of the divan in the middle of the room. Her arm was throbbing so deeply that it had to be bruised to the bone. Darkness was almost complete now, but her eyes kept shifting anyway, darting from the hall door to the windows to the entryway door, over and over again.

Carefully, she laid the gun down and crawled to the stand for more ammunition. She brought the box with her this time, even though something inside her screamed there was no need. If those bandits stormed each door and each window at the same time, which, of course, they would, she'd never have a chance to use more shells than she already had.

She settled against the divan again, pulled the gun across her lap, and held her breath to listen.

The drumming of horses' hooves still sounded, but from farther away. The wind was picking up out there, cracking the branches of the big live oak by the porch. It was shockingly loud, because an eerie silence was filling the house.

No one could help her. Even if Oleana had seen Cade go down, she had her children and the other women and their families to see to. Most raiders set fire to the ranch buildings and murdered their inhabitants.

They might have set fire to this one, too.

She strained her ears to the utmost, let herself take in enough air to smell whether it reeked of smoke. Nothing.

She sank into a heap and bent over the big gun, cradling it uselessly in her arms. She was going crazy—crazy with fear. And crazy with grief.

Cade!

Her heart cried out his name so loudly that she thought she could hear its echo in the huge, high-ceilinged room. An uncontrollable trembling took her; it grew and grew. The shaking spread through every limb while she huddled there, utterly helpless, unable to move.

She flinched when the reports of two shots sounded, muffled by distance and the walls of the house, but she didn't get up, didn't prepare for her defense. Soon, very soon, they'd be shooting into this room, shooting at her, maybe shooting through the doors or the windows before they burst in, hoping to kill her before they had to risk facing her Sharps.

Let them. Let them kill her. They had already killed Cade.

She jerked to a sitting position and threw up her head. No. Let *them* die, the low-down, vile horse thieves! They were getting away with her darling Joanna, but they wouldn't get away with killing Cade!

Tears filled her throat, came pouring down her cheeks until she could barely see. Her hands still shook, but she made them slide over the gun, checking to see if it was loaded, ready to fire. She made her eyes strain through the tears to see the dim outlines of the windows.

Boot heels rang on the porch. The front door crashed open and hit the wall. There! They'd be coming in from the front entrance.

Unless it was a trick. Of course it was! She swung around to try to see the door to the hallway, tears flooding now, choking her. She pulled up her knees to prop the gun on them and set her elbows against her sides to try to stop the shaking in her arms.

Something rattled the window, and she ripped the muzzle around to point in that direction, frantically trying to see the danger. But it came from behind her. A swift kick against her wooden barricade shook her to the bone.

She leaped to her feet and turned to meet it, her hands slipping, sweating, on the Sharps, her finger on the trigger.

The chair she had set beneath the knob

broke as easily as a brittle stick. A man roared through the hallway door and threw himself onto the floor, coming at her, sliding. Maggie, her arms waving beneath the weight of her terror, dropped the hammer and fired.

The red glare of the gun tore the dark apart, revealing Cade's face.

Chapter 11

S he kept screaming, unable to stop, shaking from head to toe, as if she was caught in that dreadful moment forever. She had killed Cade.

"No! No! No!"

Hard arms went around her from the back, and the gun slid from her hands.

"Maggie. It's all right. Maggie."

Cade's voice. But it couldn't be. She had killed him. The thieves hadn't killed him, but she had.

Shock stopped her screaming, but the shaking and the crying didn't even slow, even when he pulled her tight against the warm bulk of his body.

"What a lousy shot," he said, his breath hot and thick in her ear, his lips brushing it once on the way to finding her mouth.

He turned her in his arms, into his hard chest, and pulled her even closer, murmuring against her lips, "I thought I taught you better aim than that."

"C-cade!" she moaned and lifted her shaking hands to cup his face.

"Damn, Maggie, when I saw these doors closed I thought one of them had gotten into the house . . . that he had you . . ."

Their lips couldn't stay apart anymore, not enough to whisper another word. They kissed with a need so deep and desperate that he cradled her head in his free hand and pressed her mouth closer while she wrapped her arms tightly around his neck.

Finally, he broke the kiss, dropped the gun onto the divan, and held her close. He tucked her head into his chest, rocked her back and forth. Through his shirt, through her thin wrapper, she could feel the blood raging hot just beneath his skin.

"He *did* get in!" she cried. "One of the raiders did! He grabbed me and tried to drag me away, and I thought you were him coming back."

She grabbed a ragged gulp of air as she ran her trembling fingers over his chiseled features.

"It was awful, Cade. I was so scared!"

His arms tightened around her.

"Damn the horse thieves, anyway!" he said. "How'd you get away?"

He squeezed her closer to him, bent down and kissed her forehead.

"I grabbed the door facing and pulled loose. Kicked him where it hurt."

He made an incoherent sound, then gave a grim laugh as he slid his hands through her hair. A tremor ran through him.

"Oh, dear God, Maggie," he said, and the anguish rang raw in his voice. "When I saw the red sky burning and the raiders didn't kill *me*, then I thought the sky burning meant that *you* . . ."

"I thought they'd killed *you!*" she cried. "I saw them shoot you and then you falling underneath all the galloping horses."

"No. I was hanging onto the offside of Smoke."

Then he kissed her cheeks, both of them, heedless of her tears, and set his feet apart to sweep her up fiercely into the protecting curve of his body.

"The raiders are gone now, sweet Maggie," he said. "I saw them heading south."

She tried to run her hands over his shoulders and his arms, but he was holding her too tightly. She flattened her palms against his back instead.

He laughed, deep in his throat, a sound of happiness touched with awe.

"I can't believe we're both alive and unhurt!" he said. "What a relief! Thank the Great Spirit!"

His cheek came against her face with a sharp, quick pressure, and he hugged her so hard she thought she would break.

"And what a triumph," she said, with a chuckle punctuated by one last sob. "We've had our first raid and survived!"

"Maggie," he said. "Oh, Maggie. You're a brave woman."

A deep warmth filled her. She loved hearing him speak her name in his low, smooth voice.

"Another great thing about you is the way you kiss," he whispered.

Then the soft strength of his lips started putting her back together, healing her with silent, hot kisses along the line of her jaw.

She turned toward his mouth and their lips met with a flash of fire.

The heat traveled the length of their bodies like lightning striking two trees entwined. Cade slid his hands over her back, down to caress her hips, and she felt the hard thrust of his manhood through his jeans.

Her heart beat wildly against the cage of her chest, pulling her body closer to fit hard against his, to explore his shape and nestle into him. She slid her hands up under his shirt and took possession of his iron-hard muscles, made sure he was truly alive and unhurt.

He deepened the kiss until her hands finally went still and her breath stopped.

But even with no air she was suddenly, exquisitely alive, saved from danger—the danger of not knowing what it was like to really live.

Her mouth melted into his. A shiver ran through her, a hot, bursting excitement like a shower of sparks from fire blown on the wind. Her tongue met his and embraced it in slow, dizzying, throbbing caresses.

Please. Please don't stop. Please kiss me forever just exactly like this.

Then his hand found her breast.

A long, snaking line of bright pleasure streaked through her, fired every vein. Every pore of her skin opened to him, and colors flashed on the black of her eyelids.

"Cade . . ." she whispered.

But she could no more talk than she could pull away from him. His hand fit around her breast perfectly, just the way the rest of their bodies fit together.

He knew exactly how to pleasure her, exactly what she needed without her saying a word. His thumb found the straining peak of her breast already waiting for him. He caressed it with a sure, callused touch that, even through her thin wrapper, carried her away, set her adrift, lost in a sea of sensation.

Then she was floating off into the sky, as he untied the belt of her wrapper, slipping both hands inside to caress her skin. She pulled back a little to give him room, to let her body fill with the ecstasy that his palms spread down her sides, over her hips, onto her thighs. His hands then came up to her waist and up higher yet to cradle the aching mounds of her breasts.

The cool air brushed her tear-stained face and swept over the length of her skin as the garment fell away.

But Cade's hands held a fire that drove off the chill in an instant. Maggie moaned and grasped his huge wrists with both her hands to hold his where they were. To hold them there forever.

After a last, wild kiss, he tore his mouth free and swept her up into his arms, carried her to the big divan and set her down. His lips found hers again.

But only for a short kiss, one so hard and hot it seemed meant to brand her, then his mouth was moving down her throat, licking her bare skin now and then with the tip of his tongue but traveling fast and sure on a trail of quick kisses down and down. Maggie couldn't breathe.

He bowed his powerful neck and took her nipple into his hot mouth. She cried out with the first indescribable delight, then fell silent with wonder beneath his slow, laving tongue, his supple, suckling lips.

Never, ever had she even imagined there could be a sensation so wild and so deep.

Her whole body arched up to him, opened to him. Her languorous hands lifted to caress his hair, to cup his head and hold it. He smelled like horse and sweat and he smelled like her Cade.

Finally, he left her breast bare to the sharp air and brought his passion back to her mouth. He used both his big hands to tease and tantalize her, and suddenly they were tumbling together deeper and deeper into the soft leather nest. She helped him tear free from his boots and his clothes.

But they never broke that victorious kiss

and, when they lay naked at last and triumphantly tangled, the kiss became slower, more full of passion, until Maggie fell, lost forever into the hot and wonderful world they were making.

Her tongue and her lips begged him, demanded of him, for what came next. Cade slid his huge hands beneath her hips and cradled her, lifting her to him as she stroked his muscled back.

He slipped one long, muscular thigh between her knees. He brushed it against the weeping heart of her womanhood, and then he broke the long kiss to drop fleeting ones on her throat, her eyelids, the tender place at the edge of her hair.

He entered her slowly. She gasped, galvanized by the new, overpowering sensations, by the growing joy and pleasure in this closeness with him. He filled her and she held onto him, her face buried in the hollow of his neck.

She melded herself to him, inside and out, she moved with him on instinct, on happiness, in the sensual rhythm that was old as time, clinging to the rock of his importunate body.

"Cade," she whispered, and tasted the salty sweat on his skin, "Cade."

He answered with a long, heated thrust that took them, exploding over the edge of the world. They flew out into the fiery sky and through it, straight into the power of the sun.

For a long time afterward, they lay still, letting their souls settle, letting their bodies melt together in pure joy. Alive. Together.

"Maggie," he said, with wonder in his voice. "Maggie."

He rolled onto his side, bringing her with him, and tucked her head beneath his chin. She snuggled into the crook of his arm. He reached over her to draw down the serape to cover them both against the autumn night chill.

The last embers of red light were reflected in the windows as they died out in the sky. Maggie touched Cade's face.

"What did you mean a while ago when you said you thought I was dead because the sky was burning?"

He went completely still.

He didn't answer for so long that despair began to rise in her breast. She had offended him in some way. She had ruined it all.

"My Choctaw name is Red Sky," he said, in a voice she hardly recognized.

She knew, in that moment, that he had never told anyone else. That truth was in his tone, in the way his flesh touched hers, in the way he paced his breath.

"I ran away from Haynes's academy when I was fourteen summers," he said, "because Talihina Tuskahoma killed herself."

He paused, and she waited until he was ready to continue his story.

"I loved her, although we had never even talked alone. I saw her come out of Haynes's office that day with her face gray as ashes and her soul dying in her eyes. I didn't know then that the abuse he'd subjected her to was sexual. I was too naive to imagine such a thing."

He moved a bit beneath her, settled her more surely against his hip.

"When the girls found her hanged in their dormitory, I went crazy with rage. And with guilt because I had done nothing to protect her. I ran away, but not to home; instead I went deep into the mountains of the Kiamichi."

"Why?" she whispered.

"To be a Choctaw and a man. Haynes's purpose in life was to see that I never became either."

She laid her hand, palm down and flat, in the center of his naked chest, tilted her head to flash him a flirtatious glance.

"I'd like to testify that he completely failed in that," she said.

When he grinned, she saw a bright flash in the dark, and happiness seized her.

"I had been at the school for six years. I had forgotten a great deal, but I survived off the land. And I tested myself in every way. I jumped off bluffs into the rivers, I climbed mountains at a run, I raced panthers through the woods."

He hesitated, then gave a great, ragged sigh.

"One morning, an old Choctaw wise man, Moshulatubbee, stepped out of the woods into my path. He told me that no spirit, including my own, could speak to me and that I could find no peace unless I could be still."

"Did he know what had happened to you?" Maggie whispered.

"Yes, he said an eagle told him. I admitted to him that I was searching for the experience that would give me my Choctaw name. He told me to sit still on a stone seat high on the mountain, fasting, until night came."

"And you did."

"Yes, I did. At sunset, the sky caught on fire, burst into flames and burned red and rolling, the way it did tonight. I saw a white cloud in the shape of a buffalo, but Moshulatubbee said that was of no significance; he said that my Choctaw name is Red Sky."

He was tensing again; his muscles against her back had knotted.

"Two days later when I went to my home, my father had just died in a wagon wreck and my mother was distraught. Two months later she died having Cotannah."

Neither one of them breathed.

"And the buffalo had been long, long gone from the Kiamichi. So, to me, the red sky burning meant death and destruction."

Maggie's heart broke for the boy he had been.

"Most of the time," he said, "I won't let its memory into my mind, but tonight, when I saw the sky blazing, on fire as it was all those years ago, it took me over and I fully expected to die."

He dropped a soft kiss on the top of her head.

"Then, when the raiders were riding off and I was alive and unhurt, I had the hellish thought that the burning sky sign had meant you, that they'd gotten in the house and killed you."

His arms tightened around her in a paralyzing grip.

"Instead, it meant life, deeper than I've ever known it, when you came into my arms. That is why I tell my name only to you, Maggie."

Her very bones melted against him. She lifted her hand and caressed his cheek.

The sound of a rattling knock, then of an opening door, blew through the house on a wild gust of wind.

Maggie went still in his warm embrace.

"Somebody's coming," she whispered.

"Yes," he murmured, already pulling away. "Let me up, darlin'."

The endearment sent a rocketing thrill through her, clear down to her toes. She ran her hand over the broad sweep of his shoulders as he sat up and felt for his jeans.

"*Senorita! Senor!*" a young voice called.

"*Jorge!*" she cried.

Then she realized the state she was in and sat up, fumbling to wrap the serape around her.

"Oh! He mustn't come in here . . ."

"I'll meet him in the hall," Cade said. "Maybe there's more trouble."

He stepped into his pants and, without bothering to button more than the waistband, reached for his pistol. Maggie's hands went still as she stared at him in the light of the rising moon that poured through the windows.

Cade. Every graceful, powerful movement was that of a primal animal who would not be denied.

"Maybe some of the raiders came back," she said.

But she didn't believe it, and she didn't feel any fear. She only wanted to hold him there with her a moment more.

"I'd have heard them," he said, moving silently toward the door. "Even with you breathing hot in my ear, Pretty One."

Maggie soaked up that endearment, too, although she liked *darlin'* better.

"*Senorita! ¿Donde esta?*"

The footsteps sounded light and quick, only one set.

Cade stepped into the hallway.

"She is here," he said. "What do you need?"

"My mama says to see if *la senorita* is all right now that the raiders are gone."

"Yes, she is. She is with me."

"And you, *senor?*"

The eager little voice was closer now, edged with excitement.

"I am fine."

"A miracle!" Jorge said, from just outside the doorway. "You, *senor*, you fight *muy bien*.

Everyone is saying that you are *mucho hombre*."

"*Muchas gracias* to everyone," Cade said, a tinge of amusement in his tone.

"*Senorita Margarita?*" the little boy called suddenly.

Maggie clutched the woven serape to her chest.

"I'm here, Jorge, and I'm fine, thank you," she called. "Is everyone all right *a las casas de los vaqueros?*"

"*Si, senorita!* And nothing is on fire. Those raiders, they took only a few horses south and *senor* Bascom, I saw him behind them chasing them farther away."

"Good. That's wonderful. Now, tell your Mama, please, that I thank her for her concern and I will see her in the morning."

"I will say that."

"*Gracias, Jorge,*" Cade's deep voice said. "*Buenas noches.*"

But the child shouted at Maggie again.

"Shall I light a lamp for you, *senorita?*"

She laughed.

"No, *gracias*, Jorge," she called. "Run home. Your mama will worry."

"*Buenas noches, senorita. senor.*"

The light footsteps faded away, and Cade stepped back into the room.

"He didn't trust me, the little rascal," he said. "He had to talk to you himself."

"He wanted to *see* me, too," she said, laughing, as his long strides brought him back to her across the cold, dusky room.

Cade laughed, too.

"Shall I light a lamp for you, *senorita*?" he mimicked.

"No, *gracias*," she said, and threw the serape back to welcome him in. "You are all the light I need."

She lay on her side, propped on her elbow, looking up at him.

He dropped to his knees beside the divan, reached out to run his thumb along the line of her brow. His hot fingertips on her temple set her pulse to racing all over again.

"How about a fire in the hearth?" he offered. "The night air is becoming *muy frio*."

She reached out and began unbuckling his gunbelt. Her hand brushed the masculine bulge beneath the unfastened fly of his jeans.

"No, *gracias*," she said, smiling at him in the moonlight.

She touched him there again.

"I have Red Sky," she teased, ". . . burning. You are all the fire I need."

"Then I would suggest," he said, chuckling as he crawled in beside her, "that you teach Jorge to call you *senora*."

Those words came back to haunt Cade as the first rays of light reaching in through the windows fell across him and Maggie. *Senora*, he had said. His *senora*.

For a year. Was that what he had meant?

Did he dare believe that he could stay with her longer than that, that *the feeling* would stop tormenting him forever?

Did he dare believe that the red sky burning meant that much good for him?

Thank God Maggie hadn't been killed. Or hurt.

His arms tightened around her slight form. She snuggled closer, curving into him like one spoon into another.

"Cade," she murmured, sleepily.

It made him smile.

The truth was that this felt perfectly natural to him, this waking up with her on an old leather divan in the middle of the living room in a house that he'd never seen until a few weeks ago. And making love with her had seemed the most proper thing in the world.

That thought made his whole body hurt, *ache*, to make love to her again. He had known since the moment he saw her that she would be like a flame in his arms, all passion, all fire, even if she was a very young, innocent lady. The thought pierced his heart.

What if he *couldn't* stay? What if *the feeling* came over him like a tornado one day, ripped him loose from her arms and blew him a thousand miles away? What would happen to her then?

"Damn you, Chisk-Ko," he muttered to himself.

He propped his head up higher on the

rounded arm of the couch. On his fist. To keep his hand off Maggie's satin skin.

"Damn it all."

Did he dare believe he could settle in and stay in one place for the rest of his life and love her?

He had known and liked a lot of women, he had lived every day of his lifetime since he'd run away from the academy, but he had never known a woman like Maggie. And he had known she was different when she'd stepped up to his cell in the Van Buren jail.

Even seeing her standing in the window of that store with her curls tumbling wild in the morning sunlight and her fiery blue eyes burning a hole in the glass, he knew she was a marvel even through all of his troubles.

He lay still and watched the light grow yellow and bright in the room while the elation and the worry grew in him. She had wanted so much to make love to him that happiness rushed through him to remember it. But he might have gotten her pregnant. The tie between them felt deeper and more wonderful and completely permanent now. But he might not be able to do right by her.

He took a long, deep breath, a lingering sigh. All he could do was be honest with her and let her decide which way things would go.

The sharp, high whistle of a vaquero calling up a horse, and the answering, trotting hoofbeats sounded from the yard just outside. It was first light. The *rancho* was waking for the day.

He looked down at her, sleeping with one hand trustingly tucked into his bent elbow.

"Maggie. Time to get up and get dressed."

She stirred but didn't wake.

He tugged at the serape, but he didn't jerk it off her as he'd done that first morning of their trek together. He didn't dare. Even now, desire was rising in him like a river raging.

He could not allow himself to touch her again until she knew the truth.

So he slipped free of her, sat up, and reached for his clothes. He dressed and stomped his feet into his boots, but Maggie slept on.

Finally, he picked her up, wrapped in the serape, and started out of the room. As she began to wake, he stopped and picked up her discarded wrapper.

"You'd better get dressed before your little friend Jorge comes looking for you," he said.

Her eyes opened and she gave him a lazy smile that picked up his heart and turned it all the way over.

"How can I get dressed if you're carrying me around?"

She slipped her warm, soft arms around his neck. A thrill so strong it made him shiver ran down his spine. He wasn't thinking when he picked her up. He should have known better, and he should have stuck to his plan to not touch her until he'd had the chance to talk to her. He lengthened his strides, hurried into their room, and set her down.

"Maggie, remember I told you I couldn't stop running until Moshulatubbee told me to be still?"

Startled by his abruptness, she stared at him, wide-eyed, clutching the wadded wrapper to her breast.

"Y-y-yes."

"I only stopped for that little while, until he gave me my name."

He dragged in a long, ragged breath.

"Maggie, I'm still running. I've been running ever since I was an eight-year-old boy, since the first time I rode in through the gate of the academy and my body and soul screamed for me to run back home."

He turned away and went to the washbasin where he poured water into the bowl and then splashed it on his face. He snatched the towel from its wooden spindle.

"It's like I have to run and keep running until I reach home, but home isn't where it was anymore. This urge comes over me—I call it *the feeling*—and there's nothing I can do but pick up and ride out. It fills me with a terrible, prickling, burning restlessness, and moving on is the only way I can get any ease."

"Oh, Cade," she said brokenly.

He dried his face and forced himself to look at her.

She was coming toward him, to comfort him.

He shook his head and held out his hand as a signal for her to stay where she was. She stopped.

"What are you telling me, Cade?" she asked softly.

"That after last night the bond between us is strong as the sun," he said. "But *the feeling*, when it comes, may be stronger."

He stopped and swallowed hard, trying to keep the anguish out of his voice.

"I don't know, Maggie. I don't know if I'll be able to do right by you. This *feeling* is stronger than I am."

She stood there and looked at him, her wide blue eyes cleared of sleep and bright with pity. He could not *bear* to be pitied, especially by her.

He tensed and waited for what she would say.

"I don't know how anything could be stronger than you," she said calmly. "You rode through gunfire and wild horses last night to save Joanna. You brought me straight here, fast and safe."

She took a deep, raw breath and gave him that wonderful smile, the one that made his heart turn over once again.

"You're a hero, Cade. You can do anything."

Her eyes blazed with belief in what she was saying. With belief in him.

"How about if we take one day at a time,"

she said, "and face *the feeling* together if it comes?"

A life-giving warmth began to spread all through him. Hope. He felt hope for the first time in forever. And happiness.

"You can do anything, Cade."

They stood still, staring into each other's eyes for a long time.

She thought he was a hero.

She thought he could do anything.

He felt a smile coming over his face.

Now, blast it all, he'd have to live up to her expectations, even if she was a fluffy white girl.

Chapter 12

Maggie sat at one end of the long breakfast table trying to keep her gaze from
lingering on Cade, who was sitting at the other
end. Bascom sat on his right and Luis on his
left, talking with him about the raiders and the
ranch defense, while the vaqueros filed in at
the back door carrying the plates Oleana had
filled outside in the separate kitchen. Cade's
face was expressionless; he gave no sign of
what he felt about the night that had just
passed.

How could he seem so . . . at ease? She was
still shaky from the intensity of their encounter
an hour ago. It had cost him so much to put
his self-doubts into words that she felt completely wrung out. And she still had a warm
languor in her blood and a weakness in her
bones, not to mention a bursting joy in her
heart from their lovemaking. She didn't want
to think about ranch business or those awful
raiders today, she wanted to go back to bed
with Cade.

But Cade had his mind on business.

"Men, we'll meet at the corral when we're

done with the meal," he said, as the vaqueros began pulling back the chairs down both sides of the table. "We need to talk about defense."

Some of them nodded to show that they'd heard, and some simply sat down and began to eat their breakfast of steak, eggs, tortillas, biscuits, and honey. Oleana came in with the steaming coffeepot and began moving from person to person, refilling the tin mugs.

Maggie took a sip of the scalding brew and glanced at Cade again. Presiding at the head of the table, he looked more imposing than Grandpa ever had. His crisp, white shirt set off his copper-colored skin like white clouds against a sunset. His black hair, tied back in a rawhide thong, gleamed.

He looked so handsome she could hardly bear it. He *was* wonderful, and it killed her to think how he had suffered so long from restlessness, from *the feeling* to keep running, searching for home. She crossed the fingers of her left hand. Maybe it would never come over him again.

She took a bite of steak, then laid her fork down.

If it did come, would he tell her? Or would he just step onto Smoke and ride away? The very thought made her heart stop.

Up and down the table the men ate in silence. They never talked while they ate, whether in the long dining room or at a cow camp on the range. Eating was a serious business, and most of the time it had to be done quickly. They worked hard and went long hours without food, and they lived by Grandpa's admonition, "Always eat your breakfast—you never know where you'll be when dinnertime rolls around."

She had to use these few minutes to pull herself together and put her mind on the *rancho*. During the last few days, she and Cade had decided it was time to take over some of the authority from Bascom, who was deferential and informative with the two of them, but who was still giving all the orders. Cade had called this meeting this morning; evidently he was about to begin.

Bascom and Dunham and Ferguson left first, and then the other men started scooting back their chairs, a few at a time, going outside to smoke. When Maggie and Cade were the only ones left, they stood up and walked toward the door.

"I told Bascom I'd be the one to talk to the men," Cade said, "and I think you ought to say a few words, too, Maggie."

He took her hat from the rack and handed it to her, then reached for his. She stood there for a moment, close to him.

"So they'll start realizing that they have an Indian and a woman to work for?" she asked lightly.

He smiled.

"That's the message."

On the way out of the house and down the back steps, they walked very near each other.

She was aching to reach out and touch him; he smelled of soap and his own cedary scent. She *wanted* to touch him, not caring if the men were all around. But she jammed her hands into the pockets of her old riding jeans she'd found in the armoire and kept her gaze straight ahead.

The ranch. Las Manzanitas. She had ridden eight hundred miles to take control of this *rancho*. She had to set her thoughts on it right now.

Some of the men were already at the corral. Others were drifting toward it. Cade stepped up on the bottom log, which was set high enough into the posts for a man to roll beneath it if a crazy horse should come after him. He turned and held out his hand to Maggie.

"Want to sit up top so you can see everyone?"

"Yes, thank you."

His hand closed around hers, and her heart melted. The warmth went all the way through her.

The ranch. Put your mind on the ranch.

Cade's strength lifted her, as if she were weightless, to the top rail of the fence. His big hands burned into her waist. His dark, hot eyes lingered on hers for a long moment, then he let her go and turned to face the men.

Bascom watched them, and his eyes narrowed beneath the brim of his hat. The big Indian had surprised him at breakfast—he would have bet anything it would be another

week or two before Chisk-Ko knew enough
about the ranch to start trying to take control.
There had barely been enough time to get to
Ferguson and Dunham and tell the other boys
to catch up a bronc.

Bascom waited until the very moment the
red bastard was opening his mouth. Then he
stepped in front of him.

"Men," Bascom said, waving his hand for
quiet, even though they were mostly paying
attention. "Men, Mr. Chisk-Ko has some
words for all of you. As our new boss."

Then, since he had his back to the Indian
and to Maggie, he pushed up his hat and
winked before he stepped out of the way.

In a loud, booming voice, the Indian began,
"My wife, Margaret Harrington Chisk-Ko, is
the sole heir of Captain Macroom. We've come
here to live and to take over management of
Las Manzanitas from her father. In these past
few days while we've been looking the ranch
over we've decided to keep some of the captain's ways of doing things and change others.

"The way I see it in light of the raid last
night, our first concern needs to be defense.
First, I'm adding to the patrols on our southern border."

Bascom turned and looked at Ferguson.

"Where'll you get the extra men?" Ferguson
called out.

Maggie looked to see who had spoken with
that undertone of disrespect in his voice. For
a minute, she couldn't remember who he was,

then she realized he was one of the two who had met them on their way into the ranch. The one who hadn't had the nerve to call Cade an Indian to his face.

"Hire more men," Cade said.

"No offense intended," Ferguson drawled sarcastically, "but that may not be easy to do. This here outfit is already diff'rent enough— first one I ever rode for where we eat with the Mexicans—and I don't reckon a redskin boss'll help it much."

Maggie's jaw dropped as she stared at him. She wasn't shocked by his prejudiced attitude, but the open hostility surprised her—out on the range he acted civilly toward both of them. Then she realized that it was because he felt safe in the middle of a group that he could express his true feelings. And he hoped to turn many or all of the men against Cade.

Probably just to give himself a feeling of power that he could make running a ranch harder for an Indian.

Never mind for a woman. Even though Cade had said they'd both be bossing the outfit, the men didn't even see her. She had inherited the ranch, she was a woman, she had a husband. Therefore, Cade would be their boss.

Her pulse stopped. They had to have vaqueros, and lots of them, for the winter. The more fence they completed, the more defensible the ranch was, and building that fence took many men away from the regular work that still had to be done. The extra patrols would require still more hands.

Cade gave Ferguson a curt nod.

"If workin' for a different kind of outfit bothers you," he said, "you can draw your pay anytime."

Ferguson nodded as if to say he would when he wanted. And he would want to, Maggie thought, when he'd stirred up enough of the other men to take a whole bunch of them with him.

She would not let him do this!

"You're right to say that Las Manzanitas is different from other outfits," she said, loudly and clearly from her perch up above them. "My grandfather, Captain Macroom, treated all his men the same regardless of their color and that's one of the ways of doing things that Mr. Chisk-Ko and I will keep."

She pushed back her hat so they could see her eyes.

"Grandpa used to say that all his vaqueros sweated under the same sun and slept on the same hard ground; they all bled red blood and had flesh that tore on the same thorny brush."

She felt Cade's approving gaze as he turned to look at her, but she didn't look at him.

"The captain also paid his men more than average and built homes for those who married. My husband and I will do the same, and we will pay bonuses in cash money if the Tules pasture is fenced by spring."

She stopped talking and waited.

Finally Dobe Jones, one of the older Anglo vaqueros who had worked for her grandfather, spoke up.

"I'm stickin' around," he said dryly. "I might take a notion to marry someday and I'd need me a house."

Chuckles and laughter rolled through the group.

"Besides," Dobe said, glancing around at others in the group. "Winter's coming."

Nobody else mentioned leaving. Yet, somehow, the tension wasn't quite broken.

"Glad to have you," Cade said to Dobe.

Then he swept his confident gaze over the crowd.

"Anybody else have anything he wants to say?" he asked. "If not, we'll get on to the business of assigning the work."

"Uh, boss . . ." one man said.

Maggie saw that he was Dunham, Ferguson's partner the day she and Cade had arrived.

"Some of us was wonderin' if you might care to try that mustang there in the pen behind you," he said. "Just to get the kinks out, you might say."

Maggie whirled to look. Sure enough, a rough-haired wild horse stood snubbed to the post in the middle of the corral. Already saddled! Fear rushed the blood to her head.

He looked mean as a snake. And if the men had picked this horse as a test for Cade, they would have made sure he could buck with the best. Probably he was, as the cowboy song said, "a sunfishin' son of a gun."

Cade could ride Smoke like a Comanche. He had been a mustanger and he had broken wild horses. But this was bound to be an extremely bad horse, and the popular saying was true: "There never was a man who couldn't be throwed."

However, the companion line, "There never was a horse who couldn't be rode," dropped into her head when she turned and looked at Cade. He was smiling a rakish smile, looking as if he'd been hoping for this.

He and she both knew they had to earn the respect of these men before either of them could start giving orders. The sooner she and Cade proved their worth, the sooner they could get on with business.

"I'll try your Texas horse," Cade said, and he began climbing the fence, ready to go over it. "Looks like he might just be the pride of the Wild Horse Desert."

She caught at him as he swung his long, muscled leg over the top and stuck the toe of his boot into the other side of the rails.

News of whether he rode the bronc or not was going to be all over the Nueces Strip on its eternal, invisible, grass-roots grapevine. It would start to form the reputation of the Running M under their ownership.

He stood there for a heartbeat, straddling the fence, looking down at Maggie. She shaded her eyes with her hand and looked up at him. He had never looked more handsome.

"You can do it, Cade. You can do anything."

Her heart was pounding, hard and fast.

He laughed.

"Sure hope I don't disappoint you, darlin'."

He started climbing down the inside of the fence.

She reached out and touched his hand.

"You won't."

He met her eyes, smiling that smile that could break her heart, and squeezed her hand before he jumped to the ground. He landed lightly on the balls of his feet, lifted both arms, and pulled his hat down hard, front and back. Then he spun on his heel and tilted his head to flash his glittering, dangerous gaze up at her from beneath the brim.

She blew him a kiss.

He touched his hat to her. Then, he turned, and without looking back, strode toward the center of the pen.

"You can ride him, Cade!" she shouted, fiercely. "Remember—you can do anything!"

He was doing this for her, risking his life again as he had done last night, so that the vaqueros would stay and she could keep her *rancho*. But he was doing it for himself, too. For his reputation, for his splendid pride.

Cade always had to do this kind of thing, do more than a white man would, be better than a white man, all his life. Suddenly she was watching him through a haze of tears.

He reached the horse, who laid his ears back

and struck out with one back foot. Two Anglo vaqueros hovered nearby—one ready to untie its head, the other poised to take the hobbles off its front feet. Cade motioned that they should go ahead.

They hesitated, said something to him that she couldn't hear.

"Get *on* him before they turn him loose!" called another white vaquero, standing in a cluster of them against the fence.

Several of them laughed.

"If he don't know no more'n that about ridin' a bronc, he'd best quit now," Ferguson shouted.

Maggie smiled grimly. She couldn't wait to see their faces after the ride.

Cade made a single, commanding gesture, and the vaqueros in the middle of the corral set the wild horse free. Somehow, when he jumped back, the halter rope leaped into Cade's hand.

Maggie blinked and looked again.

Why didn't he get on him? Even Cade's huge strength couldn't hold a horse that wanted to break away.

But this one didn't. The horse stood still and so did Cade, looking completely at ease with the animal. The horse lowered his head and Cade raised his.

They stood that way for a long moment, while the horse's sides went in and out. They appeared to be . . . breathing at each other!

Maggie gaped.

Could that be? She had never heard of such a thing!

But that's what they were doing, blowing into each other's nostrils. And Cade was *talking* to him!

All the vaqueros fell silent, staring.

Finally, Cade moved. In his fluid, deliberate way, he laid a hand on the horse's neck and rhythmically stroked him, once, then again and again. After a little while he moved, with a slow grace almost like dancing, along the horse's side, still patting him, still talking. He reached for the saddle, and a cheer went up from his audience.

The next instant, by the same magic that had placed the rope in his hand, the saddle was coming off the horse, dropping to the ground. The noisy men went deathly quiet, no doubt wondering, as Maggie did for one half-second, whether Cade was going to do the unthinkable, cowardly thing and turn the horse loose.

"What the *hell*?" one vaquero cried.

And then Cade flew from the ground to the back of the mustang. He sat him as imperiously as a king. Or a Choctaw chief.

A war chief.

Maggie smiled. This *was* war, and Cade was winning.

But in the next breath she thought he would be killed before her very eyes.

The horse dropped its head between its legs and began to pitch like she had never seen any other horse do in any of her childhood visits to the ranch. Cade's big body whipped back and forth in the wind until she thought it must surely break right in two.

The bucking wouldn't stop. That was the most horrific thing. The horse absolutely wouldn't give Cade a chance to take a breath or get his balance, and he had no stirrups to support him, no saddle to hold him in.

That didn't matter. Every move he made was sure and sensuous. He rode the bronc as if their bodies had grown together, held it between his legs with his long thigh muscles, one dark hand lifted in the air for balance. Maggie's gaze followed his white shirt, bright as a moving beacon, in the cloud of dust.

The wild horse bucked halfway around the circular pen, then stopped and reared so fast that the movement was nothing but a blur of motion. The curtain of dust fell away and the bronc stood there, its forefeet stretching higher and higher, reaching straight up, striking for the sun.

Cade wouldn't stay on, he couldn't hang on—nobody could against the force of gravity. Maggie dug her nails into the rail of the fence, praying that the horse wouldn't fall over backwards and crush him.

But Cade stayed on. He threw back his head, his chiseled face set against the blue sky. Then the horse came down hard—forward, thank God—and kicked its hind feet so high that it reached the top of the fence, bucked sideways the rest of the way around the pen, and then began to run. It flattened out and flew around the enclosure at an out-of-control gallop for three full, terrifying turns.

Finally, when Maggie thought she would never breathe again, Cade shifted forward on the bare, sweating back, tightened the grip of his knees, and leaned forward along the horse's neck. He nodded to Ferguson, who was near the gate.

"Outside!"

Then the gate was hanging open, batting back and forth against the fence with a dull, wooden thudding sound, and Cade and the wild horse were gone. Hooves thundered off into the distance, and a rolling cloud of dust drifted back to the corral.

Maggie sat, staring to the west, where Cade and the horse had vanished into the vast expanse of the Wild Horse Desert. If she could move, she'd go up to the house and cry.

No, she wouldn't. Whatever gripped her went too deep for tears. A weird, terrifying tension, a thrumming knowledge had begun to build inside her.

Not because of the danger. Cade would stay on the horse, she knew that now. And he would control him. He had already proved that he could.

Not because of the Running M vaqueros. They were climbing up on the fence, standing to see where Cade went, waiting for him to return. Many of them had expressions that had already changed from skeptical to respectful. Even if some of them left, there would be enough to keep the ranch going until they could find more men. Word of this bronc ride would spread, and, at heart, the tough people who were settling Texas judged a man by what he could do more than by the color of his skin.

She stayed very still, there, on the top rail, in the steady heat of the November sun, trying to understand her feelings.

Forever. It seemed like forever that she sat there, holding the mysterious panic inside her, waiting for Cade and the wild horse to come back. The men climbed higher and strained their eyes, looking and waiting.

Finally, from far in the distance, came the faint sound of drumming hooves. The dust came blowing toward her. And, after he'd been gone a lifetime, Cade rode over the horizon and back through the gate of the pen.

He rode with the same easy seat, the same arrogant tilt of his head, the same supple rhythmic power as always. He took the horse straight to the center of the corral, rode it in a circle around the snubbing post, and brought it to a stop with only his seat and his legs and his voice.

Most of the men whooped and yelled and cheered and shouted, most of them gathered around, but at a respectful distance from the mustang. Cade accepted the congratulations with a wry smile, then raised one hand in the air to signal for quiet.

"I met a rider coming in to La Casa," he said, speaking loudly for everyone to hear. "Name of Raul, says he rides for us."

A general murmuring confirmed that was true.

"Raul and I talked while I sat my horse and let him blow," he drawled, deadpan, and the murmurs changed to raucous laughter. "You know how this old boy tends to push too fast, and I didn't want to wind him."

He waited for the laughter to die down.

"Raul says we need to get out on San Leandro Creek and dig some cows out of the brush. Some wild cattle stampeded two hundred head of our tame ones—including twenty of Captain Macroom's fine crossbreds—into the mesquite last night. Probably the raiders scared them."

He stopped and glanced around the circle of faces.

"We're riding out within the hour, since Raul says it'll take us until dark to get there. Some of you best brushpoppers step out here."

"Boss, you gonna ride your fast horse, or reckon he needs to rest up a little?"

"Better take him, he'll fly through the brush too quick for the thorns to get you."

"Name that booger Wings," somebody else called. "Not only can he fly, but he's a little *angel,* too!"

While the good-natured jesting was going on, more than a dozen vaqueros in the pen stepped out to volunteer for the hard, rough task. Ferguson and Dunham and several others held back.

Somebody in that group yelled, "Any o' us coulda rode that widow-maker, too, if we knowed a little Indian magic. All he done was cast a spell on him, blowin' in his nose and all."

The other vaqueros ignored that remark, and so did Maggie. She clapped her hands together and smiled like a silly person while her tears began to flow. There was more to a man's strength than tyranny and barking orders; Cade had just shown her that. His strength of character was as great as his physical build.

He had bested the situation in every way. Not only had he ridden the bronc—without a saddle, no less—but he could also chat and joke about it. He was nodding to one, then another, then another of the vaqueros, his aristocratic profile seemingly sculpted from bronze. His smooth, powerful gestures, the careless way he sat the horse, made him look like a god of the prairie, ruling his home, ready to ride on the wind.

Then he glanced up to find her, still sitting on the fence, and even from that distance his black eyes held the heat of the sun.

Her heart overflowed and her throat filled. With love.

That was the feeling she hadn't been able to name, the feeling that had stalked her. The feeling she'd been trying not to recognize because it held such power.

Love overcame her, overwhelmed her. She smiled at him.

She loved Cade Chisk-Ko with all the passion of her being, loved him as she had never loved anyone or anything else. And she had known it when he'd disappeared over the horizon.

The thought froze her where she sat, her hands grasping the rail.

No. He would never leave her. This morning, he hadn't said he loved her, but he'd said he wanted to do right by her and didn't that mean that he wanted to stay with her always?

Yes. Because *the feeling* that always made him move on was what he feared would prevent his doing right by her.

She gave a great, ragged sigh of relief. He would never leave her. Love like this was powerful enough to overcome any other feeling.

Chapter 13

Maggie pulled her hat down low against the afternoon sun and glanced around at the vaqueros. They were warming up their restless brush ponies before they charged them into the brush along the San Leandro again.

"This time I'm going in, too," she blurted. "I don't care what anybody says."

Toby burst out laughing. He was the fifteen-year-old Anglo vaquero whom Luis had assigned to help her hold the cattle being brought out of the brush that morning. Maggie twisted around in her saddle to glare at him.

"And just what is so funny?"

"A woman can't be a brushpopper," he said.

"A woman surely can," Maggie snapped.

She stood in her stirrups.

"Julio," she called, "come and take my place, *por favor*."

Julio signaled his partner to finish their chore of driving the used horses toward the *remuda* and swung his mount around to lope toward her. Immediately, she clucked to her cow horse and sent the pony at a fast trot toward the shade of the chuck wagon where Luis, Cade, and Bascom were drinking coffee and resting a moment before they went back into the brush for another chase.

Cade came to meet her.

"What is it, Maggie?"

"I'm going in this time,"

"You are *not*."

"You and Luis have been saying, 'Later, you can go in later, Maggie,' all day long!" she said. "I just realized you intend to stall me and stall me until dark!"

She jumped down from her mount. Cade threw his coffee out across the dusty ground, and he threw the cup into the dishtub, where it landed with an angry clatter. He followed her as she marched around to the wagon's tailgate, where the protective clothing lay in a pile.

"*Senora!*" Luis called. "Miss Maggie, I beg you to stay out here, *por favor!*"

"You're *not* going in there, Maggie," Cade growled.

She chose a pair of leather leggings, the smallest she could find, held them up to her, and started buckling them around her waist.

"You are insufferably bossy," she said, as he came around the corner.

"If you want to talk about bossy, look in the mirror," he said. "Julio was doing his job when you told him to do yours instead."

"Maybe so," she said, "but somebody has to help Toby because I won't be there."

She tied her hat down tighter and grabbed one of the heavy poplin jackets meant to save the brushpoppers' arms.

"Please, Maggie," Cade said, trying and failing to keep the impatience out of his voice. "You're a good rider, very good, but the brush is a whole different world. These ponies go hell for leather in there and you can't control them. I nearly got dragged off twice this morning, myself."

She flashed a determined look at him.

"Yesterday you rode a bad bronc that nobody else has ridden, and now your word is starting to carry some weight around here. I can't ride a widow-maker, but I can do this."

She picked a pair of heavy gloves and started pulling them on.

"I've watched and listened to the rest of you all morning," she said. "I can do this."

He laughed.

"You *couldn't* have watched, Maggie, a person can't see three feet in there! All you've seen is us coming and going. Have you noticed, perhaps, the thorns on the riders and the horses, the bruises and scratches, the ripped clothes and enough wood caught on the saddles to build the supper fire?"

"I'm going to try it," she said.

She strode around the end of the wagon.

"Luis, would you give me a brush horse, *por favor?*"

"*Senora*, no, I beg you once more . . ."

Bascom interrupted, smiling at her.

"I think we should let Maggie try it," he said. "She's a good rider and she'll be on a brush pony that knows what he's doing."

Surprised, Maggie stopped and beamed at him.

"Well, thank you, Bascom," she cried. "It's gratifying to know that *somebody* has some faith in me!"

She turned back to Luis.

"Luis, which pony should I take?"

Luis looked from Bascom to Cade, who was ignoring everyone but Maggie. He was wearing his stone face again. She hated that, but, darn it, he knew he couldn't order her around.

"I thought you wanted to push me to learn to take care of myself," she said.

"There's a limit on what you can physically do," he said flatly.

Even though she'd known he would try to stop her, Maggie was still hurt. She turned and started toward the waiting, saddled horses. Luis signaled the vaquero who was holding them to bring the grulla. Maggie mounted, then looked at Cade again.

"I was hoping that you'd encourage me," she said.

Something inside was making her do this, even though she was scared to death. She had heard brushpopping stories wild enough to curl her hair every time she had visited the ranch, but today she had to go in—she had to prove her worth and earn the respect of her men.

Maybe, too, she had to prove to *herself* that she was capable of surviving anything, the way she had done at the cave. The bad thing was that now, instead of pushing her to be independent, Cade was holding her back. It made her feel lonesome.

"I encouraged you with the bronc," she coaxed.

He walked up to her horse and laid his hand over hers.

"Maggie, don't," he pleaded. "You don't have to do this to get the men's respect. Once they get to know you well, they'll have a high opinion of you."

She closed her heart to the worry in his eyes.

"But I won't think well of myself unless I do this," she said.

"Suit yourself," he snapped and stepped back. "Just let your horse make the decisions."

He wheeled and strode to his own brush pony.

"Remember to give your pony his head," Luis said to Maggie, moving around her mount, adjusting her tack here and there to lessen the chances of its catching on the brush. "And pull your hat down tighter over your hair, *senora*. It's very dangerous to catch your hair."

She did as he said. He left her and mounted his horse.

"We have only enough light left for one more run today," Cade called to all of them.

"Raul says he sighted some crossbreds at the bend of the creek."

He started in that direction, and suddenly the other horses were moving fast, following eagerly, picking up more and more speed on their own. Maggie's breath caught—she'd never before ridden a horse she couldn't control, and nothing Cade or Luis had said had prepared her for this sense of helplessness. Brush ponies loved the challenge of the chase above all else, and these were fresh and ready for action. She had better get ready, too. They started moving faster and faster.

She tucked her elbows close to her sides and got a good grip with her legs. Then they hit the thicket head-on, running flat, tearing a hole in the tangle of *huisache* that lined the creek. She gasped, and then had no chance to breathe again, no hope of thinking. Instinctively she ducked her head and stretched out along the pony's neck.

She gritted her teeth and hung on, tried to set her feet more firmly in the stirrups behind the long, swinging *tapaderos* that kept her toes from catching in the brush. They ran through it for a short distance, then her mount stopped, so fast she could barely stay on. He lifted his head to listen. Maggie clung to the saddle horn and worked at catching her breath.

A long minute later, she and the pony heard the pop and crack of a cow in the mesquite just ahead. He leaped into motion again. He swerved to one side of a bush, bounded up to jump the next one, and crashed straight into another impenetrable-looking thicket. She threw herself low along his neck and hung on, but not before a branch tore at her leggings and another nearly put out her eye.

Her stomach went cold and turned over. She'd be knocked or dragged from the saddle unless she rode with every muscle she had. She'd often heard that a brush pony wouldn't stop, wouldn't even slow, once he took after a cow.

Her blood was roaring hot in spite of the cold fear, and her heart was thundering. This was as wonderful as it was terrible; she loved it yet she hated it, too.

She would get this cow, and then she would drive out one cow after another. The men would have no choice but to brag about her the way they had about Cade. She could just hear them.

Well, the boss of our outfit may be a redskin, but he can step right up and ride anything that grows hair.

Well, the boss of our outfit may be a woman, but she can snake them cows right out of the brush like the best brasadero *ever lived.*

Her pony made a hard right turn, ran between two impossible thickets—one mesquite, one *huisache*—and flushed the cow out into the open, running flat out. Maggie dug her fingers into his mane and dared to raise her head enough to peek at where they were going. They were headed down a crooked gully, where the wind whistled hard and the sun shone bright off the rocks. Where the land sloped so steeply that she couldn't bear to look.

Oh, dear Lord, why had she insisted on doing this? She held onto the pony's scruffy mane with one hand and got a death grip on the saddle horn with the other.

They stayed right on the cow's heels halfway down the arroyo. Then, with no warning at all, not even a twitch of her ears, the cow turned to the left and vanished into the *huisache*. The pony turned too, but Maggie went straight. She barely had time to realize she was flying through the air before she landed, bumping and sliding over the sharp-edged stones, to stop with her head an inch away from the roots of a gnarled mesquite.

She thought she was dead. She couldn't breathe. She would never be able to breathe again.

Then she gasped some air into her lungs and set her hands to the rocks to push herself up.

She had to get up and find her pony. She had to get that cow. She couldn't walk out of here into the camp and have everybody laugh because she had lost her horse. And she couldn't *ride* out without a cow to show. This was her chance, her best chance, to earn the men's respect fast. She would *not* lose it.

The sun beat down, and the wind tumbled her hair as she struggled to push herself back out from under the mesquite tree. When she had finally turned to get up, something snuffled and pushed her in the side.

She rolled over quickly and saw that she was right under the nose of her pony.

"Hey, you came back!" she cried.

Then she clamped her mouth shut, prayed she hadn't scared him, and reached for the reins. The pony's loyalty to his rider had overcome his love of the chase; it gave Maggie such joy that it lifted her to her feet. She got up and petted him, over and over.

But then she stood still and stared. The cow she had followed was gone, maybe forever. She had found it totally by accident and she had no idea where to find another.

Her arms and legs were trembling, and she felt shaken up inside. She didn't know whether she had the nerve for another wild ride. No wonder Cade had been so worried about her trying this.

She grabbed the stirrup leathers and stuck her toe in, desperate to mount in spite of her trembling body. She had to ride again, she had to prove to Cade she could do it and to Toby that a woman could too be a brushpopper.

She set her jaw and swung up into the saddle. She sat the horse, took a long breath, and turned her face up to the afternoon autumn sun. Then, with renewed determination, she stuffed her braids and the tendrils of her hair up underneath her hat. She tied it down tighter and put her heels to the pony.

"Hiyi!"

He almost jumped out from under her, but in the next instant they had plunged into the brush again. She had to find a cow and drive it into camp, then another and another. She could do it and she would!

The cracking of the brush higher up the creek rang out, and her pony skidded to a stop. He stood very still, ears pricked, nose up and into the wind. Maggie could feel his muscles quiver beneath her.

The popping and crackling came again, louder, a little closer. The pony held his head higher yet, working his ears eagerly. Maggie grabbed onto the horn of her saddle.

Once more she heard the sharp pop, closer yet, and she planted her feet deep in the stirrups. Thank God for eight hundred miles of hard riding—before then, she wouldn't have had a prayer of staying on a horse in the brush.

Pretty soon, the raking of hooves and the rattle of horns sounded right in her ear. There were three or four cattle coming, straight down the side of the creek bed, running full out. Maggie barely had time to take a better seat when she and the pony hit the brush as one.

They tore through the limbs, where the black thorns reached out to snatch at them. She peered ahead, through the bushes that had already lost their leaves, to see her quarry. The natural-born brush pony leaped ahead like a deer, heedless of limbs that would not give an inch and thorns that stabbed and cut.

He almost unseated Maggie when he whirled sideways in the next instant, but they landed right on the heels of a cow and kept chasing. More popping and breaking wood noises crackled through the air right behind them. Maggie wanted to turn and see what was there but she had no chance. It took all she had just to stay with her horse.

She was *not* going to fall off again, especially not if another vaquero was behind her.

Although she thought it would have been impossible, the cow and the pony picked up speed. To keep from having her head torn off, Maggie slid to the side of the horse and clung to his neck, the horn, and one stirrup. She tucked her head close to the horse and hung on as the surefooted pony bobbed and weaved to avoid the thorn-laden limbs—forward, back, under, over. She never tried to guide the pony at all, just trusted him to run on the best side of the next tree.

A thorn caught her hat and dragged at it. The string cut into her neck, then it broke and the hat was gone. She pressed her cheek hard into the pony's sweaty flesh and prayed. If a bush caught her hair, it would tear off her head.

After a lifetime without breathing, without air, without thinking, without peace, she and her pony burst from the brush into the open, close to the cow camp. Numbly, Maggie pulled her shaking self back up into her saddle seat.

But her blood was raging with excitement, too. She had stayed with that cow—and on her horse—every step of the way!

Then two more cows came thundering past her to join the one she was chasing. She almost fell off her horse in surprise. She'd gotten *three*!

Maggie turned to see if someone behind her had driven them, but she saw only the wall of brush. She faced front again, driving the three beautiful cows ahead of her, *her* three cows, to where the others were being held. One of the cows she'd brought in was a valuable cross-bred, one of her precious seed stock!

Her numbness drained away, trailing fire in her blood and sending all her senses to pulsing. She had done it!

"*Senora!*" Luis shouted, "you have lived through your first run and you have brought us live cattle!"

The old man was laughing, but his tone held great relief.

"*La senora esta una brasadera!*" his helper called, waving his hat in the air.

The cook was puttering around the pots heating over the fire in a trench he had dug in the ground. He straightened up and waved to show his excitement and approval. Bascom smiled and waved at her, then trotted his horse over to meet her.

But young Toby scowled and called out,

"Most likely she had some help. A woman can't do that!"

"I did not have help!" she shouted.

Toby was in the minority, though, for the two men holding the *remuda* waved and called to her, and so did Diego. A great wave of happiness washed over her. This was what she had dreamed of since her first visit to the ranch when she was a tiny girl. Her dreams were coming true!

Just before she got the cattle all the way to the herd, hoofbeats pounded behind her and she turned to see Cade, already several yards into the clearing from the edge of the brush. He was a little to the right of her cattle, keeping an eye on them. He didn't see her glance.

Realization came like a sudden, cold shower of rain. Something in his manner told her that he had had a hand in her success. He had been the one to drive these cows toward her. He had stayed on their right, out of sight, through her wild ride, herding them. He had, no doubt, been the sole reason they didn't get away from her.

And she'd been so foolish as to think she'd done all this herself! And to be so thrilled with all the praise and congratulations. Toby was right after all!

A terrible hurt washed through her.

Cade hadn't even given her a chance to see what she could do alone! *Because he hadn't believed she could do it.*

She slumped in her saddle, so disappointed

she simply could not bear it. She was tired, and all her work had been for nothing. Nothing! She blinked away the tears that stung the edges of her eyes. She had never felt such hurt.

The cattle she'd driven were slowing, trotting into the herd by the time Bascom had almost reached her. She waved at him and reined the pony, who surprised her by obeying.

"You did a great job, Maggie," he said. "I never saw anybody do better for their first time! You can really ride."

"This pony can really run," she said, and her voice was so faint she could barely hear it herself.

Cade came loping up to them. His face had a scratch that ran across one cheekbone to the corner of his sensuous mouth. How could he look so wonderful, how could she love him so much when he didn't believe in her?

"She's a born *brasadera*, isn't she?" he said to Bascom, but smiling at her. "We can leave this brushpopping to her from now on."

"True," Bascom said, laughing, as he turned to ride away because someone was calling to him. "That'll free up some hands for some other jobs."

Maggie looked at Cade, who said, "What's wrong? I thought you'd be happy to bring in three cows."

Her throat knotted. It felt so full that she couldn't speak. Finally she managed to murmur, "I would be if I'd done it by myself."

He glanced around and saw that no one was close enough to hear. She just looked at him, fighting to keep the tears back.

"Toby doesn't know what he's talking about," he said. "You know that."

"I don't," she said brokenly. "I don't know if I could've gotten those cows or not because you didn't let me find out. I saw you, Cade."

He laid one arm across his saddle horn and leaned on it. He smiled.

"Maggie, what are you so worked up about?"

"You didn't believe in me," she said. "You didn't even believe in me as much as Bascom did!"

He pushed back his hat and let it hang from the strings. The cut across his face made his intriguing face even more fascinating. He leaned closer to her.

"Maggie, you should not have gone in there and you know it," he said, raising his voice a little as some more cattle came running by. Maggie felt the vaquero's curious glance, but she ignored him.

"You had a great run, though. You did great for your first time."

"Not as great as you led me to *think* I did!"

She bit her lip to keep from crying, and he reached out to touch her cheek.

"Don't touch me," she said, jerking away, backing her horse up.

He moved his horse closer and whispered hoarsely, so the men wouldn't hear, "Be practical. Think like a Choctaw for once! Men who have cowboyed for years on the plains can't drive out cows, can't even stay on a horse in the brush! You did it! Well, except for that one time he threw you . . ."

Anger flashed to life through her hurt.

"You didn't have to spy on me every minute!" she cried, feeling her cheeks go red.

"You got up and got right back on," he said calmly. "You showed a lot of guts, more than many a man I've known. *Think*, Maggie! You were hoping to do the impossible—*I* never got a cow until noon and I was at it all morning."

"Something about that sounds really conceited, but I can't put my finger on it exactly," she said.

His hot dark eyes moved over her, slowly, serenely. They called to her blood, set it leaping in her veins, as he gave her his wonderful grin.

"Not conceited," he said. "*Practical*."

Laughter began to bubble up in her, yet a tear escaped and ran down her cheeks.

Cade sidestepped his pony closer.

"Maggie," he said softly, and leaned still closer to her, nudging his horse nearer. "I was only helping you. It's no disgrace to get some help once in a while."

His voice was a rich, warm wonder. Like heavy cream on a peach cobbler. Like the stroking of his hand on her skin.

"Oh, Cade . . ."

He reached out and cupped her face in his

hand, wiped away the tear with his thumb. His rough palm grew warmer against her cheek. Gently, very gently, he touched the burn on her neck that the hat string had made.

"All the vaqueros are watching us," she said, smiling.

"Let 'em," he said, his voice growing deeper.

She lifted her gaze to meet his beautiful eyes, dark and liquid and hot. They were pools of sweet, warm chocolate she could fall into and drown in. They looked at each other for a long time.

His hand grew even gentler on her face. He grinned again and said, "But tonight let's *not* let 'em watch, let's move our sugans to the other side of that nice, big rock there, what do you say?"

"I say that's the most practical suggestion I've heard today," she said, grinning back at him.

Later, when supper was over and the sky was dark except for the far-flung stars and the yellow-white moon, when the horses were tended and the vaqueros were singing around the cookfire on the other side of the rocky outcropping, Cade and Maggie worked together making their bed. With the sun's setting, the cold was sweeping quickly over the land.

"Wouldn't you know this'll be our coldest night yet this fall and we're miles and miles from the house?" she said.

"Complain, complain," he teased. "I never would have thought it. As I recall, when we started this trip, you were talking every day about how tough you were."

Maggie laughed as she smoothed the bed-roll's canvas cover against the ground.

"I *am* tough," she said, looking up at him. "Oh, Cade, I never would have thought I could feel such fear and such exhilaration both at once as I did chasing those cows!"

"I know."

"I was so scared I thought I would die of fright but at the very same time my blood was pumping and my heart was racing with the thrill of it," Maggie said as she unfolded the extra quilt. "It was the most exciting thing I have *ever* done."

He looked at her.

"Ever?"

His eyes stayed on hers.

Heat rose into her cheeks and she said, "Except for . . ."

"Except for what?" he asked, giving her his most tantalizing grin.

He reached across the bedroll and traced the shape of her mouth, murmuring, "Except for what, Maggie?"

She nipped at his fingertips.

"Oh, let's not make a judgment quite yet," she said. "This brush-running partnership we created today may lay every other collaboration of ours in the shade."

He raised one black brow and held her gaze

as he drawled, "I'll lay *you* in the shade, *senora*, and in the sunlight, too. That's a promise."

He bent his head to kiss her as she threw her arms around him and pulled him down. He moaned as he tumbled onto the bedroll full length with her. He reached to unbuckle his belt with his free hand, while dropping quick, hard kisses on the side of her neck, her cheeks, her nose.

"Cade," she said.

She cupped his head with both her hands, drove her fingers into the black silk of his hair. He began unbuttoning his shirt.

Maggie blew into his ear and kissed it, moved her lips down the hard line of his jaw. She kissed his face once, twice, three times, moving her mouth slowly, carefully, inexorably back to meet his.

He went still as midnight waiting for her to kiss his mouth. Her whole body thrilled to know she held such power.

"Maggie," he whispered. "Maggie."

What was in his heart showed in the way he said her name. Her eyes filled with tears.

Her lips caressed the corner of his mouth. Her tongue trailed over his lips, teasing, tantalizing, testing his patience, until he groaned and gave her his own tongue to taste.

Then, without warning, her power was all gone; he had taken it. She melted, helpless, into the bed, into the ground beneath them, into his arms. She couldn't bear to let even a wisp of air come between them, couldn't pull away to be

rid of her clothes nor to help him be rid of his.
She could only wish the garments were gone.

He broke the kiss.

"Let's . . . get . . . our . . . boots . . . off," he said,
his lips brushing hers after each whispered
word.

He tried to act on his own suggestion, tried
to let her go, tried to sit up and away from
her. But he couldn't, and she wouldn't turn
him loose.

Maggie finally tore her mouth from his.

"It's too cold to undress out here," she managed to say. "But we can't put our boots in the
bed."

"No we can't."

They sat straight up at the same moment
and began ripping off boots, then jackets,
shirts, jeans.

"Don't be a sissy," he said, as Maggie
screamed and dived into the blankets. "Any
brushpopper who can snake the cows out of
the mesquite like you can, can surely run
around naked in November."

"Look who's talking!" she cried, as he hurriedly crawled in with her.

They laughed and teased each other with
kisses and touches and words that had them
shivering more than the wind blowing off the
prairies to the north. Finally they settled into
the warm blankets, into each other's arms, into
heaven.

"Someday, darlin', I'm going to do this
right," Cade murmured. "I promise you that."

"I thought you did it right last night," she

said, and pressed her lips to the slight indentation in the middle of his chest. His skin was like silk, cool silk that grew warmer and warmer under the heat of her mouth. "But then I have nothing to compare it to."

"Undressing you, I mean," he said, dreamily. "Someday I want to take all the time in the world, to savor undoing every button, to kiss every inch of you as I uncover it, as I look at you to my heart's content."

His hands began moving over her, caressing the curve of her hips, stroking the length of her thigh.

"There *is* no someday," she said, her voice catching on the last word because he threw his leg over her and she felt the smooth, hot hardness of his manhood. "There is only the here and now, only tonight, my darling Choctaw."

He laughed and hooked his knee around her legs to pull her closer still.

"Then let's look at this in the practical Choctaw way," he whispered. "We can't waste tonight with its fast-fading sunset and its wind calling to us and this warm, cozy bed. Look here to me. Give me your mouth."

She did, and he rose up over her, cradling her body in his arms while he treasured her lips. They parted for him, as did her thighs, and they moved together as partners into the new, old song of life itself. Darkness fell completely, and the night enveloped the land and the creek beyond while the vaqueros played guitars in the distance.

Chapter 14

During the next two weeks, Maggie and Cade worked harder than either had ever imagined they would on the *rancho*. They spent much time learning the cattle and horses, the men, and the land with its scattered sources of water and its grasses and brush and sand. Making the necessary management decisions was an equally exhausting task. A few of the men did leave, but, surprisingly, Ferguson and Dunham stayed on while continuing their mutterings. Bascom continued to be generously helpful. He acted as their foreman and followed their wishes to the letter, except for the time he took two days to ride to Corpus Christi for fencing supplies precisely when they couldn't spare him. Cade and Maggie both stayed in the saddle for hours and put their hands to nearly everything the vaqueros did. They were beginning to feel well accepted by most of them.

One morning, Maggie woke in Cade's arms, snuggled deep in the middle of their big bed. She shivered from the cold air that filled the room, scooted closer to his warm back, and hugged him. Today was the first of December she remembered, and they had been together two whole months!

She stared past his shoulder at the sky lightening with the dawn. A month ago Pierce had sent her a telegram telling her of his impending arrival. But he wasn't here yet, and Cade was.

Resolutely, she relived yesterday to try to ease her worries. She and Cade and Luis had ridden out to the Saltillo pastures, named for the crumbled huts of the family who had held the original land grant, to see how much water remained in Turkey Creek. They had hardly talked at all on the way. The ride through the bright, breezy day had filled all their senses to bursting. Long lines of live oak had waved at them; deer and antelope had run away from them through the stirrup-high, rustling grass; the turkey flocks that gave the creek its name, and coveys of quail had come surging out of the thickets, wings beating.

The biggest thrill of all had been a herd of wild horses. First seeing the banners of dust, and then the manes and tails and the stretched-out, running bodies not very far away had brought Maggie's heart leaping into her throat and had made Cade cry out with pleasure. They had stopped to watch the mustangs disappear into the hazy blue sky while they rested their mounts.

Maggie shivered a little and scooted even

closer to Cade in their bed as she remembered exactly how it had been.

Cade had rubbed Smoke's shoulder, then he had hooked one leg over his saddle horn as he said, "It's a hard, lonesome land, this border country of yours, Luis. But it draws a man to it like no other place I've ever been."

Her heart soared again with the memory. She lifted her hand and stroked the huge muscle of his upper arm, then the tender skin on the inside of his elbow, hoping the gesture would wake him. Wishing he would turn to her and promise he would stay with her forever.

He stirred, and the muscles of his naked back flexed against her breasts and sent his fierce, familiar heat all through her. With no warning, he bent his arm and trapped her fingers in the crook of his elbow.

Maggie laughed and said, "I was just hoping you would wake up." She kissed his shoulder.

"So you woke me," he said drowsily, stretching out his legs to their full, considerable length, as he rolled over to take her into his arms. "And it's about time. Look at that—the sun's up."

They snuggled together beneath the flannel quilts, reveling in their island of warmth in the bitter cold of the room. It was winter in Texas.

"I wish Bascom had never gone to Corpus and brought that telegram from Pierce," she murmured. "It worries me that he's threatening to come down here and force me to go back to Arkansas."

"He can't do that," Cade said. "I won't let him." He leaned back and held her away from him so he could look into her face. "Maggie, I'll take care of you. I can do anything, remember?" he said, and he dropped a quick kiss on the tip of her nose.

She pulled away from him.

"But will you be here, even tomorrow? I don't know that, Cade, and I need to. In the last few days, I've just really been needing to know that."

He stiffened.

"Damn it, Maggie, how can you know it if I don't? How can I tell you that?"

She held his gaze and said, "Since you've been here, have you been bothered any by *the feeling?*"

His eyes went darker than ever.

"No," he said solemnly. "I haven't felt it since I met you."

A knot formed in her throat, and she could barely speak.

"You haven't?" she whispered.

"But that's no guarantee," he said, his voice very low and his face hard. "Maybe you've just entertained me so much I haven't noticed *the feeling* coming around."

He sat up, threw off the covers, and swung his feet out onto the floor.

"Damn it all, Maggie, I can't be sure that my

whole life is different and everything's changed. I can't know."

He stood up and reached for his jeans, hurriedly stepping into them.

She drew in a deep, trembling breath, praying she could keep her voice from wavering.

"Then we'll have to take life a day at a time, the way we said we would," she said. "That's all we can do."

"Right," he said gruffly.

Suddenly, he whipped around to look out the window, his head cocked, listening.

"There's some kind of an army coming in here," he said. He stomped his boots on, fast, while he grabbed a shirt and ran to the windows.

Maggie heard it then—the thunder of hooves. Many horses, coming full out. Something was wrong, very wrong. She leaped up, too, and ran to the armoire to pull out some clothes.

Soon, too soon, the hard, galloping hoofbeats reverberated in the yard, pounded closer, shook the glass in the window frames.

"Hey!" a voice yelled. "Hey! We want the Injun!"

It was a man's voice, and he sounded angry.

Maggie grabbed the first dress she touched and pulled it over her head without a thought of undergarments. That shout filled her with terror. They were after Cade!

Another, even more menacing voice,

shouted, "Las Manzanitas! Whoever's bossing this corrida, come out!"

Maggie's blood froze in her veins as she scrambled to fasten the dress. Cade was standing against the wall, looking out from behind the curtains.

"What in the *world*?" she cried.

"Twenty-five riders," he said. "On lathered horses. Armed to the teeth and carrying ropes."

To her horror, he tore back the curtains, stepped in front of the window, and threw it open. His deep, authoritative voice boomed out across the sunny, winter morning.

"Who are you?"

"Southwest Texas Stockman's Association! Vigilance Committee! We want the Indian!"

"I'll be right out."

"No! You can't, Cade!" she cried, running toward him on her bare feet. "They sound angry enough to kill you! These men are ranchers, like Grandpa, not crazy, hotheaded gun hands! If they want you, it's serious!"

She bit her tongue to stop babbling and got out of his way as he went for his guns. He checked the load in the rifle, laid it down again, and started buckling his pistol on.

She opened her mouth to tell him to go out unarmed—he wouldn't have a chance to shoot against so many—but she closed it again. She couldn't bear to see him defenseless, either.

She whirled away from him and ran to the window. She stuck her head through it and leaned out, looking over the stockmen for someone she knew. Several rancher friends of her grandfather were leading the committee. These men were respectable ranchers. They needed to know they were dealing with their own kind.

"Mr. Young!" she called to the most prominent member. "It's me, Maggie! Remember? Captain Macroom's granddaughter. You and your men please get down and come in. I'll meet you in the parlor."

His answer was a gruff "No, thank you, ma'am."

She stuck her bare feet into night slippers, unwilling to take the time to put on stockings and shoes.

"Why the hell did you invite them in?" Cade demanded. "I'll keep them out of the house and . . ."

"No!" Maggie cried frantically as he reached the hallway door. "Offer hospitality! Show them we're the owners of this ranch, and we're as good as they are. This yelling about wanting the Indian scares me to death. They lump Indians and Mexican raiders together around here and there must have been a raid last night."

He turned the knob and jerked the door open.

"Maggie, whatever happens . . ."

"I won't *hear* it!" she cried, and her throat tightened with tears. "There's got to be some mistake."

He walked out the door and she ran after him. When she reached the entry, Cade was standing on the front porch facing Mr. Young and another friend of Grandpa's, Mr. Wright.

That she could think of names at all was a miracle in itself, she thought. She loved Cade, oh, dear God, how she loved him, and they were here to drag him away.

She took a deep breath, straightened her shoulders, and stepped out through the doorway, putting on her best smile and her most ladylike Southern air. Mama would have been proud of her.

"Welcome to Las Manzanitas, gentlemen," she said, smiling directly at each of them as she offered her hand. "This is my husband, Cade Chisk-Ko, from up in the Choctaw Nation. Dear, this is Mr. Sam Young, owner of the Lazy Y and Mr. Wright of the Circle Cross. Both were good friends of my grandfather."

The gentlemen bowed over her hand, but they didn't smile or meet her eye. They had an air of terrible urgency about them.

"Won't you have your men get down so Oleana can give them breakfast?"

"Please forgive our abruptness, Miss Maggie," Mr. Young said, "but we carry bad news this morning and we ride to see justice done."

His flat, cold tone took her breath.

"What bad news?" Cade demanded.

Young stared at him with hard eyes and said, "Indian raid on your neighbors up toward Corpus Christi, the Carpenters. Family slaughtered like so many pigs, house and outbuildings burned to the ground, livestock stolen, including ten head of fine Kentucky horses and corrals and pens wrecked and burned."

He continued to look at Cade in a way that made it clear he was giving no quarter. "Some think you might know something about it, you being the only Indian around here."

"As you can see, I'm not with a tribe, Mr. Young, I'm out on my own, married to Maggie, and running this ranch. I've been right here all night and besides, I could hardly have done all that damage alone."

"Blood and red skin is thicker than water!" shouted one of the men still on horseback. "He prob'ly has some Comanche friends!"

"How do you know Indians raided the Carpenter place?" Cade asked.

"Everybody's scalped, is the main thing," Mr. Wright said. "Tracks are of unshod horses, there's moccasin tracks, and some arrows. Plenty of proof."

"Yeah!" one of the other men yelled. "Let's string 'im up! Now!"

Maggie's blood froze, and she cried, "Maybe it's false proof! Remember the 1854 attack on Roma and Rio Grande City when the outlaws disguised themselves as Indians!"

Thankfully, that struck a nerve with Sam Young.

"Could be, I guess," he said. "Captain Macroom and I rode in the bunch that hunted them renegades. We caught two and hanged them on the Roma Road with their white skins exposed."

But somebody called, "These was real Indians, all right, Sam, and you got one of them right there. Bring him out and hang 'im now—we still got to bury them other poor folks!"

Maggie's knees threatened to buckle beneath her.

"Let me look at the signs they left behind," Cade said. "I can tell if they're Comanche or not."

The two men hesitated.

After an age, Sam Young said, gruffly, "All right."

"I'll get my hat and coat," Cade said. Then, as he turned toward the door, he waved at Jorge and another of Oleana's sons, who had come to the edge of the yard and were standing near Bascom, watching the riders. "Saddle Smoke for me, *por favor!*"

Maggie yearned to follow him in, to kiss him good-bye, to hide him, to beg him to run out the back door and fly away on Smoke. But none of that would save his life as her words might.

"Mr. Young, you're a fair and decent man like my Grandfather had been," she said, fighting to keep her voice calm. "My husband is innocent—he was here all night with me. Please don't let these men hang him unjustly. You know yourself how people believed that Indians raided Roma until you and Grandpa helped prove it was white outlaws!"

"We want justice done, not just a lynching, Miss Maggie," Sam Young said. But that was all he would say.

Soon, too soon, the boys came running with Smoke, and Cade was back, shrugging into his coat, kissing her once on the mouth, strong and hard. He was off the porch, then, and down the steps to his mount. The boys held his reins while he stepped up onto the stallion.

He looked at her for a long moment—until they surrounded him and rode away.

Cade's thoughts threatened to strangle him as the white men did. He knew they wouldn't shoot him in the back because they were honorable men who lived by the stern Texas code, but if he couldn't convince them of his innocence they would hang him. They might be the ones who would make him know that that burning sky long ago—and the one he'd seen over Las Manzanitas—truly had foretold disaster for him.

He closed his eyes. At least he had had these weeks with Maggie.

His heart twisted at the thought of her. The memory of her face, filled with agony as she stood holding onto the porch pillar, was unbearable. He felt his lips curve in an ironic, bitter grin. Now he didn't have to wait for *the feeling* to come over him. Sam Young and his men were taking him away from Las Manzanitas.

They rode hard, and they arrived at the burned-out homestead within an hour. A pall of smoke hung over the whole, desolate scene, and small flames still burned in the hard timbers. Bodies of both men and women lay where they had fallen, scalped but not mutilated.

"Well, there you are," Sam Young said grimly. "There's your Indian signs that anybody could see."

Cade looked around questioningly before he got down. One or two men nodded for him to go on and look for himself.

"You'll hang, Injun," somebody from the back of the group called in a soft voice that was worse than a shout. "Right here in a minute."

Sam Young dismounted, too, and he and Cade walked closer to the house.

"The Comanches haven't been this far east in years," Cade said, making sure that his voice stayed steady. "And look here, look at these moccasin tracks."

He sat down on his haunches and looked closely at the track in the spot of earth that had been moistened when the water bucket outside the back door was knocked off its shelf.

"Comanche moccasins have long fringes in the back to wipe out their tracks as they walk," he said. "This track wasn't made by a Comanche."

He stood up and looked at Sam Young as

he said, "You've fought Indians, Mr. Young. See what you think of this."

His blood was pounding, hope was rising in his heart. Surely they would let him go. Surely.

Sam Young agreed the track did not look Comanche, but others in the group were grumbling, already dismounting, already getting a rope to throw over a tree limb.

"We can't bring this man back to life if we hang him unjustly," Sam Young said loudly, walking back to the group of men who were busily tying a knot. Let's not do anything until we've looked around a little more."

Those men stared at him silently for a moment while Cade dared not breathe. Finally, they shook their heads and went back to work, saying, "We're wasting time. No telling where the butchering bastards are by now."

Then another man, on the edge of the group of riders, gave a cry and stood in his stirrups to peer toward a clump of mesquite growing not too far from the house.

"Hey! Hey, there! Help me, now!"

Everyone on the place turned toward the hoarse shout. Cade and Sam Young ran on foot toward the sound.

A man was staggering out of the mesquite thicket waving both arms and yelling, blood, some dried and some not, all over his face. He had a terrible wound, apparently from an axe or a hatchet, on his shoulder.

"Who is it?" Cade asked.

"That's Carpenter!" Young said. "Looks like we'll get t' hear right now who done this."

In between wails and curses as the men laid him down on the ground and gave him water, Carpenter managed to tell bits and pieces of the raid. In the middle of the night, the dog had started barking and woke them—then, almost immediately, strangers were inside the house. Four of them had herded the Carpenter family out while the others began setting fires.

"They wanted to kill us outside so's we wouldn't burn up and you'uns could see we was scalped and all," he said. "But they was white men. No doubt about it. They didn't even dress like Indians."

"Well, this here's an Indian that dresses white!" cried the man who'd been picking a limb from which to swing Cade.

"They was white, I tell you!" Carpenter croaked. "I seen 'em all. Didn't even bother to cover their faces."

"The horses was unshod," another stubborn man said.

"There's thousands of unshod horses in the Wild Horse Desert," Sam Young said, as he started running his eyes over the group again. "Split up," he called, "into groups of three. Fan out and find these killers!"

He left two men to care for Mr. Carpenter, two to dig graves, and then ran to his horse. When they were all mounted, he turned to Cade.

"They left a dozen different trails, but we

lost every one of them in the brush earlier this morning," the Texan said. "You being Indian, you may be a better tracker. Want to ride with me and Mr. Wright and see if you can follow one of them out?"

Cade answered with a curt nod. Then Sam Young spoke again.

"Mr. Chisk-Ko," he said, loudly, so that the others would hear. "Every man here owes you an apology. I hope you'll accept mine."

Cade looked into his eyes, and acknowledged his sincerity.

"Apology accepted."

They shook hands before they rode out. Cade rode beside him, amused that Young was taking the precaution of keeping Cade with him until they found the raiders, just in case he was wrong in believing Cade innocent. It didn't matter, Cade thought, drawing in a deep breath. Nothing mattered except the fact that he had escaped hanging one more time. He was going to live. He would see Maggie smile again.

Three miles north of the Carpenters' place, Cade lost the tracks he had chosen from the layers of crisscrossed hoofprints in their yard. Cursing silently, he circled fruitlessly again and again, then he pulled Smoke over into the shade of a live oak tree.

"I want to look around a little," he told Sam Young and Mr. Wright. "Why don't you all ride up the edge of that draw and see if you can spot anything?"

When they were gone, he threw one leg over the horn of his saddle and tried to get the feel of the land. He had picked the thickest bunch of tracks, the ones that showed the thieves driving the Carpenters' horses ahead of them. Where they had split, he had followed the ones heading for the softest ground, but they had disappeared on the dry earth. Instinct would have to guide him now.

He pulled his hat down and started a great, sweeping search of the western and then the northern horizon, looking for a faraway cloud of dust, although the thieves had probably gone to ground before daylight. The huge border country spread out around him, an open wilderness, yet a closed one, too, with oak mottes and thorn thickets scattered everywhere, some as green in December as they would be in June. The endless, blue sky arched over it all, the breeze blew brisk and tart. Like Maggie.

He pushed the thought away because thinking of her would fill his senses and keep him from doing this job, which had to be done. No ranch on the Strip would be safe until these men were caught, so he began searching the vast, rolling land again.

He stopped his gaze on a movement, a faroff stirring on the open prairie. The motion came closer, and he caught a glimpse of horns. Cows. A couple of wild cows, perhaps running from the horsethieves. He stood in the stirrups and raked the land with his eyes, but saw nothing else moving except for the leaves on the brush and trees rustling in the wind. The prairies rose and rolled a little, and sand blew from the side of a hill. Cade tapped Smoke's sides with his heels and reined the horse toward it. That spot might be soft enough to hold some sign.

It did. Its tracks led him around the hill and into a narrow, dry creek bed. It was rocky, and once he came out of it, the soil hardened again, but occasionally he could see tracks. He angled across to a place where he could see Young and Wright, whistled and called them to him with a wave of his arm, then started following the trail.

It led him straight to a *sendero*, a clearing, where the tracks of a dozen or more horses converged again. The thieves had separated only temporarily to try to foil pursuit. That was good. Now, perhaps, the stock they had stolen was gathered somewhere nearby waiting for a buyer or for a drive to a far market.

It took him only ten minutes to find the place, a narrow valley where a creek pooled naturally, a valley filled with a hundred head of horses, but no cattle. He dropped back below the ridge line. Then Cade, Wright, and Young left their horses and crept closer to look.

There they found the Kentucky horses, their long, tall thoroughbred toplines still covered with sweat and dust, at the edge of the bunch. The horses shifted a little, and closer into the herd, another horse, familiar somehow, caught his eye.

He looked again. A white mare with a gimpy leg. Foal by her side. Running M brand.

Two vaqueros, one Mexican, one Anglo, rode up and down, circling the herd from opposite directions, waiting for the new arrivals to mix in with the old ones and all of them to settle down. There was another man with his arm in a bandana sling near a small campsite by the pond. He might have been the one Cade had shot during the Las Manzanitas raid, but he couldn't be sure. That man, too, had a Mexican partner who was helping him build up the fire for the cooking pot sitting beside it.

"That white mare and foal were stolen in the raid on Las Manzanitas a few weeks ago," Cade whispered.

"There are horses here wearing every brand registered in the Nueces Strip," Sam Young said.

Suddenly the Anglo rider herding the horses stood up in his stirrups and shouted at the men by the fire.

"Hey, Gimpy! Pedro! Is Bascom coming back today?"

"Who knows?" Gimpy yelled back. "Bascom's the boss, he can do what he pleases!?"

"Bascom!" Wright muttered, and the three men exchanged significant glances.

Cade's blood froze, as did the breath in his lungs, but his brain began working fast. His suspicions had been right all along—the something that he had sensed wrong about Bascom was that he was a horsethief, setting up raids, gathering horses to drive to faraway, lucrative markets. He didn't want to leave this country, didn't want to give up his sweet little setup: So that was the reason he'd been so welcoming, so eager to work with Cade and Maggie!

"What an irony," Cade murmured as the three men looked at each other again. "When I saw Bascom down by the stable as we were leaving, I thought he was saddling up to come with us."

Then he just lay there, on his stomach, staring into Sam Young's gray eyes.

His heart lurched and began to race even faster than his mind: Bascom had organized a raid in which Maggie had been attacked, and he had organized this one to have Cade hanged. Bascom had not come with them.

The hair on the back of his neck stood up.

Maggie was alone with Bascom on the ranch.

Chapter 15

M aggie had been staring out at the same empty yard, at the same bare-limbed trees—now throwing their long, early winter afternoon shadows—and at the same blank blue sky for so long that she felt her eyes blur. It was past noon and she'd still had no word! She had thought about Cade from the moment he left, afraid and miserable that he might be dead somewhere.

But if that were true, she'd know it, wouldn't she? Wouldn't her heart know? Maybe not. Her heart was hurting so deeply that it might not hear Cade calling out to her, so deeply that she would surely die. Oh, dear Lord, how could she live without him?

She walked outside, walked up and down the porch. The wind drove her into the house again to pace the parlor, back and forth in front of the windows. She stared into the far distance, strained her sight to see as far as she could see down the Corpus Christi Road. But Cade wasn't on his way home to her.

"Senora?"

Maggie turned to find Oleana at her elbow with a napkin-covered tray.

"You must eat," she said softly. "I have made enchiladas."

A wonderful, spicy aroma confirmed that.

"I'm not hungry, but thank you, Oleana."

Oleana calmly set the tray on the table.

"They will not hang him," she said. "He is a good man and they are good men. They will find the truth."

Maggie smiled at her and paced back to the window to look out again, despite her awareness that only seconds had passed since she'd last looked for Cade.

"*Gracias*, Oleana."

"I go to my children now," Oleana said, "to *mi casa*. But I will come to you anytime you need me."

"*Gracias*," Maggie said, without turning around.

A moment later she heard Oleana leave. She stood there and looked out the window for a while longer, then she turned away and began to pace the length of the room and back again. Perhaps if she didn't look, he would surprise her and come galloping in on Smoke.

"Oleana is wrong, did you know that?"

Maggie's heart leaped into her throat, and she whirled to look behind her, at the doorway to the entry hall.

"Bascom, you scared me!" she cried.

Then she realized what he had said and

added, "What do you mean she's wrong? Wrong about what?"

He came into the room as he answered—in the same cordial tone he had used to welcome her to the ranch a few weeks ago. "About Cade. I'm sorry, Maggie, but they've already hung him."

Her pulse stopped, but she was able to cry, "How do you know? Were you there . . ."

Something, someone, God or Cade perhaps, whispered in her ear that Cade was alive. If he was dead she would know it in her bones. They were one soul, and she felt the bond between them as strongly as she felt her breath.

Bascom walked across the room to her, holding out his hands to take hers, saying, "Now it's just you and me."

She clapped her hands flat against her sides. Her pulse started up again in a hard, quick rhythm. He had a strange look in his eyes.

"What do you mean?"

"I mean we can share the *rancho*," he said. "I deserve half of it, at the very least, you know that."

"Then why didn't Grandpa leave half to you?" she countered, trying frantically to think.

She walked around the end of the big leather divan, putting it between them.

"He was besotted by you," he said, following her, his green eyes gleaming. "And, to tell you the truth, Maggie, so am I."

Cade had been right all along, Maggie

thought. There was something definitely not right about Bascom.

The room was full of weapons, but she'd never get one of the Sharps out of the stand and ready to fire before he jumped her. If only she still carried her knife in her pocket as she had done all the way to Texas! Then she remembered that Grandpa had kept a loaded pistol in the old oak secretary desk sitting at an angle in the corner. Maybe Bascom had forgotten that. Maybe she could get to it first if she needed it.

Maybe it wouldn't come to that, maybe she could hold him off with words until Cade came home.

"I think you have feelings for me, too," Bascom said.

"Bascom, how can you say such a thing when you have just told me that my husband is dead?"

He crossed the distance between them in an instant.

"You're not weeping," he said. "You don't care if he's dead because you love *me*. You've always loved me, Maggie, so you might as well admit it."

"Bascom, go away," she said, forcing herself to look him in the eye, "and leave me to grieve. I need my privacy."

"You need *me*," he cried and grabbed her by the shoulders to jerk her into his arms.

The tight hold she had on her nerves snapped. She screamed, "No, I don't, you repulse me. You've always repulsed me! Get your hands off me!"

She bucked and fought against his embrace, kicked and butted him with her head. He drove his hand into her hair, twisted it full, and yanked her head back until her neck was painfully arched.

"If I repulse you, then we can't share the ranch," he said, mournfully. "I'm so sorry, Maggie. Now you'll have to sign the whole place over to me."

He thrust his face even closer to hers, his mouth stretched in a thin ghost of a smile.

"I have the papers already prepared," he said. "Now you see why I had to make that trip to Corpus. Sign the papers, Maggie, and prepare to die."

Her whole body chilled.

Then a knowledge came to her in a lightning bolt from the sky, in a wonderful, cleansing, warming fury that struck her in the heart and began to burn. A fury full of power.

She wasn't going to let Bascom win. He might be bigger and stronger than she, but he'd forgotten that she wasn't a little girl anymore. She had grown into a strong, tough woman who dared anything. She had risked life and limb to ride eight hundred miles in three weeks, she had risked them again chasing cows out of the brush. She had risked her heart and her soul loving Cade.

If he stayed with her, this *rancho* would be their home. If he didn't, it would be all she

had left and she would run it, she would make
her dream a reality. That was more than most
people ever accomplished in a lifetime.

She forced her body to relax.

"This seems like old times, doesn't it, Bascom?" she said, with a light laugh. "I declare,
you were always pulling my hair."

He loosened his grip and let her stand up
straight, but he didn't remove his hand.

"Let me see the papers you've prepared,"
she said, gritting her teeth to keep from claw-
ing at his arm to get him away from her. "And
then let's talk. Keeping half the ranch would
be better than dying."

He took his hand away then, but as he did,
he slapped her cheek lightly, disdainfully.

"I didn't think you'd be so easy to manage,"
he said. "But then, I guess living with that arrogant savage has you whipped into submis-
sion in your private life."

He gave her a terrible smile and said, "Was
he a savage in bed, Maggie?"

"Sit down here, Bascom," she said, smiling
back at him, "and I'll get a pen and some ink
from the secretary."

He gave a satisfied chuckle, low in his
throat.

"That's my girl," he said. "Why don't you
bring me my slippers, too?"

Laughing, he dropped down into the deep,
leather-covered cushions as he reached into
the inside pocket of his coat. Maggie glanced
back at him as she moved toward the desk,

trying not to run, trying to make a decision. Her instincts were screaming for her to open the window, leap out onto the porch, and take her chances. She didn't even know if a pistol could fire after lying loaded for four years without being cleaned. She did know, however, that it could misfire and blow up in her face.

When she reached the desk, she looked over her shoulder again and froze. *Bascom was holding a gun on her!*

He smiled at her over the top of it as he held it in both hands, propped on the back of the divan; held it trained steadily on her.

"No offense," he said, "but ever since the war I always carry some help in my pocket. Don't even look at the windows, get the pen and ink and bring them here."

"Of course," Maggie said coolly, "I'll get the pen wipe and the blotter, too."

She set her jaw and made herself turn her back to the muzzle of his pistol so she could block his view with her body. She rattled the glass inkwell, then pulled open the drawer. The gun was still there!

Shifting her stance to shield it from him, she lifted it out, praying that it would kill him instead of her.

"Hurry up," he said, and then his voice dropped into a lecherous tone. "We'll go into the bedroom and have some fun when our business is done."

"I'm hurrying," she said. In the next instant

she whirled around to face him and fired. The pistol was loaded and it fired correctly.

He screamed and fired, too, but his shot went crashing through a window, and his pistol clattered to the floor behind the divan. Maggie ran to pick it up.

"You little *bitch*," he yelled. "You've torn off my shoulder!"

"I'm going to tear off your *head!*" Cade roared, as he launched himself through the door, reaching for Bascom with both arms outstretched, his throat choking full of the desperate urgency to kill him.

It blocked all his other words, it kept him from yelling to Maggie, it consumed him. He would not be able to breathe again until he bashed Bascom's face in, until he beat his whole body into an unrecognizable pulp, until Bascom was dead, dead, dead. Bascom, the son of a bitch who had tried to kill his Maggie.

To Cade's delight, Bascom had surged to his feet and began throwing punches with his good hand. One of them hit Cade in the face, and it stung because Bascom had the power of sheer desperation. Wonderful! Maybe the sucker could put up a fight! Cade drew back his right fist and hit him back.

Bascom fell and Cade fell onto him, barely aware of anything but the bastard's face and the satisfying thud of his fists driving into it. Then he grabbed his horse-thieving neck with both hands and started choking him, pounding his head up and down on the floor.

Dimly, he became aware of Maggie's voice.

"Cade! Stop it, Cade! Cade, Mr. Young and Mr. Wright are here. Cade, stop it!"

Then strong hands were pulling at his shoulders, and the fire in his gut began to die down.

"We'll take Bascom now," Sam Young said. "He needs to hang on the Corpus Christi Road so he'll be an example to other horsethieves passing by."

Cade shook his head. Slowly he stood up, first on his knees and then onto his feet. He swung his hazy gaze from Young to Wright.

"Did you follow me?"

"The best we could. That gray horse of yours can run a hole in the wind."

"We wanted to make sure we had the raiders' leader," Wright said. "Now we'll go get the rest of our men and round up his hired hands."

"So you didn't trust me again," Cade muttered. "What'd you think, that I'd let Bascom go after he'd attacked my own wife?"

Between them, they started dragging the completely limp Bascom toward the door.

"We'll bring him to before we hang him," Young said. "He needs to know his own fate."

"That's Bascom's horse saddled in the yard," Maggie told them. Then they were gone.

Cade shook his head and looked around the room. A big pool of blood was spreading, soaking into the adobe-colored rug that lay beneath the divan, staining the wooden floor.

His stomach turned. He felt he was a disgusting excuse for a human being, wreaking this kind of havoc inside a house, a home, Maggie's home, causing her to see this kind of brutality, trying to kill a man who couldn't even defend himself. For God's sake, Bascom had only had one hand he could use to fight!

"Cade?"

He couldn't turn, couldn't look at her. He wasn't good enough for her, he was just as uncivilized as she had once accused him of being, beating on a helpless man, lusting to kill him when he could have simply hanged him.

And he *would* have killed him, too. He had already killed Mr. Haynes. He was a savage murderer, and Maggie deserved better than that.

"Cade!" she cried, and touched his battered hands. "Cade, what's the matter?"

He jerked back from her touch and looked straight past her without saying a word. He could feel her eyes on him, though, and when she finally turned and walked away, toward the windows, his heart died in him.

He had to be completely away from her, had to cleanse himself somehow. He turned and stormed out into the yard where he could move, where he could breathe, at least.

But out in the yard he didn't know where to go, what to do. All the turbulence of his entire life was roiling in his guts. Civilized and uncivilized meant nothing—look at Haynes, who was both "civilized" and educated. Look at Moshulatubbee, who could not have been called "uncivilized." He was sick of it, absolutely sick of it all, especially of white men who put him down.

Young and Wright were decent, fair men, yes, but even they hadn't trusted him to bring Bascom in after they'd *known* Cade wasn't the criminal they wanted. He felt his mouth twist in a bitter grin because they had been right. If they hadn't followed him, he would have killed Bascom dead on Maggie's parlor floor.

But he had killed his soul instead. Now that Maggie was disgusted with the sight of him, she wouldn't want him anymore—she'd made that perfectly plain when she'd turned and walked away. Now he would die of loneliness.

Maggie watched Cade from the window, wanting to hold him, aching to hold him, *dying* to hold him as she had wanted to a few moments ago. She had needed to hold him so much she had thought the need would kill her.

But his face had been so magnificently terrible that she hadn't dared. He had worn his war chief's face, and his eyes had flashed lightning. He had needed something else besides her, then, and she didn't know what it was.

It must have been *the feeling* coming over him, that was all she could think. She sighed and slumped into the window seat, pressed her forehead to the glass. What a naive one she had been to think that her love could hold him when his old nemesis would come to take him away!

And what an irony that it had to descend upon them now, after she'd been staring out these windows all day, praying to see him there in the yard. Now she was seeing him getting ready to leave her. *The feeling* must have come at this moment, at least partly because his own neighbors had threatened to kill him.

What would keep them from galloping into the yard again, like a bunch of raiders, any morning of the year to capture him and hang him if a crime had been committed anywhere for a hundred miles around? He would never feel safe here anymore.

She caught her breath. He had stopped pacing and was turning around. Then, with a long fluid stride, he marched toward the house. She watched him until he went out of sight on the porch.

He was coming to tell her good-bye.

He opened the door, closed it, came across the entry hall and into the room. She wouldn't, couldn't look at him.

"Are you all right?" he said hoarsely.

She glanced up, but she couldn't meet his eyes. And he couldn't meet hers.

"Yes. Are you?"

"Yes."

"He didn't hurt you?" he asked, his throat sounding raw.

She tried to answer, she tried to form words,

but instead she burst into tears. Sobbing, uncontrollable tears, a weeping so strong that she pulled her knees up, dropped her face into her hands and let the sorrow take her.

"What's wrong?" he said, his voice nearer now. "Maggie," he cried, "if he didn't hurt you, what's wrong?"

She let her arms fall, jumped to her feet, and stared at him.

"What's *wrong*? As if you don't know! You're leaving me, *that's* what's wrong!"

The surprise that filled his face shocked her into silence and stopped her tears.

"*You* left *me*," he said. "You turned around in disgust and walked away from me because I am such a brute, beating up a helpless man."

She stared at him while her heart began a deep, throbbing beat of hope.

"Bascom deserved every blow he took," she said. "He would have raped and killed me and stolen this ranch."

He held her eyes with his.

"If that's the way you feel, why'd you walk away from me?"

"Because I thought *the feeling* was upon you! I thought it had come because your neighbors nearly killed you and you wouldn't feel safe here anymore."

"I haven't had a trace of *the feeling* since I met you."

She watched his face while she fought back the longing to run to him.

"But it *might* come!" she cried, wringing

her hands. "Cade, what if it does come, someday?"

"You told me one time that there is no someday," he said, and her heart turned over. "But I want to ask you this: Can you go through life with an Indian, risking scorn and prejudice?"

She didn't answer, she only looked at him.

Outside, the wind strengthened. A whole cloud of brown leaves on the big tree let go of their limb and flew like angry birds against the windows.

This was the death foretold by the red sky burning—the death of his soul.

Her clear, steady gaze never wavered, and he refused to let his slide away from it, although every muscle in his body screamed for him to go, to turn away from her and go, to step onto Smoke and ride before she told him no. He *ached* to run from that.

No spirit, including your own, can speak to you unless you can be still.

Cade stood still.

He had to have faith. The second time he had seen it, the red sky burning had brought Maggie into his arms.

Yet, having faith took all his strength. She wasn't smiling at him. She looked solemn enough to tell him bad news, but her right hand was clasped around her left, her fingers twisting his ring.

Her silvery voice rang clear.

"My father is still a threat," she said, "and

I've put your life in danger too many times already. You wouldn't have gone through this horror today if I hadn't brought you here."

She stood with her spine straight and her head held high.

"Maggie," he said, "if you're willing to put up with me and the dangers I bring to you, I'm willing to do the same." Then he grinned. "Besides, I can't go. You said you'd shoot me if I rode off and left you again."

Still she didn't smile at him.

"I love you, Maggie," he said. "I love you with all of my heart and I want to live with you forever. If you feel the same way, together we can handle anything the future throws our way."

She never moved. She searched his face, his eyes. "I do feel the same way," she said soberly, "but I'm scared you'll feel you can't stop running."

His heart lurched in his chest.

"We'll face *the feeling* together if it comes someday. But for now I know I've finally found home."

She smiled then, like the sun coming up, and threw herself into his reaching arms.

Epilogue

Las Manzanitas
October, 1871

Maggie straightened her back, took a long, deep breath, and a better purchase in the bed of straw with her knees. She nodded at Cotannah, kneeling beside her to help pull Joanna's foal.

"Now!" she cried.

Working together, they gave a mighty pull, and the small head and shoulders came sliding out, following the soft nose, tiny hooves, and long, long legs. They fell back to give the foal room, but Maggie kept trying to touch its slick, messy hide, kept trying to see every inch of it, almost before it was completely born.

"A filly," she cried, her voice shaking with excitement. "Gray like Smoke and with spots like Jo. Beautiful! Oh, Cotannah, look what we did—we brought this filly into the world all by ourselves!"

"Except for a little help from Joanna," Cotannah said, in her serious way.

They both burst into laughter. Then, exchanging gratified glances, they went around to pet Joanna's head and congratulate her before she started scrambling to her feet and urging the baby to do the same.

"*Senora, Senora* Maggie!"

Jorge's calls were punctuated by his pony's drumming feet, growing louder and more urgent as he neared the stables. He clattered up to the wide door, grinning broadly.

"Your family is coming! From Ark-an-sas, *senora* Maggie! I met them on the road, they will be here soon."

Maggie's joy turned to consternation, then she felt the old fear.

"Is my father with them?"

"They have outriders," Jorge said, "but no man in the coach. Only two beautiful ladies!"

"Go!" she said. "To the branding pen and bring *senor* Cade. And ask Luis to send someone to keep an eye on Jo and her foal."

"I'll watch these horses," Cotannah said, as Jorge wheeled his pony and went galloping off.

"No, come with me," Maggie cried, as she searched for the toweling they'd brought out of the house. "You're my dear sister now, and I want to introduce you to my *other* dear sister, Emily! Let's get washed up and run down to the road to meet them."

They hurried, but by the time they left the stables the coach was coming fast into the yard. Maggie linked her arm with Cotannah's and ran toward it, her heart pounding. Pierce would never let Mama and Emily come here without him! Had they, by some miracle, rebelled against him, too?

She knew the answer as soon as the coach door swung open and they began climbing out. Both were dressed in black from head to toe.

They didn't mention Pierce at first, though, as they embraced. Finally they stood just looking at each other in the fall sunlight, holding their arms loosely around each other to make a circle of four while the big tree waved its brilliant red and yellow leaves against the blue of the sky.

"Your father was shot dead a month ago when news of the court corruption got out," Maggie's mother said. "In an altercation of some kind among the conspirators. I never inquired into it—the least said about such disgraceful happenings, the better."

Maggie looked at Emily and said, "But what about Asa? I thought you'd have been married to him for a year by now."

Emily smiled and said, "You inspired me, Maggie. I refused him at the altar. When the preacher said, 'Does anyone know a reason this marriage shouldn't take place?' I answered—loud and clear as you would've spoken, Maggie—'I do. I am being forced into it against my will.' "

Maggie stared at her in disbelief, then they all, including Amanda Louise, burst into gales of laughter. They were still laughing when

Cade came thundering into the yard on Smoke.

When he'd gotten down and been introduced, when he had heard their story, Maggie said, "What do you think, darling? Could you bear living with two more women?"

"I love living with beautiful women," he drawled, putting an arm around Maggie and one around Cotannah, "but it's a sure deal if your mother and Emily will take charge of Uncle Jumper and Aunt Ancie. If they plow up any more of the ranch to plant in tomatoes, we'll have to haul water all the way from Red River."

He smiled at all of them, his dark, warm gaze slowly moving around the circle of their faces. It lingered for the longest time on Maggie, so long that she almost forgot that the others were there.

Then he looked at her mother and Emily again.

"Welcome," he said, softly. "Welcome to Las Manzanitas. Welcome home."

Avon Romantic Treasures

*Unforgettable, enthralling love stories,
sparkling with passion and adventure
from Romance's bestselling authors*

LADY OF SUMMER *by Emma Merritt*
77984-6/$5.50 US/$7.50 Can

TIMESWEPT BRIDE *by Eugenia Riley*
77157-8/$5.50 US/$7.50 Can

A KISS IN THE NIGHT *by Jennifer Horsman*
77597-2/$5.50 US/$7.50 Can

SHAWNEE MOON *by Judith E. French*
77705-3/$5.50 US/$7.50 Can

PROMISE ME *by Kathleen Harrington*
77833-5/ $5.50 US/ $7.50 Can

COMANCHE RAIN *by Genell Dellin*
77525-5/ $4.99 US/ $5.99 Can

MY LORD CONQUEROR *by Samantha James*
77548-4/ $4.99 US/ $5.99 Can

ONCE UPON A KISS *by Tanya Anne Crosby*
77680-4/$4.99 US/ $5.99 Can